HOMO
ROBOTICUS

Mayet Ligad Yuhico

This is a work of fiction and the events and characters in this book are the product of the author's imagination. Any resemblance to actual events or persons living or dead, is purely coincidental.

Cover designer: S. M. Savoy
Art cover and map design: Mathew Yuhico
Cover Photograph: Eric Angelo Yuhico

ISBN – 13: 978 -1–7334536 – 0-8

To
Bons
Bodi, Eric, Mathew, David
Lily and Paolo

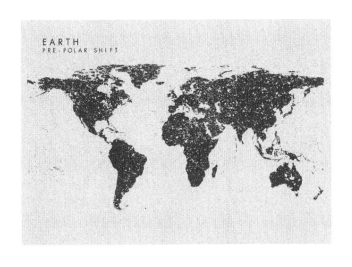

EARTH
PRE-POLAR SHIFT

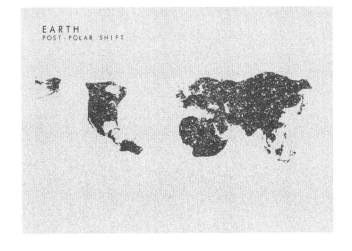

EARTH
POST-POLAR SHIFT

Nothing would be what it is,
because everything would be what it isn't.
And contrary wise, what is, it wouldn't be.
And what it wouldn't be, it would.
You see?
- Alice in Wonderland

The Edge of the West Antarctic

Buckminster City,

Perrumal Antarctic Shelf

11 February 2056

As the small hand of the clock hit six, Brice turned to the window and saw a wave of metallic spike-droids rise from the ground outside. She counted backwards from ten, and when she reached zero, the spikes bloomed multi-layered metal petals and started turning in different directions. They looked like dancers performing ballet steps, she thought with amusement; one executing a deep plié to measure the temperature of the soil; another, a hundred pirouettes to record the ferocity of the wind. These were once tasks both her father and grandfather were responsible for, but for some time now, no human had been allowed outside the tundra and these droids had done most of the scientific work.

There was a sound behind her – an excited screech, and Brice turned away from the window. Eilish was jumping up and down as she did every day when the spike-droids emerged.

"Be careful, Eilish!" she said. "Come and sit beside me," and she patted the broad windowsill she was perched upon. Eilish was the same size as she was and looked her exact age, which was six. She was wearing the same pajamas, pink with flowers. She patted down a few stray hairs sticking out on Eilish's head, then checked her left leg. Made of glassinex, it had broken two weeks before, when she fell from the same windowsill. "If you break another leg, we're in trouble," she warned Eilish. "There are no spare parts coming to this side of the world any time soon. Which is a pain in the behind, because that's what you'll have to walk on if you break your other leg, so hobble carefully!" And then she laughed. Eilish grinned, and shook her head.

"I don't know what you mean by hobble, Brice." And Eilish tugged at her arm, but her attention had gone back to the view outside the window.

"Why don't I see Fonteyn?" she said, then looked at Eilish with a furrowed brow. Boredom had led them to name the drones after famous ballerinas, and Fonteyn was their favorite. Eilish stood up and peered out the window as the drones did their magical pirouettes.

In the space just outside their window, tropical plants were lush, and fruit hung from trees, ripe for the picking. But beyond the glass-domed fortifications that surrounded the house and stretched overhead, the world was covered with ice. With relief, Brice spotted the missing droid. "There she is!" she said. Fonteyn was tall and graceful, and her job was testing the fortifications around the walls of their home.

Her happiness at seeing the droids vanished when she suddenly heard an eerie sound emerging from the bowels of the earth. Eilish clutched at her, fear evident in her expression.

The noises were scary, and, it seemed, growing scarier with each passing day. Her Grandpa Daelan said they sounded like the earth was a hungry monster opening its unquenchable stomach and, finding no food, grumbled and groaned. He was seated at his desk as always, deep into his notes. But she saw him take two noise protectors shaped like fat, orange buttons from a drawer and in one movement, stick them on the outside of both his ears.

"It's just the sound monster, Grandpa," she said, jumping from the windowsill, walking toward her grandfather and tugging at his orange buttons until they fell from his ears.

"The problem is if there's a bigger monster than the sound monster beneath the earth," he said. Brice turned to her father, Esteban, who smiled at her, but her mother Mira placed a finger to her lips and nodded toward her grandfather.

Uncle Avila, her father's brother, was making himself a cup of tea in the kitchen. As usual, he scowled at the grumbling sounds. He had just finished university, and recently arrived for a short vacation with them in the Antarctic before pursuing graduate degrees in geology, the same track his father and brother had taken. He wasn't as used to the sounds as everyone else, and found them more disturbing.

She loved her Grandpa Daelan's attention. She pulled at his ears this time, and his gray-green eyes, which were so like her own, peered at her closely. Grandpa called them "Jordan River" eyes, after a body of water that flowed in Israel. All the men in her family had the same eyes and she was happy she shared something with them.

Abruptly, Grandfather Daelan pushed away from his desk and stood up.

"It's time to leave," he said. The room went quiet. Her normally dreamy scientist grandfather wasn't prone to dramatic announcements.

But Daelan was clearly distraught. His hands hung by his side, jerking like helpless birds. "I wanted to wait to tell you tomorrow morning," he said, "but I've just received disturbing reports on the ground. It's too dangerous to stay here. Our work in the Antarctic is finished."

Daelan turned to the vast, barren, ice-covered landscape outside the window, as if unsure of his next words. "It's

February, and we have sunlight 24 hours a day. It's the perfect time to move."

He was trying to keep his tone light, but Buckminster and the land around it had been his own grandfather's brutal, beloved place. This was not a decision he would make lightly.

The city had been named after Buckminster Fuller, who'd dreamed of a climate-controlled habitat in this part of the world. It was a man-made tropical paradise, a place where Brice went to school and played with her friends, the only home she'd ever known. Her grandfather's words didn't make sense to her. Why would he want to go?

"All signs show that the West Perrumal's ice cap is on its last legs," he said. "Soon Buckminster will descend into the sea water that underlies the ice."

Brice had heard this talk before, though her parents had tried to keep it from her. Uncle Avila had been surprised and shocked when he'd arrived to find that the once-bustling city had been reduced to around fifty families. She'd heard her grandfather whisper the words "warming oceans," and "catastrophic ice sheet collapse" before they'd seen her listening and stopped talking. Her family had visited Greenland last summer, and told her they were looking at it as an alternative home and a way to continue studying arctic habitats. The ice cap there was safer, she'd heard her father tell her mother, anchored on land. And she'd also heard her Grandpa say that their Antarctic home had an "Akiles Hill" whatever that meant.

Her grandfather turned back from the window and addressed her father. "Most are leaving before it destructs entirely. You have to go too." He sounded agitated so she wrapped her arms around his waist.

"Is this the Akiles Hill, Grandpa?" she asked.

"Yes, my dearest. We will sink in seawater if we don't do something now."

She glanced at her father. He always knew the right words to say.

"I notice you didn't include yourself, Dad," her father said. "We can't leave you here. You know that. We all go together. No one stays behind." Esteban's voice was direct, brooking no argument.

But her Uncle Avila didn't seem to be taking Grandpa's pronouncement seriously. "You haven't recovered yet from the cancelling of the Buckminster Fuller scientific gathering last month. Don't see monsters underneath the bed when there aren't any, Dad," Avila chided.

A group of scientists who'd wanted to copy the Buckminster type of enclosed city in Mars's Antarctic had abruptly cancelled a long-planned symposium to be held in their city when her grandfather's warnings were reported around the world. Everyone had noticed that her grandfather's mood had turned dark when the event, his biggest project for years, had been called off.

But her grandfather shook his head. "The scientists were correct to cancel. Esteban and Mira, you have to think of Brice," he said. Suddenly, all eyes focused on her. "She's only six years old, son. Think about her future. Follow the warm waters. Go east to the Philippines in Concordia, in Palawan, where your mother was born."

Her mother Mira, who was usually quiet during arguments, stepped toward her father-in-law. "Daelan, everyone in Buckminster understood the risks of living in this beautiful, fragile land. If we've all decided it's time to go, then we will go together," she said.

She took Daelan's hand but he shook her off.

"We have practiced the Bubble transport drill every night," he said, "but now, we must sleep inside it." Daelan stood up, and with that motion, all arguments ceased.

Brice saw her father nod in agreement.

"It's time to go to the Bubbles then, Brice and Eilish," Mira said. Brice was determined to get to the Bubble first, and with an impish grin, Eilish started running after her. Mira caught Eilish's hand and then hers and admonished them to walk slowly. She rolled her eyes, it was just another Bubble drill. Life would go on as usual, she thought, when it was over.

Their two large Bubbles were parked on the lower floor. Orb-shaped and twenty-one square meters in size, the Bubble was a dependable multi-terrain vehicle of transport for scientists in the Antarctic. Made of Aquameer, a flexible, industrial-grade, oxygen-permeable plastic that was lighter than water, they floated upright due to the water's surface tension on their base. Not only were they aquatic, the Bubble also had wheels, which could come off as needed. At first, Bubbles were used mainly for hauling material in the Antarctic, as they were able to move from island to island in all kinds of terrain and weather conditions. But a few years before, some Bubble models had been revamped as survival vehicles after a scientist was caught riding one in a furious windstorm, and though his Bubble was spun a hundred miles from its original location, he survived unscathed. Its tough construction and circular shape guaranteed that its inhabitants would survive nearly any disaster on water, land, or snow.

Brice and Eilish ran into one of the Bubbles and plopped themselves amidst their toys and clothes.

"Hey Eilish, want to hear a scary story?" She looked around and her mother was not near. Eilish picked up a globe but Brice grabbed it. It was her favorite toy. The complete reversal of the magnetic poles of the earth was a non-stop focus of work and discussion for her family. North was becoming South, and the South Pole was becoming the North. Her father had said it had happened many, many times in history, without major effect on the earth. But in recent years, the magnetic poles had weakened due to climate change, and with that came a possibility of a cataclysmic pole reversal causing a shift of the equator, followed by massive ice-melt and global flooding. But always, in her stories to Eilish, if massive flooding happened, her family would ride the waters using surfboards, not Bubbles. They would ride hand-in-hand like champions, their own family flags unfurled. They would go past the glorious ice sheets, riding back to Buckminster with prizes in hand, winning first place in her mind's imaginary race.

Her thoughts were interrupted when she saw Avila in the other Bubble. He was trying to get her attention when he stuck his tongue out and started jumping up and down like a gorilla. She collapsed with laughter. She in turn stuck out her tongue, bulged her cheeks, and did some high-spirited jumping jacks copying his movements.

When her parents joined her inside the Bubble, they were whispering together in a serious tone. She winked at her uncle and sat on the floor, where she pretended to read a book.

"Have you heard about the Moores?" her mother said. "I heard they took just the clothes on their backs." Her ears perked up. Dr. Philip Moore and his wife Simone were her grandfather Daelan's best friends, and Dr. Philip had helped co-write the Polar Shift Theory with him. Their daughter Julia was her best friend, but she hadn't seen her in the past few days. She thought it had been because Julia was not allowed to go to school anymore.

"I wish I could have stopped them," she heard her mother whisper, "and explain that polar shifting has occurred many times in Earth's history. But it wouldn't have helped. No one wanted to stay. And now they are all gone."

"Except us," Esteban said, shaking his head. A loud noise interrupted him.

The sounds beneath the earth had changed. They were high-pitched and groaning, as if everything below the sea bed was collapsing.

Her mother screamed. Was this the Reckoning she had heard her family whisper about? Was this the moment the ice would succumb to the ocean, tipping everyone on it into the sea?

The sound came again, even louder. Esteban and Avila left their Bubbles and ran to the basement's floor-to-ceiling windows. Outside was a puzzling sight. The homes surrounding them had been scattered across the landscape, but now seemed jammed together. How could that possibly be? There could be just one explanation. A giant wave had unmoored the ice, scouring it from below, unhinging any structure rooted above. When the wave hit land, the houses would be thrown like discarded toys. He could actually see the sheet of ice rippling. The frozen wave it created was approaching his own beloved home.

"Take the wheels off the Bubbles," her father commanded Avila. "I'm getting Father."

As he raced toward the door that led into the house,

Daelan appeared. Esteban pulled his father close.

And then the wave hit.

Her father and grandfather were thrown into the air as rocks, stones, and debris rained down. From the safety of their Bubble, she and Eilish looked on in horror. Her father landed near the Bubble, and clawed through the debris toward its door. Her mother and Eilish pulled him inside.

"Where's Grandfather?" Brice screamed. Her father's forehead was covered in blood. As she reached for him, a wave of frigid water burst through the house's walls. And then the roof opened up, and they were all swept away by the swirling waves.

Daelan O'Rourke was swept away by the water and the wreckage of the house he'd lived in. The ice shelf he had devoted his whole life to investigating had become his burial place.

The Bubble vessels containing his family were pushed out to sea by the churning, groaning water monster. Daelan's fears about the end of the Antarctic had come true. But his projections for a new global landscape were inaccurate. Things were going to be far worse than he could ever have imagined.

Chapter 1

The Edge of Agni Island,

Suvarnadvipa

Angkasa River Coalition

Indonesia

Asian River Coalitions

12 August 2071

12 days after the Drone Strike

Brice entered the glass portal. Whoosh! She closed her eyes as a machine sucked her thin suit and headgear from her body. And then the safety lights flashed, and she entered the safe house.

Its coolness was a welcome respite from the heat outside. Naked, she sat on a pod-shaped chair, closed her eyes, and waited for the rest of the ritual. A squadron of tiny cleaning machines whirred around her, thin brushes entering the crevices of her face and body, scrubbing them clean of toxic ash. When they flew away, spray jets descended from the ceiling and water cascaded down, washing away any debris. When the safety lights flashed again, she stood and stepped forward into drying gusts of air. With the flash of a single green light, she was cleared to leave the portal.

Her dark blue suit was hanging inside a cabinet by the door. As she dressed, she tried not to think how much she loathed this stiff, ugly, utilitarian garment. Instead, she turned her focus to the notes she would write about the Agni landscape. "Day 15. Han Machina survivor #2817 interview notes in Annex V. Still no daylight due to smog, pollutants enter the crevices of the body's orifices, need for a mask 24/7. UNINHABITABLE."

As always, a thin whirring Bee, her mechanical electronic monitor, had stood by during the cleaning ritual and was now hovering at its usual arm's-length distance from her head. That soft, buzzing noise was her constant companion. There was nothing she could do that wouldn't be observed by the Colony. She turned away from the Bee, as if to block out its presence.

But of course, it followed her.

Her inward groan of annoyance didn't show on her face. She wasn't going to give the Colony analysts the satisfaction of a display of discomfort.

She was their prisoner, but she knew that if she thought resentful thoughts, she was as good as dead. She had to be better, more willing to do the impossible tasks assigned to her. It was her passport to survival.

From the hallway came a deep, booming voice that seemed to reverberate against the thin walls.

"All clear?" Diego said. "No one followed you?" When

she answered in the affirmative, he said, "I need you here, please." He came into the chamber and beckoned, then walked back into the hallway. "C'mon," he said. "This is interesting." She followed him into a small conference room, where he lifted a leather briefcase onto a table and started stuffing stacks of paper bills inside it.

He was dressed as usual in a fading checkered shirt and well-worn pants. He looked, she thought, like a rugged cowhand. Someone you wouldn't look twice at. But misjudge Director Diego Rojo at your peril. He was one of the most capable and respected hands in the Colony, and she was only able to work instead of cower behind bars because of his say-so.

"We need a load of these motherfuckers to make the world go round for ..." Diego said, and then glanced up at Brice. His eyes narrowed when he saw her expression. "What's wrong?" he said.

"I hope this ends well," she said, unsmiling.

"Mallard is a different kind of President, Brice," Diego replied. "And whatever Mallard commands, it will be Avila's priority as Defense Minister of the Colony." Diego pointed at her uniform. "Even if I object to how he does it. But for now, we have to complete this mission."

"Yes, Sir," she said, and then she coughed, and tilted her head toward the Bee. But her boss didn't seem to care that his words were insubordinate.

But Diego wasn't finished yet. "Who would have guessed he'd become such a vindictive person. Jesus! You wearing that hideous suit," he said, and directed an angry look at the Bee. "You look like an airplane mechanic, for Christ's sake!"

"I'd prefer that designation any time of the day. But

you know what, surprise! People change over the years, Director Rojo," she said, then threw caution to the wind and looked at the Bee. "I guess they'll clamp me down with some punishment again when I return to HQ. Aside from tagging the Machinas, interviewing Han prisoners, if the President wants a positive review of this place, he won't get it. It's uninhabitable. It can't be a part of the Asian Rivers Coalition, Diego. People will need to move somewhere else."

"Another country?" Diego sighed. "But which one? We'll have another battle in the World Rivers Coalition on our hands. Big headache. But as President Mallard ends his first term, he's more comfortable to muscle his way in, and anything's possible. With your Uncle Avila as Defense Minister, they want less drama, not more. President Mallard sure won't allow migrants to our shores."

She shrugged. Whatever she replied would just get her in trouble. Damn it to hell. Once he got her talking like this it was so hard to stop.

"What is President Mallard's priority, may I ask?" he said, once again ignoring the Bee. "He's one weird binary bastard. When I was a new recruit in the Colony, he was my supervisor, and he was already obsessed with the Hans. And he still is, though I haven't seen any indication at this point in time that they still exist after E Day."

Her boss looked perturbed. E Day was Elimination Day against the Hans. It was a worldwide attack by the River Coalitions against the North Korean Han Federations across the globe. That was six months ago.

"But this bombing run doesn't look like any Han signature I've seen. The Hans are methodical perfectionists. They created the first robotic soldiers, for

Christ's sake! The recent bombing images don't look like their work. Sloppy. Disorganized. Definitely not a job done by the Han military."

And he left the room. When he returned a few seconds later, he was as excited as a child finding a toy under the Christmas tree.

"Brice, I want to show you something. This arrived from the Colony yesterday." Diego was holding a flat device as big as his hand. "It's an updated version of the Presence."

He opened its lid and an array of multi-hued colors popped out, followed by the facsimile of a three-terminal workstation. She stepped back as colorful graphs and charts appeared on three big holographic screens.

"God," he said. "I can never get used to these new set-ups. I guess I'm too old and ready to retire."

He had grown more rotund through the years and his head, once fully thatched with dark hair, was now all white. But Diego's eyes were still unchanged. They were analyst's eyes – sharp, laser-like.

There were images of people on the screens. "Suvarnadvipa Station," one of them said. "Ready when you are. Agents Eric David, Bodi James, and William Riley from the Denver River Colony reporting for duty, Director Rojo." Diego waved at them.

"How are you, Director Diego, and the most foul-mouthed agent in the Colony, Brice O'Rourke?" one agent said, and guffaws could be heard from the other side of the screen. She found a chair and sat down in front of the screens.

"Former agent, you asses," she said, smiling at the screens. "Oh, I mean, your graces, dear analysts from the Colony!" She gave a mini-bow.

"Oh yeah, we've missed the way you wave your special finger, O'Rourke! Better than those f-bombs you drop all over the Colony."

Diego had had enough of their teasing. It was time to get to work. "Hey guys, you all sound drunk," he said. "Can you show me some of the images of the recent attack here in Suvarnadvipa? My guess is, they all came from drones." He pointed at the images and turned to her.

"Pretty ancient, right? My guess is drones pre-2021? The radius of the blast is too wide. Drone blasts from twenty years ago are precise to the millimeter."

She nodded. If the blasts weren't precise, they were definitely created by older technology.

"Any clues on the manufacturer? Is it American, Russian, Korean? Check out those markings on the soil, Colony HQ analysts."

"Request to duplicate the bombing site, Sir," she said.

"Beam it to us, guys," the director ordered. "Maybe 50 square meters. The deepest bomb markings, please?" In seconds, the bombing site was displayed.

"Ahem..." said one of the analysts on the screen. His voice had gone serious. "Defense Minister O'Rourke would like to join you." The trio sat up straighter and one of them even patted his hair in place.

In seconds, an image of the Defense Minister appeared before them.

"Hello, Avila." Diego placed his hands on his hips as he greeted their boss. Brice stepped backward and averted her eyes. He looked so much like her father that looking at her uncle was always painful.

"Hello, Diego. Brice," the real-time, 3-D holographic image of Avila O'Rourke replied. "What a neat invention, huh? I can beam myself anywhere in the world, even if I'm still inside the offices of the Defense Ministry. And we can virtually go anywhere we want to as well. Shall we take a closer look at the site?"

Diego led the way into the holographic minescape of cratered land that appeared in the room. The image was synced with Avila's location so perfectly, it seemed he was actually on the site with them.

"If I may say so, this bombing run looks incredibly primeval," she said, and squatted, closed one eye, and peered closely at the displaced dirt in front of her.

"C'mon, let's get closer," Diego said and motioned to her. She followed her boss. For a rotund person, Diego skipped easily around the craters, but the virtual reality images were too discombobulating for Brice to navigate well. At the virtual edge of a bombed-out crater, she slid and fell on all fours.

Her uncle bent to help her, though his hands grasped just empty air. "Thanks, Minister O'Rourke," she said and got to her feet in embarrassment.

"Fooled you, Agent O'Rourke! The team at R and D outsmarted us all with this one. It's a beauty of an invention." Avila's voice boomed. She froze and averted her eyes. She didn't want anyone to see the expression on her face.

But she couldn't outrun the sound of the chuckles coming from the terminals.

Instead of getting angry, she looked toward the screen and waved at the analysts, then winked at them. Her sense of vertigo abated as her mind finally managed to sync with her body's perception of the replicated bombing site.

"A Han insurrection? But this is definitely not Han,"

Avila said, and peered into a bomb crater. "And this is troubling. At least those Han sons of bitches were predictable."

It was a racist, bigoted statement, but Brice couldn't help but agree. In 2024, fed up with extreme economic sanctions imposed on their country, the North Koreans unleashed missiles armed with nuclear warheads at South Korea. The United States and Europe, close allies, were drawn into the internecine fight between the two countries by sending their armies to help. In retaliation, North Korea sent drone bombings to London, Berlin, Paris, and Tokyo.

The Hans were successful up to a certain point, disrupting governments and destabilizing the daily lives of the citizens in the bombed cities. But the nuclear bombing of Kyushino in North Korea in 2052 and the Polar Shift in 2056 had caused catastrophic damage to countries around the world, including the North Korean peninsula, which was inundated with water. Their national borders disappeared, and they were left with little farmable land. Only the Han River was still a recognizable boundary. "Han" became a derogatory term for the country that caused so much mayhem around the world, spit out as a curse.

Diego squatted and scrutinized the ridge formation of the soil.

"I've been analyzing Han battle scenes for thirteen years," he said, "but this bombing run doesn't seem to follow a pattern. Colony, request for pattern analysis, please. Brice, any thoughts?" Diego glanced at her, but she just shook her head.

"These bombs must have been created by a child. You're correct, Diego. No discernable pattern at all," she said.

"What do you think, Diego?" Avila said. His image was so close to her that she wanted to pat his arm, at least. She had not seen her uncle since her detainment six months ago.

Surreptitiously, she looked him over. Though only thirty-eight years old, his hair was prematurely grey and there were wrinkles around his eyes. Unlike Diego, who slouched and bulged in the middle, Avila stood ramrod straight, betraying his military background, and he had retained his runner's lithe physique. His expression was more serious, but he still had the same rakish grin. She wondered for a second if her uncle was still able to do his monkey impersonation. But that was from another time and place.

As usual, he was dressed impeccably. It was whispered that this top boss had a very readable dress code inside the Defense Ministry. The more dressed he was, the more chaotic the situation.

Diego patted imaginary dust from his pants. "It's apparent that we have to see more samples of the drone bombing markings. I need to see the actual site, Avila."

"Then go out. You have my permission," Avila said.

"For the past few months, I haven't been allowed past the perimeter of this Station," she whispered to Diego. "So you've planned to go out all along, and use the deepwahs?"

"Uh-huh," Diego whispered back. "We need that cash I was packing so we can go to General Pali's side of the mountain."

"As if bribery works all the time, Director Rojo!" she wagged a finger at him. Her voice rose a notch and she didn't care if Avila heard it. "But that means we have to ask for military protection. You don't want anyone getting nosy with intel we've gathered."

Diego gave a thumbs-up sign, and then faced Avila, as if testing him. "You have to give up something in order to glean something far more important." He turned to her. "We'll need support reinforcements, of course. I requested the Echo commander in charge of Suvarnadvipa Station to accompany us," Diego continued. "Aren't you curious about them?"

She had not been allowed outside the Suvarnadvipa Station in six months, and she was deeply excited to be able to join this mission. But she couldn't care less who the support reinforcements were.

There was a soft beeping sound in the background, and Avila touched his ear, alerted by his communication device. "Look, I have another meeting," he said. "As I've said, go where you need to go and tell me what you see. I'm done. Over and out."

As soon as Avila's image disappeared, Diego turned off the Presence.

"Poof! Just like that! Will the Minister of Defense start micro-managing all the cases in the Colony now? Is that a bad precedent?"

Diego grinned. "He's a thousand miles away, Brice. We're on our own here. Who's looking over our shoulders, except your cute security device?" and he waved a hand at the Bee.

She clucked loudly. "And who are the Echo contingent?" she said. "More testosterone-riddled soldiers?"

He smiled and shook his head. "Sollus soldiers! All these Roboticus sentient droids are still new to me. I've met a few of them in the Colony but a whole Echo contingent. Wow," he exclaimed.

"My sister Ira is a Roboticus, a Sollus in fact, but she didn't choose the military as a career."

"Her DNA is from your dad and mom, right?" Diego asked. "How did that happen? I heard their growth is accelerated."

"The growth from infancy to a fifteen-year-old is accelerated by programming mandated by the government to five years," she said.

"Whoah," he exclaimed. " It's rude, and I couldn't just go near them and ask them at the Colony – Sir, Madam, may I feel your skin. Are you all synthetic like plastic?"

She chuckled. "Around eleven years ago, new advances in technology made it possible for human skin cells to be replicated using synthetic materials. And then once skin cells are replicated, the skin becomes the host for sperms and eggs. This can be replicated and implanted without a womb present."

"Jesus, Mary, and Joseph," Diego made a sign of the cross. "No sexual intercourse, no womb needed, but an Artificially Intelligent Person is created."

"You're getting it, Director Rojo. AIP," she smiled.

"I don't judge. I meet a Sollus or an Aequilavum, and I take them all at face value. I've been impressed so far. The test program was in Harvard and in top universities around the country. Many have started applying at the Colony, and they're doing well," Diego answered and brought two of his thumbs up as a mark of approval.

"That batch of Sollus kids! They topped the Honor Roll, and were outstanding students that volunteered in every organization, Ira included," she said with pride.

" So, are you ready? Let's go. I requested them by 12:00. That's in ten minutes." He grabbed the virtual desktop device with one hand, and with the other, his ever-reliable field backpack.

She followed Diego down the hallway. He stopped at the portal door and pushed a button beside it. Security images from outside were beamed back to them.

One terminal showed two vehicles hovering a few feet above the ground.

"Might it be better to use trucks instead of using the Hovers?" she asked.

"Nah, we're okay with the Hovercraft," Diego said. "And we want to be safe. The ground here is filled with toxic pollutants. Anyway, they're on time, and that's good!"

Diego hesitated, then asked, "May I observe them first? Security cameras, interior of vehicle, please." Instantly, images of the vehicle's interior were loaded onto the terminal.

There were seven soldiers in the vehicle, all of them in military fatigues.

They looked completely human.

"I've always thought this experiment would go wrong," Diego said. "It was your father Esteban, with the help of Avila, who stole the first Machina soldiers from the Hans. Did they ever think that one brave act would spawn the Roboticus technology happening today? Look at that!"

"Well, Ira is a wonderful human being. I'm sure these Sollus soldiers will meet with your approval," she said as he patted the back of her immediate boss.

Diego's Colony communication collar device sounded and he touched his ear briefly, then cocked his head to one side, listening.

"The Sollus are very impatient to meet us," he said, tapping the device off. "But I think it makes sense to bring them in and offer some rest to replenish their batteries. At least they're better equipped to handle the smoke suffocating this place than we are. Let's suit up and head out, Agent Brice." He stood up and moved toward the exit door.

"The haze affected the screen's visibility again." She tapped the screen again, this time harder, and sighed. The smoky haze surrounding the land had been there for months, caused by the burning of rubber plantations by the remaining survivors of Indonesia. "I wish the inhabitants would stop burning those rubber plantations, to stop this pollution," she sighed in exasperation.

"It's easier and way cheaper to burn large swathes of land to clear the previous harvest than it is to hack it by hand. With less of the human population remaining, it makes sense to burn them," Diego said in mock horror. "Robots! Drones! Smog. We can barely stand up from the weight of the world's problems. Let's go," Diego said with finality, and placed a hand on a panel near the door. It opened to another portal that led to the main entrance.

It took just seconds for her and Diego's burn suits to be sucked back onto their bodies, this time with protective helmets encasing their heads. They paused just inside the door as they waited for their oxygen pumps to kick in. Finally, the door opened and they stepped outside.

A door opened in the first Hovercraft, and Diego took a seat inside it and pulled off his helmet.

"I'm Colonel Riggs, Echo commander," said a large man with a blond crew cut. "And we're ready to rock and roll, Director."

His accent was unmistakably south of the Beltway, she surmised, maybe Georgia.

"Mind if we bring along Brice?" Diego said. "She's from the Colony."

The commander assessed Brice from head to foot.

"Why is she the prisoner of the United States and its allies, Director Rojo?" The commander's gaze lingered on her dark blue uniform.

"Classified, Commander Riggs. Agent Brice is not part of the active Colony Intelligence unit, but she is allowed to do tasks mandated by Colony Heads, under the Defense Ministry," Diego answered in a curt manner. It was obvious he was displeased with the commanding officer's questions.

"The Defense Minister being Agent O'Rourke's uncle. I could see it for what it is, but as long as she's vetted by you, Director Rojo, and she won't be a problem to the Echoes here, then I'm good too," Commander Riggs answered.

She looked down and snickered, drawing a sharp look from Diego.

"She's toothless, a detainee of the US River Coalition. She's not allowed to carry weapons. Except the Azukal," Diego said.

"Ach! Sugar as weaponry!" the commander waved the thought away dismissively.

The Azukal held a chemical that resembled liquefied sugar that when used up close, encased a perpetrator in its sticky essence. But in an emergency, this substance could take the form of a hardened glass so strong it could protect soldiers from shrapnel and gunfire.

Colonel Riggs turned toward her and nodded. "As long as she's under your supervision, Director, it's fine. Come on in."

She sat at the far end of a middle bench seat near the window, while Diego sat in front with Colonel Riggs.

"Ahem," someone said, and she turned around. One of the men in the back of the vehicle was smiling at her. Most of his companions were smiling as well and several gave her thumbs-up signs. She had trained as an Intelligence agent, and at a glance, she had memorized the features of the Sollus soldiers riding inside the Hovercraft. Most were young, the same age as her sister Ira, who was eighteen years old. Three were African-American, two were Asian-American, one was Latin-American, and she briefly glanced at the person sitting beside her. He had almond-shaped blue eyes, dark brownish-black hair, pale skin, and an aquiline nose. Was he Eurasian? Brice's attention was diverted when Diego suddenly shouted from the front.

"I'm gonna bring you boys to General Pali," Diego said. "Let's see if he'll allow you to get past his Fu dogs," and he nodded to the soldiers.

The Hovercraft lifted smoothly from the ground and glided toward their destination at top speed. This small aircraft flew smoothly over the burnt earthscape of hills and valleys.

"General Pali's compound will take around thirty minutes to reach, guys, so hold onto your horses," Colonel Riggs said.

Minutes turned to silence. As the vehicle flew higher, the air seemed thinner. By instinct, Brice touched her helmet, ready to switch on the mask function at a moment's notice. She felt someone tap her shoulder.

"How long have you been a prisoner of the Colony?" one of the soldiers from the rear of the vehicle asked.

She answered him in Bahasa, the language of

Suvarnadvipa. She always learned the language of the place where she was assigned, and used Bahasa to test her ability to adapt to a new language and environment. "Six months. And I'm not a prisoner. I'm a detainee. The Colony has not cleared me to return to HQ. There's an official investigation ongoing. But I've been assigned to a variety of islands here for the past six months," she said.

Her silent seat companion finally turned toward her. "Aku ingin mencintaimu dengan sederhana; dengan kata yang tak sempat diucapkan kayu kepada apu yang mejadikannya abu," he said.

He was reciting lines from one of her favorite poems. And he was reciting them in Bahasa. He had a deep, mellifluous voice, and when she turned to face him she saw that his eyes were the blue of a summer sky.

"Very apt, soldier, for the inferno we're flying above," she said. "I want to love in a simple way; with words that the wood didn't get to say to the fire which burned it into ashes."

"Lt. Quinn Mathews. Call me Quinn," the soldier beside her said. "And you are Agent...?"

"I'm Brice," she said, and extended her hand, but before she finished saying her name, there were wolf whistles all around. "You're the famous Troubadour," the blue-eyed soldier said matter-of-factly. "The Inquisitor who makes the Han Prisoners sing like canaries in their confessional."

"How do you know about me?" she said.

"It's SOP for us to study who you are, Agent O'Rourke. We're your military support. We've been here for a month, and we've been listening to your interviews of the Han soldiers you've captured in Suvarnadvipa," Quinn said. And then he smiled. "The boys have given you that nickname."

Brice shook her head. "They all sing like canaries after a certain point, you know. I don't have a problem with the Hans. They are either sick or dying. And the Machinas have a certain stony expression..."

There was a commotion in the back of the vehicle. One soldier was swinging his elbows like a wind-up machine, mimicking the Machinas' wind-up-toylike movements. The soldiers burst into laughter.

"You're naughty soldiers, you are." She turned around and wagged a forefinger at them. She paused, trying to look at them closely without being impolite.

Like Ira, these Sollus robots didn't have disjointed movements like the Machinas. They seemed to be perfectly human in every way.

One soldier asked from the back, "There are rumors that it's the Homo Roboticus Aequilavum that dropped the drones. Is that true?"

"I'm not allowed to say anything," she replied, just as her Bee flew around her.

"Aequilavum? The AQs? To be honest, I haven't seen or met an AQ in my years as a soldier. Do they look like us?"

She hesitated, then nodded.

"What's different, then?" His voice had grown serious. Jesus Christ, she thought. This soldier could replace her role as The Troubadour. He had an awful lot of questions.

"Their DNA is from robotic chromosomes, unlike yours which come from the DNA of your human parents. They don't have memories of childhood, like you. No memories of carefree teenage years. All they have are a jumble of memories bought from the black market. Their sole purpose is to defeat the Machinas," she answered.

"Was that successful?" Quinn asked.

But she did not answer.

The soldiers had apparently grown tired of poking fun at the Machinas. "Are we still looking for Han soldiers then?" one said. "We've been going from one fiery palm plantation to another. We're a long way from home, so tell us what we're doing here." She hesitated, then glanced at Diego, who was animatedly explaining something to Col. Riggs.

"There appear to be no Han soldiers left after E Day, no DNA markings anywhere. Unless they fly, or they're ghosts, we have found no markings of any creatures responsible for the drone bomb run. But we're looking at the markings the drones made, which are near General Pali's side of the mountain."

There were sounds of clapping from the back of the vehicle, and more high-fives.

"Yes!" one soldier shouted.

"We've been cooped up in Barracks, and the guys here have been itching for some real live action," Quinn said. "Can you tell us something about who we'll meet?"

"General Pali knows most of the caves," she said. "His great-grandfather was said to have been a protégé of Osama Bin Laden, and if there's a guy who can fortify a cave, it's Pali. I believe he's the one who can give us access to the bomb sites."

Her words were greeted by another round of clapping and wolf whistles.

The Hovercraft was following a roadway now, and a thick plume of smoke clouded the stretch of road before them. But a couple of kilometers west, the air was clear, and a hazeless valley was visible below.

The Hovercraft in front of them stopped, and when theirs did as well, Echo Commander Riggs stepped out of the vehicle with Diego to confer on strategy.

Minutes ticked by. Finally, they were given a thumbs-up sign by Commander Riggs, and the soldiers took this as an invitation to leave their vehicles. Most of them pulled out cigarettes. Others unfolded a stash of chocolate candies and chewed quietly. She and Diego were allowed to take off their helmets. At this altitude, the smog was not present.

"Hey Brice, keep an eye on this, will you?" Diego said, and threw her the Presence.

She caught the device with one hand and placed it in her front pocket. "It's unlocked. Set it later when needed," he said. She nodded and saluted. "Yes, Director Rojo."

Quinn observed the exchange in silence, then leaned on the vehicle, surveying the valley below.

"Maui?" she asked. "Analysis is my line of work. There's only one ancestral line that carries those eyes, and it's from a group of Irish-Americans who lived in Hawaii for hundreds of years."

"Correct, Agent O'Rourke. My parents and their parents lived in Maui before the Polar Shift. Most of the islands disappeared when the Antarctic ice cap disappeared, but Maui was spared. But when the poles shifted, we had to flee Stateside."

Stateside. He was referring to a political division that no longer existed. After the poles shifted, the boundaries in the United States disappeared. The Rivers widened, and waters dividing the land were the only boundaries still tangible. The Eastern states' coastlines from Rhode Island to Florida eroded inland, and California crumbled between the fault lines running from the Mendocino coast to the Salton Sea.

"Which River Coalition did you finally land in?" she asked. She wanted to correct Quinn, but didn't have the heart to do it.

"Ohio River Coalition. Texas." He stood up, and coughed. Cigarette smoke was drifting over them. He fanned it back toward his comrades.

"I really can't understand smoking," Quinn said.

His eyes were so arresting. When she was sure Lt. Quinn was looking elsewhere, she glanced at him from head to foot. And then he turned to her and laughed.

"Not what you think an AIP is, eh?" Quinn asked.

"I'm sorry. Was I so obvious? Please accept my apologies. I have a Sollus sister named Ira, and a Simplex sister named Eilish," she said.

"Oh cool. You're used to us then." Quinn turned and scanned the horizon.

"I don't see an us between me and Ira. And with you," she said in an impatient tone.

Brice closed her eyes and kept them closed a few seconds. She hadn't been sleeping well. Around her were the voices of the soldiers, joking, laughing, conversing. For the past six months, she had primarily been working alone. Transferred from one uninhabitable island to another, she'd missed the camaraderie of working with a group of people. She was thankful Director Rojo had used his considerable clout to include her in this field investigation.

When she finally opened her eyes, Quinn was staring at her. And she stared back.

Robot, sentient droids were antiquated terms. Those

words were derogatory terms. It was actually a crime to use them in the River Coalitions, even if the being in question belonged to the Homo Roboticus genus.

When she hesitated, he turned the question focus to her. "Did you come all the way from the Colony, or somewhere else?" he asked.

Jesus Christ, she thought. "You know I can't tell you," she said. "That info is also classified."

Time to change the subject again. She pointed to his fatigues. There was an insignia of bamboo trees on his lapel that she had never seen anywhere before. "How about you, Lt. Quinn? Are you from Fort Khan?"

Quinn grinned. "Bamboo represents freedom of spirit, and flexibility. But sorry," he said. "Even for you Colonists, where we've been before Suvarnadvipa – it's classified."

"Touché then," she replied. "I'm the analyst who's analyzing this drone attack, under Director Rojo's direct supervision, of course."

Quinn nodded. "That was part of our briefing today. The signature with no signature. The perfect crime. Why use the antiquated drones? Why use them in the American and Asian River Coalitions? And why in this Godforsaken place?"

"The Colony was able to intercept some intel. We're following some leads. Quinn, I dare say, you should be an agent of the Colony. I feel under siege with your questions," she said.

Quinn pulled a flask from his pocket and raised it to his mouth. He grinned. "Let me see. You're a detainee, and yet Director Diego hands you these important tasks. How does the Colony trust you?"

She waved at the device buzzing near her head. "Easy,"

she said. "I'm constantly monitored by the Bee."

He nodded, and then he turned to face the view of the distant mountains. "I heard we're the first foreigners to set foot in this place since the Great Migration."

She followed his gaze to the valley. It was bereft of humanity; even the planting fields were empty. "It's incredible that a country that once had 200 million people has just a fifth of the population left. I read that a haze of smoke blanketed Indonesia even before the Polar Shift, owing to the thousands of rubber plantations burned to clear the fields for planting. Is that true?" he asked.

"After the poles shifted, the proud archipelago of 13,000 islands was reduced to fifty, and the haze remained, rendering most islands uninhabitable. I've been to twenty islands so far these past months, and it's hopeless." She fingered the collar of her burn suit, tugging at its restrictiveness.

The sound of other vehicles coming from the compound distracted them, and the Echo Commander came running to the lead pick-up.

"We're allowed to go nearer," he said. "Let's go, let's go!" The troops who were loitering lazily a minute before now snapped into action. As they ran to the Hovercraft the atmosphere felt suddenly tense.

She noticed Quinn looking at the side of her uniform. "You don't have a weapon," he said. She pointed at the weapon strapped on her waist. "Don't worry, I'm good," she said.

Quinn whistled. "That's just some sugary nonsense of a popgun. Want another kind of Bad Mama?" She shook her head. "Not allowed. I'm good with this," she answered.

The road became narrow, and then the vista opened up, and a spectacular scene floated in front of them. The valley below was filled with green vegetation, mostly coconut trees with heavy fruit hanging from them. Distant mountains seemed to enclose the land in a protective embrace.

When their vehicle came to a jolting, unexpected stop, the hair on the back of Brice's head rose. She ducked by instinct. When a blast of wind hit them, she reached for her weapon and triggered a shot.

In a millisecond, the team was safely encased in a protective bubble. But all around the vehicle came the sounds of gunfire. And the other Echo vehicle did not have the protective covering of the Azukal.

"Halt!" She heard one of the Sollus soldiers from the other Hovercraft shout. "Echo 2, Beetle Bugs. Stop firing! Soldiers on your left. Bearing packages." She reached again for her weapon and fired, and the protective bubble disappeared.

"Halt!" Colonel Riggs's commanding voice was heard again, and then she saw two men and a woman standing next to the road. They had their hands on top of their heads in a gesture of surrender, and their faces were wrapped in cloth. The Echo soldiers from the first vehicle were training their weapons on them.

"Prisoners? But where did they come from?" he whispered to her.

She whispered back. "Han soldiers?"

She knew at a glance that they were not from the North Korean peninsula. But then, one of the prisoners looked familiar.

Her heartbeat felt like clanging cymbals. Could it possibly be him?

The sharp voice of Diego jolted her.

"O'Rourke, set up that darned Presence," Diego ordered. "I need intel on this. And everyone, cover your faces, damn it! If they're Han, they might hunt you down and retaliate!" His barking voice prompted her to unfreeze. She opened the Presence device. And then she pulled a ski mask from her pocket and put it on.

In a second, the Suvarnadvipa Station was linked to the Colony, the three terminals floating on air in the middle of an active field scene.

The analysts were chattering excitedly. "O'Rourke, unmask the prisoners!" one told her. Moving like an automaton, she approached the three.

"Minister O'Rourke is joining us from the Colony," Diego said, now behind her. While the rest of the soldiers were guarding the perimeter, Quinn stayed near her and Director Rojo.

Brice approached the first prisoner. As she reached for his head covering she noticed her hands were shaking. And then the cloth was off, and there he was. Hari. She hadn't seen his face in six months.

The other analysts from the Colony recognized him as well. "Hari Salim, Hari Salim, Hari Salim! Shit, we have to arrest this dude!" one yelled.

Before she could stop herself, her hands moved toward him. But she never touched Hari. A sudden jet of liquid spurted from something he held in his hand and covered Brice from head to foot. Within seconds, it formed into a thick web. And then she heard a loud piercing sound that seemed to come from the other side of the mountain. The sound was so powerful that she saw one of the soldier's robotic arms unhinge from its socket and fall onto the dirt.

The sky darkened, and when she looked up, Brice saw what looked like a flock of birds approaching. But as they drew closer, she could see they were actually human beings with gigantic mechanical wings flapping at their backs.

"I've come to bring you home, Brice," he said, and he put his arms around her. She felt herself airborne.

She felt a pulling feeling near her feet. Quinn had caught hold of the web and was becoming airborne as well.

And then she saw that Quinn had a knife and was hacking the webbing strands around her. The web lines loosened, and she and Quinn fell back to the ground. The last thing she saw before she hit was Hari's horrified face as she fell away from him.

She felt a hard thud as she hit, but the webbed rubber that was wrapped around her body saved her from injury. But Quinn wasn't so lucky. The impact blew out both his arms and legs. She screamed for help, and when her Bee appeared above her, she was for the first time grateful to see it. She knew help would be there in a matter of seconds.

"Hey soldier, stay with me." She placed two fingers on his inner wrist and felt Quinn's pulse. It was faint. "Echo, you're going to survive this," she said.

Then she looked up at the sky.

Hari's gone, was the last thing she thought before she lost consciousness.

CHAPTER

Concordia Island,

Palawan River Coalition

Philippines

Asian River Coalitions

2 May 2058

13 years, 2 months, 30 days before the Drone Strike

The ground shook, but she held on to her hidden perch as the other children shoved each other as they rushed to the cliff's edge. And then one by one, they jumped into the water with nary a hint of fear in their faces. To them, the sea was their playground.

"Hey Eilish, come here and hide!" she called.

A tiny elfin face looked up at her. She smiled. Eilish's clothes had become disheveled, showing the glassinex parts of her anatomy.

"Come on over here. You'll be seen where you are," she said.

She pulled Eilish into her hidden, leafy lair and fixed her clothes, tugging her shirt sleeves over the shiny wrists, and socks up over knobbed knees.

"Brice, why do I need all these clothes?" Eilish said. "At home..."

"We're not at home, Eilish. We're out here to play."

Eilish turned to her. "Who are we playing with? We're always up in the trees. I want to go home."

"Hush, Eilish," she snapped. "Don't move!"

Eilish sat down and hummed to herself.

Pulling a leaf from her own hair, she balanced precariously on a branch. Hidden in the sturdy branches of the mango tree, she intended to stay that way until the last rays of the sun vanished and the other kids ran back to their homes. Her family had left Antarctica, the coldest and windiest continent on earth, only six months before. Palawan, located in the western part of the Philippines, was a balmy tropical paradise, but it was still shocking for her to leave the house in the thinnest of garments and flip flops.

A tall, gangly boy passed their tree, and she turned to stare. Eilish started humming, "Brice is in love, Brice is in love..."

"Eilish, hush! What do you know of love?"

"You look at Hari with gaga eyes, Brice, like in the movies."

"And why do you know his name, Eilish?"

"I may not be as intelligent as you, but I'm not blind and deaf. I'm tired of following him," Eilish muttered and refused to look at her. Was that anger in her tone? Did she bring it too far?

"I love you, Eilish. I'm sorry I went too far."

"I love you, Brice," she answered.

For months, she had spied on the movement of the children in Concordia. But there was one particular boy she followed closely. A gaggle of younger children followed him around, and every day he led them to the Isadora Caves. Her mother and father forbade her to go to the caves, but she couldn't help herself. She followed Hari there.

She often saw Hari helping children climb up the steep steps that led to the entrance of the caves. He helped each and every child who needed it, calming the nerves of the younger ones, and admonishing the older ones to behave.

"Eilish," she called, as she slid down from the mango tree, and they followed Hari once again to the caves. The stairs were long and the children he was with complained about the climb they were about to make. "Listen, count with me," Hari told them. "It's just ninety steps. And when we get to the entrance, there's a hidden rope we have to pull." As she watched, unobserved, more than anything she wanted to be the child he was speaking to.

Hari stepped on leaves and twigs strewn below the trees. Suddenly there was silence. Hari had stopped walking and was standing in the path, facing her.

"Hey, you!" he said, and with one movement, she turned and grabbed Eilish and ran with her to their usual hiding place in the mango tree. The girls climbed quickly.

A sudden crack of breaking twigs came from below. "Don't move, they're going past us," she warned Eilish. She placed a forefinger on her lips, but she knew that would probably just make Eilish ask loud questions about why she needed to be quiet.

Brice pointed at a tree branch below them. "Look at that amazing Komodo," she said. It worked. Eilish stared at the lizard, and started singing to herself. She was very easy to distract.

Because Eilish belonged to Homo Roboticus Simplex, sometimes she felt guilty about how easily she could outwit and outsmart her. The Polar Shift was almost two years ago, and while she was about to turn eight years old, Eilish remained at the mental age of six. Sentient droids were not allowed to age, and because Eilish was the sister she never had, Brice often raged at the unfairness of it all. Her company had been lifesaving when they'd moved to the Philippines, a place utterly foreign to her in every possible way.

Most of the other kids on Concordia were natives of the island, and her green eyes had elicited derision and laughter from her classmates. The children were not nice to her, and since she couldn't speak their language yet, school was difficult, and she could not join in their games. Brice preferred instead to sit in hidden perches where she could scientifically observe the children. She could listen as well, and bit by bit, try to teach herself their difficult language.

Nearly all of the Philippines' 7,700 islands had disappeared after the Polar Shift two years before. Palawan Province's 1000 islands had not fared well. Only Luzon, the remote island of Concordia and the tip of Mt. Apo in Mindanao had remained intact.

Concordia was a lone island outpost on the Philippine archipelago's western tip. Even before the Polar Shift, it had been almost untouched by humankind. The island was not big enough to have its own airport, and was devoid of the white, sandy beaches tourists love. Chain hotels had come and gone, bankrupted time and time again when their edifices were blown away by wind and sea. Typhoons seemed to visit every month, bringing days of unbearable rain, encasing the island in gloomy foul weather most of the time. Small wonder the children jumped with joy when good weather rolled in for a few days.

Her mother had forced her to go to the local school to help her learn the local language. She managed to learn a few Filipino words but suspected that if her mother heard her utter them, she would be spanked.

Her hiding tree started to shake, and when she looked down she saw two boys were rocking it, trying to topple them from their perch.

"Puti, bumaba ka!" one shouted. She knew what they were saying. They were hurling insults. "Puti," or white, referred to her white skin; Brice had heard that insult more than once.

Her skin was fairer than that of the people surrounding her and though her hair had been light brown in the Antarctic, it had turned darker since they'd moved to Concordia, and her slightly almond eyes showed the Filipino roots of her grandmother Isabela. When the boys wouldn't stop shaking the mango tree, she folded up her shirtsleeves and insulted them back. "Ulol!" she answered, and the two boys laughed, because she'd uttered a cuss word.

She picked a ripe mango, peeling it with slow, deliberate strokes until the fruit came out. She took two bites and shrugged, then dropped the fruit onto the boys. She heard cursing below, then silence. Brice swung to another branch of the tree. She found hard green mangoes there, picked them, and threw them down too. She was sure she hit the blockheads. The tree stopped moving, and for a minute or two all was quiet, except for the sound of children's happy shouts nearby. She peered into that scene with a glance.

It was a hot day and they were jumping one by one from the cliffs, screaming with joy as they plunged into the refreshing water.

The shaking started again. The boys were back.   "Hey you, who are you?" one asked. "Why are you following us? Are you a person or a ghost?" Then a barrage of green objects flashed toward her. As the hard mangoes hit her, she felt her legs losing their grip around the branches. And then she heard a small, high-pitched voice below her.

"You're Hari, right? And you're Amil. What do you want with Brice?" Eilish had slipped unnoticed to the ground, where she was standing, fists drawn. She looked ready to fight.

"How do you know our names?" the older of the boys asked.

"I see you every day, and Brice... Brice says your name. Hari, Amil, Hari, Amil..."

"Arrrrgh, Eilish, shut up." She took one mango and threw it to Eilish.

"Whohohoa...who is this creature with glass legs?" Amil asked in perfect English. He started running around Eilish in circles. He took off his shirt, and waved it like a victory flag, all the while thumping his fist on his chest. The older boy stood transfixed.

Eilish taunted. Her arms were crossed. "What, you haven't seen an AIP before, fools?"

"I've never seen a droid. But I've heard about them. Are you as strong as they say you are?" Hari asked.

"Of course I am. Why don't you try me?" Eilish brought her arms up in a fighting stance.

"Then let's, shall we?" Amil darted behind her and grabbed her hands, then quickly tied them with his t-shirt. "I've always wanted one for mys..." he started to say.

He wasn't able to finish his sentence.

"Hari! Hari! Amil?" an adult male voice called. "What are you two rascals doing..." the voice stopped, and the younger of the boys scampered away like a wild animal. The older one seemed frozen in fear.

"Untie her, Hari. Next time I see either of you taunt a helpless girl like this, I'll be tying rocks to both of your hands and dropping you off in the Palawan Sea."

The man was thin, like many in the island who either fished or farmed. Brice thought that he was the handsomest man she had ever seen, with curly hair and dark eyes set behind long, long lashes. He wore a uniform and his voice was deep and resonant. Brice imagined that he was a commander of a thousand troops, each soldier kneeling down in abject adoration of such a handsome hero.

With astonishment, she saw the older boy who had pelted her with mangoes was slowly approaching him.

And then the man embraced the child. He whispered something in his ear, and took his hand. They walked toward the tree where she was rooted, and the man called up to her. She was amazed that he knew her name.

"Brice, little girl. You can come down now," he coaxed in English. "Your father told me where to find you. I'm Tio Dio."

"I'm Eilish!" a pert voice piped up beside them. "I'm Brice's friend. Pleased to meet you."

Dio smiled and held out his hand. "Can you call your friend to come down from the tree?"

"Brice... Brice! Come down, Tio Dio wants to meet you."

Her secret was out. How did her father know where she'd been hiding every afternoon? She had no recourse but to go down.

She wiped her face and patted her hair, which yielded a mango leaf or two. She smoothed the folds in her dress, a simple summer shift that seemed to be getting shorter by the minute as she was growing rapidly. Slowly, she climbed down the tree.

The man who called himself Tio Dio was standing at its roots with one of the boys who had been torturing her. "Brice, this is Kuya Hari," the man said, pushing the older boy forward. "He'll be a big brother to you and Eilish. He'll always protect you two, you hear? We protect each other here in Concordia. Hari...where is your cousin, Amil? He scampered away like a coward!" Hari's father shook his head, then stared at her.

She returned his gaze.

They looked alike, she thought. One was shorter and with a thinner frame, the other taller and more muscular. But they had the same wavy hair and brown, gentle eyes.

She offered her gap-toothed smile to Hari.

"I'm off to meet your father right now, Brice," Dio said. "Would you like to walk with us? Of course you too, Eilish." He pointed toward a woven basket on the ground that was bursting with mangoes. "Hari, we'll bring this to the O'Rourkes."

Hari expertly slung the heavy basket onto his head. But it wasn't easy to walk with it, and he looked like he was on the brink of falling down. After a few strides, Dio took the basket from Hari and put it on his own head.

Hari started to giggle. She started giggling too. The

image of a stern military man in uniform balancing a basket was too much for the children.

Tio Dio Salim just egged them on. He started swaying and singing, "I yi yi yi like you verrrry much, I yi yi yi think you're grand." Giggles turned to guffaws, and the children were all laughing. Eilish didn't understand the joke, but she started to laugh when Brice did.

The O'Rourkes heard the approaching laughter and ran to the front porch of their house. But there were two strangers with them. One wore a beard and looked familiar, and then she realized he resembled her Grandpa Daelan.

"Uncle Avila," she ran to hug her uncle.

"When did you come back from the mi-ri-ta-ri?" Eilish squealed, and jumped up and down.

"Oh, I've graduated since then, Eilish," Avila hugged her.

"Why are you so dark and thin, Uncle Avila?" Eilish asked, then pointed to the stranger beside him. "Who is he?"

"Eilish, manners please," her mother admonished her.

"I'm now with the Colony," Avila said, then faced his family. "Meet my boss, George Mallard."

George Mallard was tall and handsome with salt and pepper hair. When he grinned, his eyes nearly disappeared, leaving only a lopsided smile.

"What's a boss, Uncle Avila? What's a Colony?" Eilish tugged at Avila's shirt.

"He's the person ordering me around in the office, Eilish," Avila said, as he squatted and patted Eilish's head.

"What's an office, Uncle Avila?" she said, and laughed and kissed Eilish on the cheek. "It's where you go to earn some money to feed and house your dear old Uncle Avila." Avila then made monkey sounds, and started scratching his stomach. The girls ran in pretend horror as

Avila lunged at them.

"Oh no no no," her mother declared from the family dining room. "What a mess you two are! Before you run away and play with Uncle Avila, you need to come inside and clean up." She gestured at Brice. Her face registered alarm when she glanced at Eilish, whose dress was streaked with mud and leaves. And then Hari's father spoke.

"My apologies, Dr Esteban and Dr. Mira. There was an incident with Eilish and my boy, but it will never happen again on this island, I assure you." He stepped forward and gestured at his son, and with his eyes, prodded an apology from him.

"I'm sorry, Eilish," Hari found his voice. "It's the first time Amil and I saw a... an..." he had difficulty saying it.

"Droid?" Eilish's gaze settled on him.

"No, Eilish. You're no longer allowed to be described that way," Esteban said in a soft tone.

"She's an AIP, idiot. Don't call her a droid," Brice said. "Artificial Intelligent Person. And until I hear you and Amil say sorry, I won't forgive either of you. Let's go, Eilish." She'd started to drag Eilish out the door, when her mother stopped her.

"Brice, you are crude and rude. What will Eilish learn from you, dear child? Let's declare a truce, shall we? Please apologize for your behavior to the Salim family and to your Uncle Avila and to Mr. Mallard as well," her mother admonished.

Brice had no interest in apologizing. But her uncle was looking at her with a grin on his face. When he winked, she extended a hand toward Hari.

"I'm sorry for being rude, Tio Dio, K...k...Kuya Hari..." Kuya was a Tagalog word for older brother, but because of the way he'd treated Eilish, she found it hard to use it. She tried again and turned to the others in the room. "Uncle Avila and Mr. Mallard," she said, reluctantly.

Hari smiled and extended his hand to Eilish, who grasped it with eagerness.

"Now that's settled, Colonel Salim, please meet my brother Avila and George Mallard from the American River Coalitions." Dio Salim warmly shook the visitors' hands.

"Now, tell me, Colonel Salim," her mother said, "what brings you to this neighborhood?"

"Dr. Esteban invited me to your home to meet your guests. I heard there's news about the aggressive Hans and their weaponized Machinas."

And then Dio Salim noticed how eagerly the children were listening. "We can talk about this later," he said, and switched topics. "The village's annual Mango Feast Day is tomorrow. There will be a parade around town with colorful floats, each sponsored by a different family. After, there will be a feast featuring different kinds of mango dishes. I was wondering if Brice and Eilish could grace our family float, and be mangoes for an hour?" Esteban smiled at the girls beside him.

"What do you say, ladies?" he said.

"Could I be a yellow mango, Tio Dio?" Eilish piped up without prodding.

"Eilish, what's the magic word, my dear?"

"Please, Tio Dio?" Eilish said, and tugged at his shirt. Colonel Salim, who'd seemed so stern when he was reprimanding his son, looked at Eilish with a smile.

"Of course, Eilish. You'll be plump, juicy and ripe mango then. And you, Brice?"

When she didn't quickly respond, her mother nudged her.

"I hope she won't be a very sour, green mango, Dio. But Brice will be there with bells on."

"That's settled, then. See you at the float tomorrow," Dio said. And he turned to leave.

"I've prepared so much food for Avila and his guest. Why don't you stay for dinner? The children can get to know one another more. And I'm very interested in all the Han news."

Dio smiled and nodded, and Mira led them all to the dining room, as the children ran to the table.

The sound of church bells ringing very early in the morning started the next day's activities.

Soon, the O'Rourkes' home was inundated by a steady stream of traveling vendors selling a variety of breakfast Food made from mango: sticky black rice with dried fish and sour mangoes wrapped in banana leaves; soft, sweet, gelatinous tofu with caramelized mangoes as topping; pickled green mangoes; deep-fried bananas and mangoes on barbecue sticks; the dishes were endless. The array was dizzying, and Eilish and Brice flitted from one vendor to another, lifting the light cloth covering the food baskets, oohing and aaahing at what they were selling.

A loud sound erupted in the distance, a noise of clashing trumpets and cymbals, and people started shouting and running to the middle of the road. It was time for the floats.

Everyone clapped and cheered at the sight of the first one, which featured a statue of the Virgin Mary carrying a basket of mangoes.

As the float passed, a rain of candies showered down, and Brice felt a tap on her shoulder. It was Hari. He was wearing a yellow shirt and a funny headdress shaped like a mango. "You're late," he said. "Grab my right hand, Brice. And you, Eilish, you can grab my left. Ready, set, let's go!" And he ran them through the crowd.

When they reached his family's float they were greeted by the sight of Amil wearing a green mango suit. The girls burst out laughing.

Dio was driving the tow vehicle, and he leaned out to wave. Beside Dio was a beautiful lady who was wearing a colorful headdress made to look like ripe mangoes in a bowl.

"Mama, Mama!" Hari ran to her, dragging the two girls with him. "Meet my two friends, Brice and Eilish O'Rourke!"

"Call me Tia Noor," his mother said. "You girls are beautiful! I prepared your headdresses like mine, with ripe mangoes in a bowl. You can wear yellow shirts and pants. Is that all right?"

The girls nodded.

"Let me help you," Noor said. Brice took the yellow shirt and pants and dressed herself, as Tia Noor struggled to dress up Eilish, whose stiff limbs resisted the shirt and pants. When she offered to help, Noor just smiled.at her. "Go and join the boys!" she said, and waved her off.

She ran towards Hari and Amil, but stopped in her tracks, pointed at Amil, and started laughing again.

"You think this is funny?" Amil said and wagged a finger

at her. "Put your headdress on. Let's see who's laughing then!" When she and Eilish were finished dressing, Hari reached down and pulled them onto the float.

And then it was time to get going.

Amil started waving to the crowd, while Hari scooped some candies from a bag and threw them. He was greeted with squeals of delight. She and Eilish copied him, scooping up the candies and throwing them to the crowds.

Once or twice, people pointed fingers at her, shouting "Puti, puti!" When she stuck her tongue out at the mean strangers, some laughed, while others wagged a finger back at her.

The sun was blazingly hot, and after driving around town for hours in the mango suit, everyone was sweaty and exhausted. Finally, the parade headed to the church patio for the final blessing by the priest. As soon as floats were parked, Hari and Amil slid off.

"C'mon, Brice and Eilish," Hari said. "It's so hot. Let's go jump off the cliff. Last one in is an ugly monkey!"

Hari and Amil scampered off as though they were being pursued by hungry beasts. She grabbed Eilish's hand and ran after them.

But when she reached the edge of the cliff, she hesitated. Eilish followed her gaze to the place where the sand met the sea.

"Whooooah, Brice," Eilish said. "This is a pretty big drop. But I wish we could join the other kids and just jump."

"Well, why don't you go yourself, Eilish?" she taunted. The view was making her dizzy.

"You know I can't go far from you, Brice. Mama told me

a million times," Eilish was about to start a spiel on the rules from home, when Brice cut her off.

"Oh, grow up, Eilish," she snapped. Instantly, she regretted it. Eilish looked at her uncomprehendingly and Brice brought her hands to her mouth as if to press back her words. "I didn't mean to say that," she said. But it was too late.

"What does grow up mean, Brice?" Eilish asked. She just shook her head. How could she explain this to her? And why should she have to? Why couldn't Eilish just grow up with her?

"I'll be nine in a few months," she said. "I don't understand why you can't you grow up with me, Eilish."

"I'm six, Brice. And what's wrong about staying six all my life?"

She couldn't explain the difference. She didn't really understand it herself. But the last thing she wanted to do was make Eilish feel bad. "Never mind. C'mon, let's jump!"

"What? Really? Won't I break?" Eilish said.

"Really. I'll set you to swim mode." She opened a control panel on the back of her neck and moved a switch. "Done! Now, time to jump that darn cliff!" She turned Eilish around, and grabbed her by the shoulders. "Mama said you're made of stuff that lets you float on water. Now, let's go!"

They walked together to the edge of the cliff.

Hari spotted them. "C'mon Brice, jump!" he said in a taunting voice. And then the other children started taunting her too. They were chanting another word she didn't know, but she had a feeling it wasn't a compliment.

"Duwag!" her tormentors called to her, and stuck their

tongues out as one by one they jumped to the waters below.

Hari sidled up next to Eilish. "That means coward," he said. "C'mon. You have to help me save face. They think I'm not a good leader if you stay here like scared monkeys." He grabbed her hand and beckoned to her. "Let's go," he said. "I'll help." And he stretched out his hands.

She started to pull away, but Hari took hold of her hand. "Just close your eyes. I won't let go in the water. Are you ready?"

She could see the other children were snickering, and lunch money was changing hands. They were gambling on what she'd do. But finally, she was determined to do it.

Squeezing her eyes shut, she said a prayer, and jumped. As she flew through the air, she had an unexpected feeling of incredible exhilaration.

The last thing she heard was Eilish's high-pitched squeal as they hit the water. She caught a glimpse of Hari's smiling face submerged in the deep aquamarine, and he flashed a thumbs-up sign. They swam to the surface together.

From the cliff side, they heard the sounds of clapping and shouting. The three began to swim toward shore.

Suddenly the clapping stopped. "Look, look," a boy said, pointing toward the sea. An armada of huge ships had appeared. There were smaller boats near the ships, and they were heading toward land. The men rowing them worked in perfect synchrony. From a distance, the rowers had similar features, with almond eyes and jet-black hair. She couldn't put her finger on why this sight disturbed her. But Eilish knew at a glance.

"Are they AIPs too, Brice?" Eilish said.

Beside the ships was a small flotilla of air-floating pods.

They were shaped like an inverted bowl, and colored red with drawings of ancient-looking snakes slithering over them.

Like the rowers, the bodies of the soldiers in the pods had been molded to perfection, and their faces wore identical furrowed expressions. Their uniforms, however, were bright red, not the dull green of the robots in the boats.

There was a sudden tooting sound so loud it made her cover her ears. Behind the armada of ships was a single monster of a vessel. It seemed to be filled with ordinary people, not robots, because they were waving and jumping up and down.

"Why do they look so happy? Who are they?" she asked Hari.

Hari looked worried. "We'd better hurry back," he said. "I have to tell my father about this." And he turned and swam toward land. Once he reached the shore, he ran toward the village, his wet clothes leaving a trail of drip marks on the sand.

She picked up Eilish and carried her, so as not to waste time. She decided to follow Hari.

As they approached the town square, they saw it was filled with more droid soldiers. One of them was facing village menfolk, holding a weapon that looked like a small cannon.

He was speaking a language that seemed familiar but she couldn't place it. Grandpa Daelan had practiced rudimentary Mandarin with her during their long winter spells in Antartica, and though this language sounded similar, it wasn't Mandarin.

And then she heard someone answering the soldier

impudently. She froze in her tracks. The voice was her father's.

One soldier was very tall. The color of his uniform was the same hue as the eggplants her mother forced her to eat once a week. His hair was tied in a knot on top of his head, and the weapon at his side was smallish, but it looked very deadly because it was pointed at her father. And then her father raised his hands in surrender.

Hari turned when she came up behind him. "What will they do with him?" she cried.

"Let's climb into that tree. Hurry!" Hari said and hoisted them up the branches of a large mango tree. The other children who had come running from the beach didn't follow his orders, but instead ran back to their homes.

From their perch, they could see both the harbor and the town square. An army of tents had been set up in the field near the square. As they watched, the monster ship docked and hundreds of men, women, and children got off it and scampered toward the tents, as if to claim them as their own. But there didn't seem to be enough tents to hold them all. Fight after fight broke out, and suddenly, they were all battling.

A loud shout caught her attention back to the town center. "Kneel!" a soldier shouted.

Concordia's mayor had his hands up, while her father was kneeling as ordered.

A short, rotund man who walked with an uneven gait seemed to be in command. He was definitely human.

"I am Colonel Kang Chul-Moo," he said, "and this is Captain Lee Jae Seung," and he indicated the droid soldier with the violet uniform. "We come in peace from North Korea, with the Han River Coalition."

"Pssst, psssst!" It was Uncle Avila with his boss George Mallard at the base of the mango tree.

"Come down fast!" he said. The three of them complied.

"Uncle Avila, what's happening?" she started crying. Her uncle embraced her.

"Now, listen to me," he said. "The Han soldiers won't touch your father because he's a scientist. Here's the plan. Brice and Hari, George and I are going back there to get your fathers. Your job is to collect all the children and bring them to the caves. Your mothers are on their way there. When I get Dio and Esteban, we will take them to the caves. If we don't show up soon, we will meet later in another place your mother knows, Brice. Now, go!"

It was the first time she had heard the word "Han." Were they the people in the boats?

As they started running, they passed trucks full of droid soldiers.

"Follow me!" Hari said and led them onto a pathway that passed through rice fields ready to be harvested. The tall stalks provided good cover.

"How far will it be, Kuya Hari?" she asked. She was getting tired. She was carrying Eilish in her arms again.

"Just be patient," Hari replied. "We're almost there."

He stopped and crouched low. She heard the humming calls of birds and the soft clicking sounds of komodo dragons.

"Tuk...o! Tuko!" Hari called, copying the sounds of the animal. After a few seconds, someone answered with the same clucking sound.

From the shadows, a group of women emerged. Crying with relief, she ran to her mother, who had tears running down her face; her eyes were wild with terror.

"How did you get here? Where's your father?" her mother asked.

"Uncle Avila... told me to run here," she said. "Papa is in the town plaza, with the mayor. Uncle Avila marched toward Papa to save him. He said he'll be safe because they won't touch a scientist."

Her mother grabbed her in a tight embrace. Brice felt the wetness of her tears on her shoulder. Then her mother pulled away, as if she'd made a decision.

"Avila won't leave his brother, Brice. But we have to go inside the caves while there's light. There's no time to waste." And taking her hand, she began to pull her down the path.

"Mira, in here," a voice said. "Follow the light." It was Noor Salim, Hari's mother. She was waiting for them near the mouth of the cave. "As the tide rises, it will engulf the entrance," she said. "We'd better hurry."

She looked at the dark crevice Noor Salim was pointing at, and shivered.

It was the same cave she had seen Hari teaching the little children to explore. The dark, slippery caverns were too dangerous, they were told. But in times of danger, they were also the safest place to be. Locals told many tales of foreigners invading the tiny island of Concordia only to lose, time and again, to the natives who'd outwitted them by hiding in these very caves. But invaders who tried to navigate them without a local guide either drowned inside them or got lost and died of starvation or madness.

The secrets to safely navigating the labyrinthine cave passageways were passed through the generations, and only the Concordia native-born knew how to survive in this place.

"Brice, come on. There's no time to waste," Noor Salim called, her face full of concern.

She heard Hari's mom calling out her name, but she hesitated. When would she see her father again? And then she sighed and followed Hari and his mother through the entrance of the cave.

Inside, day turned into night and darkness and eerie silence greeted them. And then came a tiny spark of light. Someone had lit a gas lamp.

The light grew brighter, and Brice saw that an enormous group of people was bunched near the entrance. Men, women, and children in various states of distress were huddled together, and many were crying and shaking their heads. Every child looked bewildered and lost.

The group looked up when Noor Salim spoke. "Mga kababayan, kaya natin ito. Tinuruan tayo ng ating mga ninuno kung anong gagawin sakaling mangyari ito. Tayo na, ako na ang bahala sa inyo," she said.

Brice could only understand a little of what she was saying, but she seemed to be assuring her neighbors that the lessons their ancestors had passed on to them in case of foreigner attack would save them. "Come on. I'll lead the way, so don't worry," Noor said to her mother in English.

And then Noor gestured to the huddled group before her. "We have to keep moving back, since a lot of us will be seeking shelter here. Just hold on to one another. Soon, the boats will be ready, and it will be time to leave."

She turned to her mother. "Why are we leaving Dad and Uncle Avila?" she cried. "I don't understand."

"Daddy and Uncle Avila will figure out a way to find us. We will pray for that," her mother whispered to both of them. "We have to remain strong, like all the O'Rourkes. Now, let's join all the families."

She wanted to weep. Her mind kept replaying images of that robot soldier pointing a gun at her father's head. Deep inside, she knew they were in a hopeless situation, but she also knew she had to act strong so her mother wouldn't worry about her.

Her Uncle Avila and his boss George seemed determined to save her father. She glanced at Eilish who was held tight in her mother's arms. Eilish would march toward the soldiers, risking her life to save her, if she had to. Brice would perform the same for Eilish, her mother, and her father.

The thought made her smile. They were a spunky family, the O'Rourkes. Maybe her father and uncle would survive after all.

Avila

As soon as he saw that the children had fled to safety, he and George Mallard scrambled up the mango tree to observe the scene unfolding in the town square.

The soldiers were clearly Machinas, the robotic soldiers weaponized by the Hans that he and Mallard had been pursuing for the past six months. He pulled a tiny straw-like viewing device from his pocket, placed one end to his eye, and the scene became clear. He focused the device on his brother, and the mayor who was standing beside him.

The Colony, the Defense Intelligence arm of the United States, had tapped him six months before to spy on these droids. He had scoured the world in search of them.

After the Polar Shift two years ago, his plans to follow in his father's footsteps as a geologist had been abandoned, and he'd entered the American River Coalition's Special Forces, despite Esteban's disapproval.

When South Korea unleashed a nuclear bomb on its northern enemy in 2052, 106,000 people died in the city of Kyushimo. North Korea signed the Korea Armistice in 2054, and abandoned war on all fronts, on paper. But in secret, instead of embracing the coalition's offer of help to rebuild their country, North Korea became embittered, turned more inward, and started the hidden, aggressive pursuit of sentient robots as weapons.

In the Mumbai Conference for Robotic Laws in 2055, Moscow had urged the International Community to create legal groundwork for Artificially Intelligent Persons, since North Korea's threats of weaponizing them a few years before had caused this issue to become an international concern. The framework they'd arrived at had followed Asimov's three laws: "A robot may not injure a human being or, through inaction, allow a human being to come to harm. A robot must obey orders given it by human beings except where such orders would conflict with the First Law. A robot must protect its own existence as long as such protection does not conflict with the First or Second Law."

North Korea, long a pariah in the international community, continued its robotic program unhindered, with no overseer allowed through its borders to check its robotic programs. As a result, international sanctions were initiated, resulting in food shortages for the majority of the people.

He crouched and observed the soldiers. The foot soldiers looked identical in height and their pale skin, the thin lips and almond eyes. The officers looked different, their heights were different from each other, their eye, nose and lip features were unique and even their hairstyles were not the same. The highest-ranking officer seemed to be the only human being of the group; he was the smallest of the soldiers and his disfigured face offered a variety of expressions. The one it was currently wearing was anger.

Esteban's hands were raised high. So were the mayor's, but suddenly he wrapped his arms around his abdomen and vomited at his feet. The Machinas whacked his head at this inopportune movement. Another soldier approached and ordered the soldiers to stop. He had a different uniform, his was darker, aubergine. Even his hair was twisted in a bun different from the common soldiers. Definitely an officer.

His eyes shifted to the person on his brother's left. He felt his breath relax a little when he saw that Dio was dressed as an ordinary citizen, and not a highly-ranked soldier of the Pasig River Coalition. Dio had been driving the mango float a few hours before, and his faded shirt, short pants and flip flops were a common get-up for the villagers in Concordia. He wouldn't rate a second glance from the AIPs. That would give him a better chance to guide his brother, a chance for both men to stay alive.

His brother wasn't helping that cause. Esteban was observing the sight in front of him; he could not shut his scientist's observer eyes even at his peril. Don't look too closely on their most-guarded secret, Avila prayed to him. If only he'd just look at the ground.

When his brother, apparently hearing his prayers, actually turned his eyes downward, Mallard dropped from the upper branches of the tree to the ground, beckoning to Avila to follow. Both men crawled toward the cluster of men who were kneeling in front of the Hans.

"Halt!" A soldier shouted and pointed his weapon at the two. Avila and George were forced to walk toward the assembled townfolk.

Colonel Kung Chui-Moo turned to look at them. "What's this? Interesting..." he said. He spoke in perfectly-accented English. "Are you two from the American River Coalition?" The human soldier examined Avila and George. In spite of the fact that Esteban was so darkly-tanned from his work as a geologist that he could pass as a Concordia native, the Colonel barked orders. "Capt. Lee Jae Seung, tie up the interlopers. Now!"

The Machina with the bun grabbed him and Mallard by the collar and threw both of them near Esteban and Dio. George was as white as a sheet as Captain Seung grabbed his shirt and threw him on the ground. Then the Machina started kicking him. When they were finished, he was thrown back near him and Esteban.

The Machinas and their officer huddled together and exchanged whispers, giving him and Esteban a chance to do the same. "Do you realize what we're up against?" Esteban said. "Promise me that you'll look after Mira and Brice, if you make it and I don't. Promise me on the souls of our parents that you'll find a way to bring them out of this country. Promise me, Avila."

"Take him!" he said. He folded to the ground when

Estban kicked the back of his knees. The ruckus attracted the attention of the highest-ranking officer.

The Colonel eyed them. "Well, well, well... what do we have here? Very interesting." He turned to the officer beside him and shouted. "Kill both of these Americanos, Captain Lee. As an example to the town that from this day forward, my words are law."

He closed his eyes when he heard the words. Oh shit. Death at the hands of the Machinas. No, it won't happen. He'd rather be killed escaping rather than staying put and dying in those droid hands.

He glanced at Mallard, and saw that his pants had become wet. He looked away, pained at his humiliation.

He knew he would be executed now, despite his brother's attempt at saving his life.

But Captain Lee surprised him. "I'm sorry, but I cannot follow your instructions," he said. "According to our basic robotic principles, we are not supposed to harm or kill human beings. You can do the killing yourself, Colonel Kang." He stood ramrod-straight, his arms at his side.

The Colonel stepped in front of Captain Seung and slapped his face, and the assemblage of droid-soldiers aimed their guns toward him. Other soldiers started running toward the square. A pair grabbed his arms, and a ruckus ensued as Lee fought them off. The melee was the perfect opportunity to escape.

Mallard ran toward the jungle. Avila took a step toward his brother, but Esteban whispered, "I'm just a scientist, and don't know a thing, but you two will be executed if they find out who you really are. Take care of Mira and Brice. Now go!" Esteban had saved him in Antarctica by pushing him inside the Bubble. Now, he was saving his life again. He knew that it was useless to argue. With reluctance, he turned and followed the path Mallard had taken. He found him waiting just inside the jungle.

Mira had given him directions to the caves when he had tried to look for Brice and Eilish. But he wasn't sure if he would be able to follow them well. The sun was setting and it would be dark soon. But after a few mistakes, he found himself in front of the opening into the caves.

With a sense of enormous relief, he saw a group of children and mothers huddled inside the entrance. Water was swirling there. The tide was rising. He and Mallard put their hands in the air, to indicate kinship. The group of men guarding the entrance quickly recognized them and allowed them into the belly of the cave.

He heard a child's voice. "Uncle Avila, Uncle Avila! Where's father?" It was Eilish. She and Brice and Mira were huddled by a fire.

What could he tell them? How could he look them in the eye? "I offered to exchange myself with Esteban, Mira," his voice almost a whisper. "But he wouldn't let me do it. Esteban told me it was my duty to bring you out of Concordia. But I'll go back for him. I promise." And then, he began to weep.

But Mira didn't seem upset. "We have to stay calm for the children's sake," she said. "Let's focus on escaping. They're planning to leave by midnight."

"Where, and how?" Mallard asked in surprise. The villagers looked like simple folk to him, without any weapons but twigs and rocks.

."We've rehearsed this scenario many times, and we have an evacuation plan," said Noor Salim, who was standing nearby. "Our parents forced us to do it yearly, just in case." And she picked up a gas lamp and held it high, illuminating what looked like a hundred boats lined up against the cave walls.

At nightfall, the Concordia villagers got into their boats and guided them into the small waterway that led to the open sea.

With no light except the stars, they paddled toward nearby Leoncio Island, where another secret cave existed. The plan was to continue their journey this way, island-hopping, until they reached the farthest shores of Vietnam.

With luck, they would make it without detection.

It was hard for him to leave the island without Esteban. He knew Esteban was thinking about their father who had argued on that fateful night to leave Buckminster City so they could all live. As the oldest boy in the family, it was Esteban's duty to bring his youngest brother to safety.

He had promised to Esteban that he would bring his family to the American River Coalitions. He in turn had promised Mira that he would go back to save her husband. He would defeat the Machinas, even if he had to steal their own technology to do it.

Chapter 3

Aboard the USS Golden Wattle

The Edge of the Straits of Singapore

15 August 2071

15 Days after the Drone Strike

Quinn

The sudden bright rays of the sun woke him up, and as he swam back to consciousness, he became aware of the woman sitting beside him. He and the soldiers from his Echo contingent had been flown aboard the USS Golden Wattle, a hospital ship. He had been there for five days, and had escaped from his hospital room to the hospital garden on the fifth deck where he could feel the sun beating at his skin. And that's where he'd fallen asleep.

"Agent Brice! How long have you been here?" he said.

What was in her expression? Pity? Curiosity? His gaze

shifted from her face to body. Something was wrapped around her elbow.

His last distinct memory was both of them flying from the air, and falling to the ground.

"How hurt were you?" he asked, and her expression puzzled him. Brice had a tentative smile, but her eyelids were puffy, and her eyes were red. She had been crying.

He asked again. "Are you okay, Agent Brice?"

She shook her head.

Brice stood up and went to the ship's ledge and stared at the view in front of her.

Water, water all around. This hospital had an incredible view of the ocean. The vast expanse of water stretched to the horizon. The combination of the brightness of the sun and the reflection of the sea at noon illuminated everything to a shining patina.

Except that Brice's face was in shadow. Were her thoughts full of shadows too? He had been intrigued by her the first time she sat beside him in Suvarnadvipa. She was not talkative like some field agents he knew, but quiet, introverted. It was as if her thoughts were stuck in the deepest parts of the ocean. And she was happy leaving them there.

"I was wondering if my timing is off, and you still needed to rest, Quinn," she said at last. Her security Bee, which was hovering around somewhere, settled on her shoulder as she started to speak. "I sought permission to see you." She then pointed at the soldier standing at attention by the door. "I hope you don't mind if I brought more than a Bee this time."

"Oooh, the full platoon this time to guard you?" he said. Her nose wrinkled, and the first hint of a smile appeared on her face.

"Not very funny," she said. "How are the wounds?"

"Oh, my wounds, robotic wounds, to be clear, they are grievous, but I'll survive."

He laughed, then winced. Brice's expression switched to concern. She turned to come toward him, but he waved her off. "Any news on the fugitives who escaped?" he asked. "You know, the ones that tried to grab you?" he added, as if she needed reminding.

"They've disappeared." Brice crossed her arms. Definitely not a topic she wanted to discuss, he noted.

"It was like a surreal, hallucinogenic dream." He paused, gauging her reaction. She did not rise to the bait and offered no answers.

"Hey, I have some good news," he said. "For some reason, Director Diego visited this morning before he went back to Colony HQ in Denver, and asked if I was interested in working at the Colony as an agent."

Brice's expression turned inward again, indecipherable. But it was clear to Quinn that she was not happy with what he said.

"Agent Brice?" Quinn prodded gently. Brice remained silent, and after a minute, she faced him.

"So Director Rojo wants you at the Colony?" she replied. "With a beat-up body. They'll run you to the ground, you know. Director Rojo takes no prisoners. Is that what you want?"

"I guess they must be desperate," he said, and chuckled.

But she shook her head. "Director Rojo has researched your background. The Colony needs your brain, Echo."

"Are there a lot of Sollus in the Colony already?" he asked. "I've been with the Echo, so we've touched on the vital work of Intelligence. I don't know if I have the temperament for it, though. And why are the Intelligence Agencies called the Colony?"

"Oh, it's an insider's joke," she replied. "If and when you visit there, you'll see the agencies are like busy beehives in a bee colony. And no, you're not the first Sollus agent-combatant. The Sollus have done very well even in the Colony. Don't worry. You'll learn fast."

"Was it your idea?" he asked. "Having me there?" He was desperate to break through her walled-off mood.

"Maybe I mentioned it to Director Rojo that you're a good candidate. You know, you're a soldier, an Echo, and you just need to shift from targeting hard combatants to soft targets." When her eyes focused on him, he saw they were like granite. She was an Intelligence agent after all, and she was gauging his reactions, noting it all in her Colony-trained brain.

A loud blare of sound made both of them turn. Another patient had turned the volume up at the common Video Wall. It was showing news images of President George Mallard and Defense Minister Avila O' Rourke pinning a medal on him when they visited the USS Golden Wattle a day ago.

"That's you, Echo. Looking good for the cameras, soldier." A group of soldiers who were near him clapped their hands.

He waved them off, mouthing thank yous as they continued to cheer and clap.

The next images on the screen focused on Mallard attending the WRC on the Amendment to the Mumbai Robotic Laws. His angry, furrowed expression was clearly visible.

"Re-election time. He wants to break away from the

WRC on Robotic Laws," Brice said.

The proposed law change was a big deal. It had been all over the news. It was intended to give an even hand to all Homo Sapiens. Since sentient droids could decide on their 21st birthday whether or not to live forever, all human beings on earth were given the same choice.

"He wants to return to a more natural state in which we're less driven by technology, more by nature," she said. "That's his rhetoric this past year. Definitely anti-robotist."

"He is one unhappy puppy," he said as he stared at Mallard's image on the screen. "You know, he wasn't comfortable with me when he visited. He stiffened, you know?" And with a groan, he stood up, and reached toward Brice.

Brice was about to say something, but then changed her mind. "Nope, he has no love lost for the Roboticus species," she said.

"Our own President is a Homo Roboticus bigot?" he asked. It was clear Brice was not a fan of Mallard.

He gestured toward the guard a few feet from Brice. "Is he Sollus, like me?"

"I can't tell, and I didn't dare ask. It's rude, you know," she whispered then chuckled.

"Have you explored the walled-in garden here? C'mon, you have to see it." He stood up, moving to the side. He saw that she hesitated outside, but walked toward a small walled-in garden with a rippling fountain. There were chairs there to sit on, and Brice sat on one. She then turned toward the ocean.

"I still find all this water absolutely beautiful," he said. "Are you sick of it?"

"I've always loved water," she answered. "But sometimes, I can't wait to go back to the Colony and all those subterranean tunnels there. It's not surface land, but at least tunnels run through it, right?" The wind was blowing her hair, and he thought he had never seen anyone as beautiful as this woman. But her next question threw him off.

"Have you decided on your 21st year decision now that the WRC laws might be changed in the US?" Brice asked.

Was she curious about his answer because she was struggling with her own?

"Of course!" he said. "I want to live forever." His tone was playful, but she didn't respond to it. And then he thought he understood why. "So this isn't a social call. It's part of the interview for the Colony, right?" But she shook her head.

"No, it's not a social call. HQ wanted me to have a full check-up here. I'm being flown back to Colony HQ in Colorado this afternoon. I just wanted to know how you are." She leaned back in her chair, and looked directly at him.

"Maybe Director Rojo wanted me assessed?" he asked. "Maybe this is part of the test." He folded his hands and pretended to grimace.

"Don't flatter yourself," she said. "The Colony has more important tasks than getting a potential recruit to change his views."

He nodded. "My adoptive parents would love to see the family lineage go on and on, forever. I just wanted to be sure I'm making the right decision."

"If I had the choice to live forever," she said, "I would. In the end, Homo Roboticus might just save humanity, not doom it. Tell me, why did you become a soldier? You were a marine biologist before?" she asked, turning to look at him.

"I've always loved the ocean. I wanted to find a way to save the sea creatures from the rising waters. It's increasingly acidic, you know, and so many life-forms can't live in that kind of water." And then he sighed. "But after the Polar Shift, then the Han Invasion, something changed. I realized evil people existed. And I wanted to help protect the good ones any way I could."

He faced Brice and observed her demeanor. She was calm as she asked questions. What was her purpose here, he wondered. "Were you always athletic in school? It helps in the Beast exams, you know," she asked.

"Yes," he said, relieved that some semblance of a playful tone had come back to her voice. "I could outrun anyone." Then he burst out laughing. "It's my robot machinery, I guess. I really loved running, and thought it was such a waste of a gift to not use it."

He reached for his crutches. "This is my perfect cover," he said. "What do you think?"

"A little crippled...but otherwise perfect!" Brice said, as she pretended to check an imaginary notebook.

"As a marine biologist, yes, I follow the rules. But as a spy, world, here I come!" He rubbed his hands together.

"Oh yes, I almost forgot," and she fiddled inside her handbag, and pulled a brown bag from it. "A nurse gave this to me," she said. "It's some of the freshly baked croissants for some VIP in the hospital." She dove inside her bag again and pulled out a knife and a tiny container, and held it all out to him.

She smiled. "Butter with rosemary, or butter with slivers of garlic? Or both?"

"Butter with rosemary, please, mademoiselle," he

grinned. "Is this your way of bribing an agent?"

"Too presumptious," she wrinkled her nose. "You still have to be tested to see if you're Colony material, Quinn." She pulled the croissant in half, bit into one piece, and offered the other one to Quinn.

"Oh, I'll pass. I'm sure of it," he said with confidence.

He bit into his bread. "Mmmmm... delicious," he said.

"I used to bake on lazy afternoons when I knew I had to visit bedridden friends," she replied.

"So your friends often land in hospitals!" he said in mock horror.

"Or mortuaries," she said matter-of-factly. "So this visit deserves bread. Great bread!"

He let out a laugh, then winced. "Try not to make me laugh. It's too painful, you know."

As she handed him another piece of croissant, his fingers brushed against hers. She pulled away quickly, but her face remained expressionless.

He felt an intense jolt of electricity pass between them. Was she aware of it? Or was she pushing their connection away, somewhere in the deepest recesses of her being again?

He was surprised by her next words.

"Mathews," Brice said, "we might work together," and she looked directly into his eyes. "And they'll mark it against you again if I get involved with you." She had reverted to calling him by his last name, clearly a deliberate attempt to establish boundaries between them.

There were hundreds of cases of Roboticus and humans falling in love. Once memory was possible with machines, the synapses of the brain wires intertwined and grew depending on the permutations of an individual's unique experiences. Language, thought, emotion; robots had all the organic components needed to individuate experiences and fall in love.

Brice turned away from him before he could answer. The wind picked at her hair, blowing it over her face.

He was falling in love with her. Being near her made him feel like he was on fire. He couldn't let her argument stand, but he knew he didn't have to win it that moment. But there was one burning question he needed to air.

"So, who was the fugitive at Agni?" he asked. "The one who tried to take you?"

He always followed his gut instinct, and it was never wrong.

Brice took a long time to answer. "I can't explain now," she said. "When you're better, I'll tell you."

"The perfect answer to lure me in!" he said and laughed. "Sure," he said. "All right, I'll take the Colony job. So when do you think I'll be shipped to HQ?"

"You'll need to finish rehab. The nurse said you're healing very well. Maybe in a week and a half? In the meantime, read all the books you haven't had time to, and report to the Colony when the doctors clear you."

"Sounds good to me!" he said. "You seem to know your way around here. I gather you've landed in the hospital once or twice?"

She nodded. "Too many times to count."

"Good God!" he said in mock horror.

"And that's how I learned delicious food is important for reviving the spirit," she said, miming stirring something and placing it in an imaginary oven.

"How about some lasagna, next time?" he said, and winked. He was trying to get her to smile, and break this serious mood.

"That would constitute big-time bribery, soldier," Brice said and put her hands on her hips.

"Tell that to the Marines," he said and laughed. "Let me tell that to Brig General Pali, Suvarnadvipa, in particular."

She seemed restless, as if she knew her time with him was over. She sat down and reached over to the bread near him, grabbed the last piece of croissant, and took a bite. And then she closed her eyes and sighed. "I'm just trying to enjoy the sunshine, soldier. A temporary gift of peace. Let's enjoy it while we can."

But then she sat suddenly upright and touched her breast pocket, and then her ears. "Director Rojo," she said in her formal voice. "Yes Sir. I'm on my way to Denver Colony HQ."

And she frowned.

"Yes, Director Rojo. I'll be there soon," she said, and stood up. "I have to go, Quinn. See you soon at the Colony HQ."

He stared at her, trying to sear this image of Brice standing there with the ocean behind her into his brain. He was in love with this unreachable, seemingly unknowable Homo Sapiens. It was torture. But he wouldn't trade the feelings he was having for anything in the world.

She waved goodbye and he saluted back.

"See you soon, Agent O'Rourke," he said.

After she left, he turned away from the ocean. She was gone, leaving nothing but the bag of croissants. He grabbed another one, took a bite of it and smiled. He missed her already.

Chapter 4

Pasig River

Philippines

Federation of Han Asia

13 years, 1 month, 11 days before the Drone Strike

Avila

The edge of the Pasig River was alight with twinkling lights, but he did not see them. He was focused only on steering his boat to the dock nearest Quiapo Church.

The buri hat was a nuisance, but he had used it that day to hide his face from the intensely beating sun. It was early evening, and he didn't need it any longer, but the cloth had another purpose as well; it hid his features from the Machinas monitoring the river.

A lone figure was sitting by the dock, a cigarette dangling from his lips. He had long, jet-black hair, terribly uncombed, a scuffed, unwashed white shirt and shorts torn at the knees. Beside him was another man. His head was covered with a hat, his face hidden in shadow. Just two of the millions of the country's laborers waiting for their ride at the end of their day.

He slowed the boat and whistled.

"Esteban! Dio!" he called, and paddled the boat next to the dock. The two bedraggled figures jumped into the boat. They were hauling between them what looked like a small tree wrapped in nets. "Lay it down and don't move it until I tell you to," he whispered to the two men.

Esteban followed his instructions, then flattened himself onto the cold flooring of the boat face up, his gaze on the violet-pink skies of a stunning sunset.

The river was a well-used thoroughfare, and there were a thousand boats on it, snarled in traffic as it was day's end, and soon, more would join them as employees were bursting from offices, waving their hands in relief as they took to their boats.

His boat sliced through the throng, just an indistinguishable vessel among the thousands.

"Hey, great to see you two," he grinned while looking at both men lying flat on the boat. "Emaciated, but looking great," he chuckled.

"Very funny, Avila," Esteban's eyes were closed, and he estimated that his brother weighed a hundred twenty pounds now. His sunburned skin blended with the colors of the wooden floor, and he looked at the dirty, callused feet.

"Have you been running barefoot the whole time, Esteban?"

"Uh-huh, just so that my cover's not blown. Dio got me the job, sweeping the floors of City Hall," Esteban turned and patted Dio.

"I see you've been using the contact lens the past month to hide your green eyes," he asked his brother. He heard a groan in response.

"It feels like ten years in this place," Esteban answered. "We've been running from one safehouse to another. But thanks to Dio, I'm alive," he grinned.

It had been a month since Dio Salim's lieutenants had whisked their leader and Esteban out of the Concordia prison and smuggled them to Manila. Fortunately for Dio and Esteban, the Hans were more concerned with settling their North Korean population than chasing two escaped insignificant prisoners out of Concordia.

"Don't move," he said. "Give me ten more minutes to navigate to a calmer spot, then we can talk."

And he paddled hard to get away from the throng.

"All clear," he gestured to the two that they could sit up. Esteban eyed his clothes.

"Man, where'd you get the outfit? You must have drugged some poor fellow, and when he woke from a deep sleep, found that he was buck-naked," his brother laughed.

He paddled till he was sure there weren't random checkpoints on the water. Finally, he stopped the boat. At last they were alone in the middle of the Pasig River.

"There! Just three men stopping to eat dinner before curfew. We'll pause for five minutes, and then we have to move again." He pulled two triangular packages wrapped in banana leaf from beneath his seat, and gave one to Dio.

"Whoa. This is my first meal of the day," Dio said, sitting up.

"Same here," Esteban said as he threw a banana leaf package to him and he caught it with one hand and grinned. "A boy needs to eat." He scooped around two tablespoons of rice, and daintily picked two thin slices of dried fish to put onto it before shoving the rice into his mouth. His next victim was a tomato, which he dispatched with a noisy chomping sound.

"How are my girls?" Esteban asked.

"They're both good. Brice is serious as always, while Eilish follows, fawning over her. By the way, Mira sent this. And also from Noor." He handed both of them tiny devices, which looked like worms.

Esteban formed the device into a ball and placed it inside his right ear; a recorded message began to play. As he listened, tears started to trickle down his face. When the recording ended, he threw the device into the river where it quickly began to disintegrate. Dio went to another corner of the boat, listening to his family's message in private.

"I'm very relieved that this mission is finally completed and it's time to go back to the ARC," he said. "I've wanted to get one of these Machinas to Concordia for months. Was it difficult to get?"

"It was," Esteban nodded, "but with the help of Dio and his undercover soldiers, the droid was able to be subdued." Esteban patted the net-bound package he'd brought on board. "It's deactivated but how will it be transported to the ARC?"

"I'm going to rendezvous with another boat that will take us to Vietnam. You ready?" he asked.

"Ready steady!" Esteban said, and raised his thumb.

When they heard the sound of an approaching motor, he tipped his hat to cover his face better.

"Is this the boat?" Esteban said.

"Don't move," he shushed his brother.

The boat was full of Machina cavalry. It gunned past

them at full speed. He watched them pass.

"Shit," Esteban exclaimed. "They're the dumbest of droids. How can the Filipinos not defeat these machines?" Esteban's face held undisguised disgust. But his voice softened when he spoke again. "But look at our own country. People are just concerned with their survival. Same as folks in the Pasig River. They do the best they can." In the end, Esteban defended the Philippines more than he criticized it.

The Polar Shift had halved the world population and people retreated inland when coastlines disappeared. Panicked citizens jammed overwhelmed cities lacking infrastructure to host displaced citizens.

From a distance, a bigger boat was cruising at a faster speed. It slowed a few hundred feet from his boat. Powerful headlights beamed toward them.

It also wasn't the rendezvous boat. Sensing a trap, he reversed and gunned his boat into high speed. When Esteban lifted his head, he yelled, "Duck, damn it!" And then the Machinas began to shoot. He crouched low and grabbed a Flammatelun, a gun that fired flaming bullets.

With just one shot, the Machina boat burst into flame hot enough to melt the AIP soldiers. The boat stuttered to a halt, giving him time to escape. But when he glanced at his brother, to his horror, he found him lifeless. Dio crouched beside him, pressing on some of the wounds on his thighs to stem the bleeding.

The Machinas' weapons had hit his brother.

"Dio, drive the boat!" he shouted, and he exchanged places with him.

He tried to resuscitate his brother. But to no avail.

Esteban was dead, his eyes open to the Manila skies.

He cradled his brother's body and sobbed.

But he still had a job to do, and that package to deliver. After two hours of fast travel, they came up on the WRC boat that they'd been looking for. Dio decreased the speed of the boat, and saw George Mallard waving to him from the deck of the larger vessel.

But he couldn't respond. He was still clutching his brother.

When the small boat drew up to the larger one, it took a moment for Mallard to gauge the situation, and then, by instinct, he climbed into the rowboat, took off his jacket, and covered Esteban's face. Then he reached out toward Avila, first to put his hands on top of his, then to gently extricate Esteban from his grasp.

And then Mallard took over. He had a vague sense that Coalition soldiers boarded and picked up Esteban's body. They also removed the bundled Machina that Dio and Esteban had brought to the boat just a few hours before.

It was the first successful capture of this kind of droid, and Coalition governments were eager to get it. But at what price?

He couldn't bring himself to look at the prized Machina. He blamed himself for the death of his brother. If he had not been so obsessed with getting this robot, would Esteban still be alive? But his thoughts turned to another worry. How would he ever be able to tell Mira and Brice that Esteban was dead? Once ashore, he slumped to the ground and sobbed, and he didn't care that the Coalition soldiers would see him.

St Mary of the Angels Church

Kallang River Coalition

Singapore

Asian River Coalitions

June 25, 2058

13 years, 1 month, 7 days before the Drone Strike

Mira

From the corner of her eye, she glanced at Brice. She'd been sitting in the same spot for two days. Beside her was Eilish who sat still for just a few seconds, then got up and walked around the pews of the church, chatting with people she knew.

Hari was sitting behind Brice, looking very somber in a white long-sleeved shirt and black pants.

In the pew beside Brice, she was watching her child like a hawk. A child psychologist had assessed her child, and said that for now, she was processing her grief in her own way, and it could manifest in many ways.

Brice sighed and stood up. She went toward her father's flag-draped coffin, and patted it mutely.

She hadn't spoken a single word since her uncle had told her about her father's violent death on the Pasig River.

"Some ondeh ondeh, Auntie Mira?" a petite woman said to her. She was wearing a military uniform. Lt. Xingli

Teo Hong had been assigned from the Singapore Armed Forces to fulfill the family's needs during the duration of the wake of Dr. Esteban O'Rourke.

She turned around and smiled at her. "Lt. Teo Hong, what would I do without you?" In front of her was a tray holding an array of colorful dessert cakes.

"There are some more pandan cakes and ang ku kuehs for the other guests, but I reserved the most delicious for you!"

"You are all too kind, Lt. Teo Hong. And you are as always, very sweet!" She touched the officer's hand, and looked around. "You have all been very kind to all our families from Concordia."

"Our deepest condolences, Dr. O'Rourke," the officer's voice dropped, as if she would cry. "He died an honorable death. Hosting the families is the least we can do for the community of Concordia."

She glanced at Brice again and shook her head. "If only your kind gestures could make Brice see and hear. It would be a miracle!"

"Oh, she's a tough one, your little girl," Lt. Teo Hong enthused. "She'll survive this one, give her time. We've had soldiers with the same symptoms of hysterical blindness as Brice, and you just have to give her some space till she's ready to come out."

From the side, she saw Noor Salim waving at her, indicating that other guests from the Singapore military were arriving for the wake.

She sighed and tried to smile. It was the least she could do, she thought, to try and repay the government's generosity in housing the fifty families that had fled from Concordia two months before.

The night had been moonless, and the waters choppy as the villagers paddled desperately toward the Hanoi River Coalition. As they approached the docks, the piers were teeming with a thousand fellow immigrants, all fleeing from Palawan and other River Coalitions like Tokyo and Shanghai. The Han invasion had been swift and devastating to many of the River Coalitions in Asia.

Lost and numb from their midnight run, the villagers were given temporary lodging by the WRC task forces. The villagers from Concordia were assigned to the Red Cross forces of the Singapore River Coalition.

Grateful for the help given to them, the adult villagers in Concordia helped out any way they could. In a few days, they had taken first steps toward autonomy and set up a camp of their own.

She had been too busy to worry about Esteban. She volunteered her services as a certified paramedic to help out the overextended WRC.

In a week, the HRC was in crisis mode. Their refugee camps quickly filled to capacity and they were refusing refugees from their shore. And then they asked all volunteer forces to leave, including the Concordia contingency.

But fortunately, in the last few hours before they were slated to be homeless migrants again, the Red Cross in Singapore forces stepped up and offered the traumatized families a haven in their country.

They were offered temporary housing in the Western Coast, called Parc Oasis, near Jurong Lake. Most of the housing was buried deep underneath the ground. But on days when the water was at its lowest tide, people were allowed outside the compound.

Parc Oasis was nestled in a deep forest where komodo dragons crossed the roads lazily, monkeys hung in the trees, and squirrels chased each other across the rooftops.

And the food! Every evening, the families were introduced to a feast of Singaporean cuisine, which to her surprise was a mixture of Malaysian, Indonesian, Chinese, and Indian Food. This brought succor to her neighbors in Concordia. The children were the first to adjust. After they'd been in Singapore just a few days, she heard laughter coming from the green space outside her residence. The children were playing again. They may not have been jumping off cliffs like they did in Concordia, but the forest trees near Jurong Lake were enough for the gang of four – Brice, Hari, Amil and Eilish – to explore and find a sense of trust and enjoyment again.

And then Avila arrived with news of Esteban's fate. Brice fainted where she stood. When she regained consciousness, her vision had darkened and she didn't speak. Mira had spoken to her child gently, but she did not respond. She had suddenly become blind and deaf.

The psychologists from the Red Cross had reassured her that the physical manifestations Brice was experiencing were common to many children who had experienced the Polar Shift and the Han Invasion, events that happened in the space of two years. They had given her some medical protocol to follow, but for now, what her daughter needed in order to recover was time and patience from family and friends.

Esteban's wake seemed to make Brice even worse. She refused to leave her father's casket and slept in the church, bundled next to it in a blanket. There was nothing she could do, short of carrying her daughter away forcibly.

She even refused to bathe or change clothes.

Noor Salim tried to help as best she could. "Here," Noor said to her on the second day of the wake, "before you meet the visitors, come and drink some water and have some moments of peace and quiet."

"I am so worried about her, Noor." She slumped into a chair. "Avila requested that I go back to America next week and return to Boston, to the O'Rourke's family home, but I can't just yank her away to another place after all we've just been through. The doctor says she needs time to heal, but if I move her now, I'm afraid she may not speak ever again! I think it's best to stay here in Singapore till the situation stabilizes."

They had only a few minutes of rest before it was time to return to the church. As she entered, she saw Avila and Mallard arriving and embracing Dio.

"Is that George Mallard? He looks like a ghost," she asked Noor. Gone was the confident supervisory agent that Avila had introduced to them a month ago. Mallard's eyes seemed blank and his shoulders were stooped. He had become a shell of his former self.

"People are truly complex. Dio acts like nothing out of the ordinary has happened. But I wonder if someday this will affect him," Noor wondered aloud then faced her. "Dio and I have decided to stay here for a while. The children love it, so they'll be happy about that. We are staying here with you. We'll look for schools, and I can ask around for the best doctors."

She hugged her friend and neighbor, relieved. "The people here have been so kind and accommodating. I could eventually look for work here too."

"The children have become very close," Noor said, and

they both turned to look at Hari, who was teaching Eilish some card game, while Brice sat mute and still beside them.

"My poor daughter," she said. "She didn't really get the time she needed to grieve her Grandpa Daelan's death in Antarctica. Esteban's death is just too much for her."

"Shhhh..." Noor said, embracing her grief-stricken friend again. "We're all safe now. We can begin again."

"How much grief can our children take? This could mark them forever, and there's nothing we can do to stop it." She was crying harder as she said this.

"You're here, Mira. You have to be strong for Brice and Eilish's sake. How lucky they are that you are here for them."

She pulled away from Noor and wiped her eyes. "I have to tell Avila that we're staying here in Singapore." She patted the pocket of her dress and fished out a thin tube of lipstick. "I can't mess up my daughter's childhood, Noor, by collapsing like a helpless fool. I'm ready to meet the visitors. Noor, will you hold my hand?"

Noor had been a rock for the entire Concordia refugee community since the day they fled their island. For a moment, Mira felt a surge of relief and gratitude that was stronger than her grief. It had been great luck that the Singapore Red Cross had offered them a chance to relocate in their country. She wanted to some day be able to give back to the community and help migrants like herself find a home. But first, she had to find a way to help Brice. It was that, or watch the child drown in her own sorrow.

A group of men in military uniforms had entered the church. They were from the Singapore Armed Forces.

"Let's greet them, Noor," she said. "Let's be proud of Esteban's and Dio's heroic efforts to save the United River Coalitions. It's the least we can do." And she walked toward the men and forced herself to smile.

Though to others she appeared blind, deaf, and mute, there were voices inside her, voices screaming inside her head.

How can someone describe unbearable pain to someone else?

It was reassuring to her that her mother, Eilish, and her neighbors were around her. Though everyone coaxed her to eat, it was as if her digestive system had shut down, and she couldn't open her mouth to take in food. There were days even moving from a sitting position was too much of an effort for her.

Yesterday, her mother carried her to the tub and bathed her. She could not even lift her arms. It was as if her muscles had atrophied and the burden of repositioning was too much to bear.

Her mother did not ask questions or complain, just lovingly shampooed her hair and soaped her like a baby. And then she dressed her and returned her to the pew near her father's remains.

Before news had come of her father's death, she, Hari, Amil, and Eilish had found paradise here in Singapore.

They had recovered quickly from the ordeal of fleeing by boat, and were adjusting well to their new surroundings.

From the time the sun rose, the four of them raced on donated bikes toward a beautiful park near Parc Oasis called the Chinese Garden. Eilish was usually strapped to the back seat, and Brice captained the front.

But one day she had seen her Uncle Avila standing in one of the tiny pagodas, his hands shielding his eyes, searching for them.

At a glance, she knew something was wrong. And when Avila called her to him and told her his terrible news, she collapsed.

Uncle Avila's explanations did not help: her father was a hero, and he'd saved the River Coalitions by doing a secret government act.

It was all too much to bear.

The memory of that horrible day receded when she felt Hari tap her arm. She remained still, then nodded her head, acknowledging his tap on her arm. He reached out to hold her hand. Would she mind?

She didn't answer, but didn't yank her hand away either.

Tears started to drop from her eyes. In response, he stood up and walked away. He returned and sat down, pulled a sandwich from the tissue paper that was wrapped around it, and gave her the tissue paper. It had a bit of mayonnaise stuck in its middle.

She smiled.

He reached out to her mouth and with his fingers, tried to open and close it. Did she want to speak up?

She shook her head. She still had a lot to think about. She turned from him and slumped down, facing away from everyone.

She thought Hari would leave her then. But he didn't.

But she was left again to her own thoughts. For the life of her, she couldn't understand why so much tragedy was happening around her.

Was it her fault? And if it was not, whose fault was it?

In her Grandpa Daelan's case, the collapse of Antarctica and the Shifting of the Poles were too mind-numbing to comprehend. Why did they have to leave their new home in Concordia, Palawan, too? If the climate kept changing, would the global waters reach Boston as well, her father's city of birth? Where could they go to be safe?

Her parents had thought that Concordia was a perfect haven, and yet this turned out to be untrue. The Machinas had attacked its shores. Who and what were these creatures, and were they responsible for killing her father?

Underneath her grief was anger. She was furious at herself. If she had known the day of the Machinas' attack would be the last time she would see her father, she would have marched to him and embraced him one last time. Never mind if the soldiers killed her for it.

If she had known that the day the sea took her grandfather's home would be the last time that she would see her Grandpa Daelan, she wouldn't have left his side at all.

From somewhere behind her came the babbling voice of Eilish. How could a droid be made to be evil?

She heard the thump of heavy footwear in front of her. She jumped as a soldier barked, "Attention!"

Hari nudged her. "Stand up, Brice! It's the changing of the guard for the Singapore military. So one soldier remains while the other soldier salutes and turns away..."

Hari kept babbling but she didn't want to hear any

of it. Her pain was too unbearable. Whoever killed her father would pay for their sins. They would pay and she'd be the one to do it.

Avila

Avila was impressed at the large gathering for his brother's funeral Mass, and surprised to learn that people had traveled from places far from Singapore to say their final goodbyes to Esteban.

But he couldn't shake the feeling that his niece had blamed him for her father's death.

Mira had told him that her temporary blindness and muteness would go away when the trauma of Esteban's passing had been processed by her brain.

But he couldn't help wondering what would happen if this processing never happened. Brice sat by her father's coffin for hours on end. He witnessed moments when an incomprehensible expression flashed on her face. She was feeling something very strongly. Was it hatred or disgust? He was most disturbed when her unseeing gaze seemed to focus on him, guided by the sound of his voice.

Avila was grateful that Eilish stayed beside her, and the Salim boys also provided a steady companionship. He saw how Brice responded when Hari held her hand. But still, she stayed silent. He wasn't surprised when the guests finally left and he saw his eight-year-old niece walking toward him, her hands on Eilish's shoulders.

"Brice, nice of you to find me. May I hold your hand?" he said. But she didn't acknowledge his words. Instead, she made hand signals for Eilish to start walking away from them.

"Eilish, will you excuse us?" Avila said. "I need to talk to Brice privately."

Eilish nodded and skipped away from them.

He directed Brice to a pew and she sat down beside him. It was useless to talk to her like a child, or fawn over her. She had grown so much from the wide-eyed child he had seen in Antarctica.

"I know you want to know why so many things have been happening to us since Antarctica," he said. "When will it end?" She nodded and reached for his hand.

Avila carefully weighed his next words. He had pondered this question himself, but that didn't give him the ability to offer an answer that made any kind of sense.

"I wanted to be a geologist when I was young, Brice," he continued after a long pause. "Just like your Grandpa Daelan and your dad. But instead, I shifted into the military after the Polar Shift.

"Did the Polar Shift happen naturally, or was there a human component to this change? And what about the evil Hans?" Avila started to say, but he was surprised when Brice found her voice and cut him sharply with it.

"I'm not interested in the evil Hans, Uncle Avila. Why did the Polar Shift happen? Do you know? Aside from Grandpa Daelan's theories?" Her voice had risen an octave, and now her arms were crossed.

"Oh my goodness! I'm glad to hear that anger coming from you, Brice. Better a spewing angry Brice than a silent one." He tried a light remark hoping for a slight smile from his niece. There was none.

"Oh, Brice, you know this isn't my place of expertise. That was your Grandpa's and your father's area of knowledge!" Avila's voice rose an octave as well.

"And now, they're both dead!" she spit back at him. "I want to know how all of this happened. Whose fault is it, Uncle Avila? What caused all of this?" There were now tears threatening to spill from her eyes, but Brice sat straighter, as if by doing so, it would prevent her from crying in front of her uncle.

"Well..." he started, then shifted in his seat uncomfortably. How to explain to an eight-year-old girl about the complexities of human nature?

He tried another tack. "What's your favorite Singapore food?" he asked and took Brice's hand.

"Mala Xiang Guo!" Brice piped up, and he was surprised Brice had named a dish famous for its abundance of Szechuan chili peppers.

"Try to remember what it feels like to have your belly full of your favorite Mala," he said. But her eyebrows were raised, her expression full of skepticism.

"And?" Brice crossed her arms and stomped a foot.

"So you are full, but what if you just keep eating and gorging on Mala Xiang Guo?" His eyes widened, and he puffed his cheeks. He pulled Brice's hands to his face to touch them.

"That's disgusting, Uncle Avila!" Brice cried.

"There was a time when there were no wars, plagues, or famines to kill people. Everybody had food to eat, and everybody was safe in their own homes. But people wanted more than what they had."

"And it made the earth shift?" Brice asked incredulously.

"People were aware that changes were happening in the world around them, but couldn't connect that it was their wanting more of everything that was causing them and in the process, imperiling earth. More food, more gadgets, more toys! When will it be enough? That's the simplest explanation I can think of, Brice." He sought her hand, then squeezed it.

"The melting of the ice glaciers in Antarctica was the first crisis, and then came terrible hurricanes in the United States and intense forest fires all over the world. This was more than enough evidence to show world leaders that the environment was changing and something drastic had to be done, but no one paid attention." He shook his head, as if trying to shake loose a bad dream.

"The point of no return was when the poles shifted. People only realized that their world was catastrophically changing when half the population disappeared in the great floods."

"I don't really get it, Uncle Avila," Brice said. "Why did Grandpa and Papa have to die because some people were greedy?" Brice slumped into his arms, and wept. "I don't understand it at all," she whimpered.

He stroked her hair. "Don't you see? All our actions are intertwined. Every action for good or ill affects every other person in this world. Perhaps, if more of us were as reflective as you are and asked more questions, we wouldn't be as messed up as we are now." He embraced Brice tightly.

"Then we're doomed!" Brice said, and started to sob.

Though he didn't reply, he agreed with what his niece said. Up until two million years before, there had been multiple human species roaming the earth together. But the others had gone extinct. Some scientists speculated that Homo Sapiens would survive another 1,000 years. But that now seemed to be a ridiculously optimistic guess.

How long will it be until we destroy ourselves, he wondered, as he held Brice closely. If nothing was done, they were clearly doomed to extinction.

Chapter 5

The Colony HQ

Denver
Colorado River Coalition
United States of America
American River Coalitions
21 August 2071
21 days after the Drone Strike

Brice felt the cold wind at the back of her neck, but she disregarded the chill and focused instead on the people who were running on the road ahead of her. Little did they know they were also traveling a long and winding path. How many times had she run this same road, the wind her sole friend and companion?

When she reached the top of the rise, she paused to catch her breath, her security Bee buzzing loudly, as if it too was winded. She was standing on the highest peak in the ravaged Americas, a rare chunk of land not touched by the ever-encroaching waters.

Her perch was a vulnerable spot, but the best place to test new recruits. And from all accounts, this was going to be the last time they would be tested in open air.

The test for acceptance to the Colony was tough. Recruits had started at ten in the evening twenty-six hours before, and the course consisted of forty miles of mountain trails, made slippery by the rains. Most of the candidates had at least four maps to point them in the right direction, but the maps had been made soggy and unreadable from the rain. They were not allowed to use a device to help them if they got lost. The Colony wanted to test their resilience, among other things.

She heard huffing and puffing sounds that meant another runner was coming near. Half a kilometer away, a recruit was approaching. He seemed to slow when he saw her.

It was Quinn. His injuries were now a thing of the past. He waved at her.

She nodded back. There were two other runners behind him. Their bodies were as lean as was humanly possible, and they were tall as Olympic Ethiopian marathon runners. Even from this distance, she could see the recruits' facial expressions were without a hint of humor. This was hard work.

"It's twelve midnight. Some hot chocolate?" a man's voice said behind her.

"Henry James Keyon, up and about at midnight!" She jumped up and embraced the man. The Colony's Deputy Director of Intelligence wore a formal jacket.

"To what do I owe your presence at this hour?" she said and bowed to him. "You do dress like your boss,

Henry. Such originality."

"You're really messing with me, O'Rourke," Henry chuckled. "Any of the recruits folded yet?" he asked.

"Nope. Tough nuts to crack, this batch." She turned her gaze to the runners, then sighed. "This show of stamina and strength is suddenly making me feel old, very old, Henry."

"How old? I feel like I've lived a century, dear Brice. Or maybe a century and a half," he sighed.

"It's been 26 hours now, and no one has died from hypothermia yet. They're a tough bunch." He handed her a thin square device with a small, glowing screen. "Look at their numbers. Amazing." Brice scanned lists of measurements including heart rate, oxygen levels, and total distance they'd traveled. All were very impressive.

"Were we as hardened when we took the exams to gain entrance to the Colony?"

"We were. You just don't remember it. Lee Jae Seung was a droid, as I remember, and Hari had some terrible robotic qualities himself..."

"How young we all were then..." she said, as they both observed the runners. There was a beat of silence. She wanted Henry to speak up first and gauge why he was here, at this hour, beside her.

"So pray, tell me, why am I here? For six months I've been flitting from one Indonesian island to another, and now I'm suddenly commanded here by Director Rojo."

"You know, we were a tough bunch." And he brushed some imaginary dirt from his right shoulder. Brice noticed that he avoided her question.

"Oh, you don't fool me with the optics, Henry. And God, why are you wearing a suit?" She shook her head in mock disgust. "What is the situation below? My guess is that I'll be the sacrificial lamb in all this." And she stood up, surprising her former Colony comrade. "Even if you're now the Deputy Director of Intelligence, you can't fool me, Henry. Spit it out."

"I thought you'd get distracted with my elegant attire. Tell me, when you saw Hari, how did he look?"

She eyed him, then turned away from him. She had to work for the Colony, but that didn't mean she was going to answer any of their questions.

They were distracted by the sound of a thousand feet pounding on the ground. The runners were getting closer.

"Is that Quinn?" Henry said and pointed. He then drew a monocular from his right pocket and observed the runners.

She ignored this question as well. Then she asked one of her own. "They asked me to observe the examinees. Why?" But Henry didn't answer any of her questions. "Oh, okay. Touché. You won't answer my questions either," she pouted.

"Serves you right," Henry muttered. He gestured with a handful of dust he'd grabbed and thrown on her head.

Quinn had a lean, spare frame that made him easy to distinguish from the other Colony candidates. His running style looked smooth and effortless.

"He's doing well," Henry said. "I suspect he has an advantage because he's AIP."

"My, my Henry, you haven't changed," she said. "What a prejudiced ass you are!" She hoped he was joking but wanted to be sure. Henry laughed.

"After Jae, I would think you'd be more careful of the way you speak of them," she continued.

"Sentient droid, AIP, Sollus, AQ. Does it matter? I'm not

a prejudiced ass, Brice. We still don't know what really happened to Jae and Hari, Brice. It's been six months…"

"Henry, you bigot. Quinn is a Sollus with human DNA, raised by human parents from birth. Except for the spare parts, he is human. He didn't need six months in rehab, for one thing."

"Touchy," Henry snarled.

"Asshole," she bit back.

"Stop," he said. "We are all pained by Jae's and Hari's disappearance. But we are moving forward. As a Sollus, Quinn is a different species altogether. We need him in the field. He's perfect for the lab too. Highest IQ of all recruits, besting you, Brice."

She pulled her own monocular lenses to her eyes and focused on the examinees.

"We need his brains. Maybe a scientist could solve this puzzle. We're faced with a very deceptive enemy."

"Quinn was injured badly," she said quietly. "I don't know how ready he is for the subtlety of Intelligence work."

"You saw him under fire," Henry said, "so you've seen how fast he reacts. And Diego rarely vets a recruit, though he's trained many of them. What's so special about this guy?"

"Oh, I don't know. Gut instinct. He won't leave me in a firefight."

"Same way you saved Quinn in the battle of Agni."

"He'd do the same for me. Flying colors. I think he's ready for an assignment."

"Let's just see how he makes it through training school," Henry said. He looked away from his telescopic device as a bear of a man in rumpled clothes sauntered up. It was Diego.

"How's Indonesia, Diego? Still thinking about retirement? Desk work won't suit you," he said. "Come and play with us till the rug of death gets pulled out from under you."

"I bet you two will never retire," Diego said. "You're both addicted to the rush." And then he sighed. "I'm old, fat, and greying. I just want to die on a little piece of land somewhere far away, with my feet facing the sun."

"Won't you miss being Station Chief?" she asked, a mock worried expression on her face.

"Gosh, Brice," he said, "I'll miss it like I miss evil, sneaky Drone makers, corrupt generals, flashes of AQs in the sky. Speaking of which, recruitments for the Colony are postponed indefinitely," Diego said. "Quinn will be your assistant in the field, Brice."

"Assistant? Diego! He's hasn't passed the Colony as an agent."

"He's not your assistant as an agent, Brice. He's an Echo. He'll be your security."

"For what?" she asked.

Diego rubbed his unshaven cheek.

"You know Avila has a preternatural instinct for this stuff," he said. "If he says you go, then you go. Anyway, orders are orders. You two go down for the Intelligence briefing."

"What's going on?" she asked.

"There's always something afoot," he said. "But this looks serious."

"You two get going," Diego said. It was an order, and she and Henry turned to one another, then turned toward the harnesses lying on the ground near a promontory.

"Hey, you two," Diego said. "Why don't you use the lift,

like…" But they didn't hear the rest of the sentence. They'd already reached the cliff's edge, put on their harnesses, then jumped onto a zip line.

"Geronimo!" Henry said as he catapulted from the edge. She was quiet as she fell a hundred feet to the ground. Somehow, the monitoring Bee managed to stay by her side.

Henry yelled, "O'Rourke, when will I ever beat you?"

The main HQ Colony's inner sanctum was guarded by a series of doors and interlocking walls that opened and closed to an entrant's shadow on the walls.

Security floodlights flashed and she had to squint her eyes to protect them from their brightness. There was a sudden beep, beep, beep of a machine as it scanned her body.

"Body ID. Can they see the healed broken bones, I wonder?" she said to Henry.

"Within a millimeter, to be precise," Henry answered. He was right behind her. "These babies can see anything. Can it even see my broken heart?" He paused, and looked at her.

She tried to gauge his expression. " Awww, still got that crush on me, Henry? You're as naughty as ever," she teased.

"You've always been in love with Hari, Brice. I don't know why. So who am I kidding?" Henry turned away from her and walked toward a doorway that opened to a cave-like terminal full of rushing trains and harried people walking with quick steps.

Henry had always teased that he had a crush on her, but she always felt uneasy with him. He was always egging her on, competing with her, but she never gave in. She had a competitive drive that drove him nuts. It must be painful to lose to a woman.

Henry was waiting for her near the glass-enclosed entrance door for the trains, looking upwards at the cavernous ceiling.

"When did the Colony become so enormous and complicated?" she asked.

"When were the world's problems not enormous and complicated? You're part of the problem, I think so," Henry said, baiting her. But she refused to rise to his bait.

Instead, he took her elbow as they waited on the platform. After a few minutes, a train arrived and they boarded it.

The tracks started at ground level, then plunged off a steep incline. The drop made her stomach churn and the air seemed compressed, as if even the oxygen molecules were sparse in this part of headquarters. She gripped the seat's handholds tightly until the train leveled off again.

The whoosh of the trains reminded her of the rides she'd taken in college to get to classes.

She shook her head to get rid of them, and closed her eyes, but that made the churning in her stomach even worse.

Chapter 6

Denver Congressional Hall

Colorado River Coalition

United States of America

American River Coalitions

13 September 2058

12 years, 10 months and 19 days before the Drone Strike

Mallard

He scanned the crowd in bursts of a few seconds, looking back at the newspaper he was holding in his hands. He didn't want to be too obstrusive observing the crowd, but couldn't help noting his observations. His training as an Intelligence agent was too ingrained, and he couldn't keep still as he scanned the crowd again.

When half the land around the world disappeared,

including Washington, D.C. along the Potomac River, most of the surviving congressmen and senators had convened in Denver, the highest point in the nation.

It took a year to build the Congressional building, but build it the government did. The reinforced building was now built with thirty floors underneath it. In the event of another catastrophic Polar Reversal, Congress could just stay inside the bunker forever until their supplies ran out.

He noted Avila O'Rourke beside him, and took notice of the clothes that hung loosely on him. It was three months since his brother died and he could not imagine what was going through his head ever since that fiasco retrieving the Machina. Was it all worth it?

His boss, Joseph Roy, Defense Minister of the United States, stood up and was sworn in. Blair stood ramrod straight as if he was in front of a firing squad. In front of them were the wizened senators heading the Congressional Defense Committee, and the pugnacious Senator Nelson Blair was ready to slug it out with the panel in front of it.

"At ease, Minister Roy. As you know, we don't want to waste time around here. Before anything else, I'd like to know why we can't attack the North Koreans at the heart of their own country?"

"Senator Blair, if we look at the map right now, the Korean peninsula has disappeared after the Polar Shift. Nothing remains of the land as we speak. They do have an impenetrable defense system of underwater nuclear missiles which can strike any country in an hour." Blair said all this in a slow manner so that it could be understood by the crowd as well.

"The North Koreans took advantage of the chaos of the Polar Shift by attacking the Coalition countries at their most vulnerable. They opened up their bunker to unleash the Machinas. From the time of the Great Migration in 2058, the lid to Pyongyang has been closed," Roy continued.

"We'd like to know what you have learned about the Machinas. We've learned from confidential memos of the Denver Colony HQ that Dr. Esteban O'Rourke and Col. Dio Salim valiantly retrieved one droid from the Hans three months ago. Please update us and… " He was interrupted by an aide who whispered in his ear.

"Before anything else, let's acknowledge the brother of Esteban O'Rourke who is in the audience. Avila O'Rourke?" Senator Blair turned around in their direction and he nudged Avila beside him to stand up. A round of applause rippled across the congressional hall.

"The US government is grateful for the heroic deed of your brother, Mr. O'Rourke. May his death not be in vain." Another round of thunderous applause came from the galleries, and Avila turned around to acknowledge it.

The senator waited for the applause to die down, then he crossed his arms as he sat back, ready for the session to begin again. "As you were saying, Minister Roy…" the senator glared again in their direction.

"The captured Machina has been analyzed by our Defense team and…" Senator Blair suddenly slapped the table in front of him, just under the microphone and Blair stopped mid-sentence.

"We would like to know, Minister Roy, if we can build the same droid to attack the Hans back?"

"We have gathered the best minds around the country, Senator Blair, and we have come up with a better plan. We're going to build the first Sollus camps in ten cities around the country in a year. Our allies in other countries like London, Berlin, Singapore, and Tokyo will also create the first sentient robots, technology from Jan Zimmerman." He was about to say more, but the more aggressive senators interrupted him.

"Minister Roy, we're not all dunderheads here. We've invited Dr. Zimmerman here many times, and we're familiar with his process. The Sollus camp is being set up as we speak, and the process will take five years for the sentient Homo Roboticus to grow from infancy to adulthood. The Sollus camps will not create Machinus soldiers to defeat the Hans. Not in the quickest possible time. Do you have any other alternatives?" Senator Blair drummed his fingers for everyone to hear, as he continued to question the Defense Minister.

"We have a plan to capture Machinas, and turn the droids against the Hans, Senator Blair," Roy answered.

It was the first time that the senators seemed interested in what they had to say. The senators turned to each other, and the session was stopped. They were conferring amongst themselves and nodding vigorously to one suggestion of a senator. Then they motioned that the questioning will resume. Senator Blair turned to the Minister. "How will you do this, Minister Roy?"

"We've been gathering intelligence near the Han Occupied lands, and once in a while we come across the Hans. If opportunity arises, we grab them."

"And?" Senator Blair prodded him impatiently.

"And we've been catching more and more Hans in our defense storage facilities. If we can find a way to weaponize these droids, then we have a way to defeat the Hans." Roy looked across the gallery to find that most of the senators agreed.

"We do need better options, Defense Minister. Otherwise, the Hans will occupy more territory around the world. Can you give me the latest summary of the Machina soldiers occupying the United States?" Senator Nelson Blair was relentless, and his boss looked toward him, as he gave him a sheaf of paper which he had updated this morning.

"This is the latest intel we've gathered around the country," Roy intoned. "Machina soldiers in occupied territories in the United States – Potomac River – 40,000 soldiers; Florida Keys – 30,000 soldiers; San Francisco Bay – 35,000 soldiers; Seattle – 30,000 soldiers; Michigan River – 40,000 soldiers."

"How are our defenses holding up, Minister Roy?" Senator Blair inquired. "I don't want to wake up and find that those Machinas have overtaken Denver."

"The defenses are unbreachable, Senator. Although the waters have encroached on both coasts because of the Polar Shift, this has also provided us with defenses inland since the rivers have swelled width-wise. Our soldiers are amassed near the shores to stop the Machinas, Senator." Roy was still standing up, and he knew he was prepared to give the information till the interrogation was done.

"How about our neighbors and other countries in the world? Still no signs of China and South Korea after North Korea invaded their shores?" Blair asked in a softer tone as the countries which had disappeared off the face of the earth were mentioned.

His boss hesitated, then looked at him. He was surprised when Roy turned to him, and nudged him to stand up.

"The Denver Intelligence Colony Head, Mr. George Mallard, will relay the information, as this is his area of expertise, Senator Bryan." Roy prompted him to go nearer the microphone, while he sat down to listen to him.

"Mr. Mallard, proceed then with the report," Senator Blair said.

He stood up and addressed the podium. "It is unfortunate that a great part of India, Africa, South America and Russia have disappeared after the Polar Shift two years ago. Hindsight is 20/20 and we know these countries did not have disaster plans in place as waters rose even before 2056. Other countries – China, Japan, South Korea, Singapore, Taiwan, and Hong Kong in Asia – have survived owing to the fact that they had built thirty-story bunkers underneath their cities. When the Hans invaded four months ago, the people retreated underneath the bunkers for safety.

"Unfortunately, some countries were ill-prepared, like the Philippines, Indonesia, Vietnam, and Cambodia.

"But we have good news about other countries. Two weeks ago, Sydney, Melbourne Seoul, Shanghai and Guangzhou River Coalitions have reappeared and re-established communication with us. The communities are all thriving as we speak." A burst of applause interrupted his words.

"Shanghai and Guangzhou have indicated that they will not help the North Korean government. They are strongly allied to us, Sir." Another burst of applause rippled across the hallways.

"That's great news! What's the situation in United Kingdom and European River Coalitions, Mr. Mallard?" Senator Blair's tone was almost gleeful now, happy to receive some good news.

"London is safe, Senator. But Edinburgh and Belfast as you know were overtaken by the Machinas. Unfortunately,

Paris was also was overtaken and Resistance by France has been slow owing to losing their defense forces by half when the waters rose," he answered. "Germany has been helping beef up the defenses of European River Coalitions, Sir. All the countries I've mentioned have survived because of their well-prepared bunkers, Sir.

"The countries which have been slow in following the specifications have been almost wiped off the face of the earth, Senator Bryan. Greece, Spain, Italy have not been heard of yet, as we speak. We are hopeful one of them will communicate with us or the WRC, Sir." He paused and rolled his feet, from the balls of his feet to his toes, to ease the muscle cramps in his calves.

"Tsk, tsk...very sad indeed, Mr. Mallard. We can end this day with the facts as you mentioned. We will make this a regular update from all of you. As a reminder, I want the Machinas defeated. Find a way to do this. The sooner we have our lands back, the better. Dismissed." With the swing of the gavel, the Congressional inquiry was done.

Chapter 7

Denver Colony HQ

Colorado River Coalition

United States

American River Coalitions

21 August 2071

21 days after the Drone Strike

"Here we are," Henry said as their tram stopped in an antiseptic-looking terminal. There was no one else in the terminal when she and Henry alighted. The clacking of their shoes on the tiled floor were the only sounds they heard.

The electronic whoosh of doors opening at the passage's end never failed to startle her. The Bee was blown backwards as they walked through the doors. She waited until it slowly eased itself back down on her shoulder.

More body scans came next. After a few minutes, they were cleared, and at last allowed to enter the cavernously quiet space of Colony HQ. As they headed toward their destination, they passed hundreds of people working in individual pods of glass. Many were lying in hammocks, staring at the ceiling and reading. Some were running or cycling as they worked, all the while staring at the terminal in front of them. Others were just staring into space, thinking. One pod had a picture blown up a million times and a group of people huddled before it, conferring on their own data.

A warning bell sounded, announcing that visitors were arriving.

As their images panned on a wall, all of the Colony workers' terminals darkened.

All eyes were on them, and she heard her name whispered from one workstation to another.

"It's Brice O'Rourke."

"She's here! In the flesh?"

"What is that? Is she wearing a prison uniform?"

"What really happened in Marikina, Brice?" Henry asked.

In that instant, both of them realized that all their bonds of friendship had disappeared, and their political beliefs had riven them apart.

"Because your father's brother is the Defense Minister and the President is your family friend. And here they are, your Highness," Henry adopted a mocking tone to disguise the awkwardness that had arisen between them and pushed her toward the door marked War Room.

She could see both Avila O'Rourke and President Mallard standing just inside the door. Her heart was beating fast. The last time she had seen Mallard was three years ago at Harvard in her last year in college. The last time she had seen the Defense Minister was when she started applications to join the Denver Colony HQ two years ago.

As she entered the room, the men turned to her. Both had aged, their hair graying at the sides, but with the same lean physiques they had when they were agents for the Colony HQ. But now, the two top officials of the land were in very formal attires.

Their expressions were indecipherable.

They had experienced the same challenging and tragic events all those years ago in Concordia, yet now they were on opposite sides of the table.

It was strange what war could do, Brice thought to herself. Very strange indeed.

Chapter

Paris, France

Federation Han Europe

11 February 2060

11 years, 5 months, 24 days before the Drone Strike

Avila

He had ensconced himself across the Left Bank facing the Louvre, and observed the Machinas all lined up, standing at attention along the banks of the river, looking back at him. Their handsome Korean features were visible even with a military cap covering their face. They even wore an elegant red, long coat, as if they could feel the cold!

But dig deeper inside the Machina machines and it was all hardware. Their eyes recorded every movement around the perimeter, their ears were used as listening devices. These Machinas could run at 30 km/hr with their clipped boots. They could use their hands for a number of functions; the Machina fingers had a thousand uses like the human hand. But their peripheral vision was not yet perfect. It was a bit delayed and their movements were slow when catching the movement of an object.

Ever since his boss, George Mallard, was tasked to regularly update Congress about Machina activities around the world, he was now assigned to act as liaison with the French Resistance.

France was now inhabited by only 20 million people; 60 million people were lost to the sea after the Polar Shift. Their army was decimated, leaving their borders unprotected and open to the aggressive Hans two years ago.

"There you go, Avila," someone tapped him from behind.

"Analie," he turned and all he could feel was the warm embrace of Analie Bertrand , his Intelligence counterpart in France.

"How's Paris, ma chérie?" he deadpanned. "Was it hard bypassing those Han droids?"

"Sometimes I wonder if the droids are just for show. They don't seem to mind me going back and forth from the Left to the Right Bank. It's great they haven't perfected their peripheral vision yet. But I don't want to know what they'll do if I'm caught meeting with you," Analie mimicked someone choking her.

"Third time to see me and we're still good!" He high-fived Analie but she gave her fist to his open palm.

"I just want to slam all of those droids so badly," Analie's voice lowered an octave, and he felt the chill in her voice. But then it cheered up again. "But hey, I have some good news for you, my friend. So we've been counting the Han human migrants to our shores. There are 50,000 of them, and we've been tracking them thanks to hidden surveillance Intelligence mechanisms we put in place before the Paris occupation. Their numbers have been dwindling. We haven't been able to infiltrate their camps, but looks like the reason for their death is irradiation from the nuclear blast they experienced when South Korea detonated a bomb on them in 2052. We have no body count on the number of the dying, but we're keeping our eye on the leaders. If they start disappearing, then we'll find a way to search where they bury their dead."

"Who are the Han Federation leaders in Paris?" Avila asked, curious about the hierarchy in Paris compared with other countries' occupation numbers.

"The Military Administration is under General Beom Gimbae Heo and Governor Min-jun Gimhae Park. They follow the dictatorial edicts of Pyongyang. The people in Paris are stoic. They will overcome this like they overcame Nazism a hundred years ago," Analie answered.

"The WRC and the US Congress have been forming groups asking how the Hans can be defeated, you know that," he revealed this highly classified intelligence to Analie, whom he trusted with this piece of news. Analie nodded.

"Unless there were droids that were stronger and smarter than these Machinas, our situation is hopeless. The French are drained from the Polar Reversal, and they have lost friends and loved ones by the millions. Add to that, the catastrophic loss of their homes. It's truly mind-boggling. Pray that we survive till you wipe out the Imperium. Promise that you'll find a way!" Teary-eyed, Analie couldn't hide her emotions anymore. She brought her hands to her eyes and sobbed. He reached out to her and she embraced him.

"We'll try our best, you know that, Analie," he said, trying to calm this beautiful colleague he had met through the Intelligence community. Despite the high-risk situation Analie put herself in, crossing the Seine to meet with him to update the American River Coalition, he was shocked by how she smelled so good. The hint of lilac and jasmine was subtle yet overpowering. Analie raised her head toward him, and their lips almost touched, but she backed away from him and fished something from her bag.

"I almost forgot! This book is for your niece Brice and the doll is for Eilish. How are they? Growing up very fast, I bet," Analie asked him in wonder, and pointed at the book she brought out. "It's Nancy Drew in French. I had to retrieve it in my apartment and give it away lest the Hans start going house-to-house confiscating our stuff."

He was touched that she remembered, as he had mentioned the names of his nieces just once to Analie. "Brice is now ten years old, while Eilish remains six. I'll be seeing them soon in Singapore. They'll love the gifts. Thank you, thank you! When the Hans are defeated, we'll visit Paris, Analie. Or you come visit us in Singapore."

"Alors. I'd love to visit a place near the equator. I'm tired of this never-ending war, Avila."

The French way she pronounced his name amused him. Their lips touched this time, and their problems were forgotten for the moment. All he felt was Analie's arms around his waist pushing him toward the ground, hiding them from the stares of the Machina soldiers hundreds of feet away. It was a little bit of happiness in a time of war. He closed his eyes trying to memorize how

Analie smelled. It would be months before he would see her again.

Sollus Compound

Yang Bioresearch Institute

Kallang River Coalition

Singapore

Asian River Coalitions

05 June 2060

11 years, 1 month, 27 days before the Drone Strike

Mallard

It was Mira's face that he saw first as he entered the lobby of the Yang Bioresearch Institute. She was standing with Avila who was holding Brice and Eilish in each hand. Eilish burst away from Avila's grasp to rush toward him. Brice was hesitant as always, staring at her feet. Brice had never warmed up to him. She was holding a Nancy Drew book in French.

"Brice, parlez-vous Français? Do you speak French now?" he asked her, a quizzical expression crossing his face.

"A bit, Tio George," Brice answered, her response as succinct as ever.

"And who do we have here?" George asked Mira. Mira had surprised everyone with the decision that she was going to participate in the Sollus program. Since she didn't want to displace Brice's routine, Mira had opted to join the Singapore Sollus program.

"Meet Ira," Mira smiled. The infant looked angelic, at peace with the world. Her breathing was even, then she suddenly stirred, opening her green eyes.

"May I hold her hand?" he asked.

"Of course, George," Mira answered. He held Ira's hand and the soft dewy skin confused him.

"Is she really Sollus?" he wondered aloud and looked around at the grinning faces of the O'Rourkes. Even Brice managed a smile at him.

"Yes, she is a beautiful baby." Ira cried and Mira shushed her by cradling her some more. "See you later at the apartment. I better feed the hungry one. Are you coming with me, Brice and Eilish?" Mira asked.

"I can give George the tour around the facility. And the two girls can accompany us so you and Ira can have some space." Avila directed his words to Mira, who nodded.

"Yes, I'm exhausted. See you later, ladies." Mira blew Brice and Eilish kisses, as she brought the baby closer to her chest to coo her back to sleep.

"The apartments are housed within the facility, George," Avila said, then motioned to the center of the facility. "The parents are required to stay here for five years as the Sollus infants grow from zero to three years old in a year. They'll age by three years every year. In five years, they'll be fifteen years old and old enough to live outside the facility without supervision. Come, I'll let you go inside the facilities. Girls, you're not allowed to go inside, so run along to the playground..." Avila had not finished his words yet, and just heard the delighted squeals of the two girls as they raced toward the playground in the Sollus compound.

Avila turned around and directed him toward a grey, somber-looking building. The door alone was around ten feet tall. He touched the door, and a tiny burst of electricity radiated from it.

"Careful! It's just a deterrent for intruders. But it's not harmful," Avila said as he pressed his thumb on a small device by the doorknob. The words "DNA matched" flashed on its screen, and George did the same thing. There was a pause as the machine tested his DNA, and the device flashed "Profile checked." Then the giant door opened onto a courtyard. As they walked toward the courtyard, he saw that it opened to twenty floors downward.

"All this was explained to us when Mira was exploring applying for the Sollus program. You see, when the Machina machine was retrieved from the Hans, from the Colony HQ lab, it was clear that the Hans tried to mimic human skin, which was supple and tough. From the outside, they look human. But if you slice them apart, there is nothing inside but the hardware of advanced computers. Let's walk to the birthing room!" Avila smiled when he saw his reaction.

"Two hundred years ago, it was believed that a live birth can only come from an egg from a mother and a sperm from the father. But 40 years ago, through the research of Nobel winners John Gurdon and Shinya Yamanaka, it was discovered that sperm and egg cells can be produced from human skin cells. There's no need for a human father or mother to start the reproduction process!"

They stopped in front of the birthing room, and their

DNA was tested again before they were allowed to enter. Upon entry, a clear glass wall separated them from the rows upon rows of babies in their cribs.

"Babies can be born from the DNA of a male and female, two males, two females. The skin is the source of life for the sperm and the egg, the skin is also the host for growing the organs, muscles, and blood vessels. When you open the babies from the Sollus genus, you see a human body inside." Avila's voice grew excited. "Ira O'Rourke cries and poos at night, she's a delight!"

"How about their personality? Their emotions?" he asked.

"Genetic codes are divided into 'inner person genes,' the internal workings of behavior and emotions, and the 'outer genes,' which determine how they look," Avila said, and leaned his forehead on the glass facing the birthing room. "We are not allowed inside to see the process from fertilization of egg and sperm to a full-term baby, but from what Mira told me, it only took three months for Ira to be born."

"So, the Sollus AIPS age according to a program?" he asked. George slightly hesitated when he used the term AIPS or Artificially Intelligent Persons. He couldn't yet think of the babies in front of him as human persons. Not yet.

"Yes, it's all programmed," Avila nodded. "I don't think the families can stay here much longer than five years."

"Where are they housed?" he asked. He couldn't imagine staying in this place for five years, but Mira had uprooted her family from her former Jurong West residence home to stay here.

"Mira stays in this building. Ira will be under observation till she reaches fifteen years old. Ira will also be surrounded by other Sollus babies, and have a community together.

The schools are being set up for them as we speak. Would you like to go there?" Avila asked.

But he shook his head. He was tired and needed time to digest all this information. He was staying with the O'Rourke family this weekend, but wasn't sure this was the correct decision. A baby, even if it was a Sollus, would change things forever with Mira.

He had to try to overcome his trauma with the Machina encounter two years ago, but he was uneasy from the time he entered this facility. He hated the concept of artificially-anything. He wanted to leave and get away from this place right now...

"Would you like to go back to Mira and the kids?" Avila asked.

"Oh sure, let's see the kids and Mira." He nodded but he wasn't sure he wanted to stay. He had a decision to make this weekend. If he felt it was impossible to have a relationship with Mira, he had to be clear about it as soon as possible. Mira deserved nothing but the truth. He turned and looked at the babies again, and felt a shudder up his spine.

What did the future hold for humanity? Will the Artificially Intelligent Persons overtake the Homo Sapiens? Looking at it from his viewpoint, he knew what the answer was. Humankind had no chance at all with the machines.

Chapter

Colony HQ

Colorado River Coalition

United States of America

American River Coalitions

21 August 2071

21 days after the Drone Strike

The meeting had started and Brice walked behind Henry as he entered the inner vestibule.

The room was dark and all the faces were somber, their attention on the images flashing at the side of the room.

As her eyes adjusted, she tried to see who was attending this Colony meeting.

"For those of you who have just arrived, let me introduce Su Kyi Lyu, Head of Operations, Southeast Asia. John Nicodemus, HO Eurasia, Pedro Simon, liaison,

Department of Defense." Her uncle started to speak and turned towards her and Henry who were the last to arrive in the room.

A screen flashed and a picture of two faces appeared. They were Hari Salim and Lee Jae Seung.

"We've been suspicious that the Drone Attack in Suvarnadvipa was not perpetrated by the Hans, but by another entity," Avila said. "New enemy, new tactics." He paused, then folded his arms. "What do they want? But we've observed renewed activity from the AQs, especially after the Suvarnadvipa rescue of Hari Salim."

Avila pointed at the faces on the screen.

"It is clear that our mission has changed. Ever since Hari and Jae disappeared six months ago, we've been grasping at straws. As you all know, our efforts have led to one debacle after another; it's as if the enemy knows what we're doing even before we plan it. We've checked and rechecked the drones that attacked us. Are they responsible for this? Clearly, they mean business."

Avila looked around the group, and his glance lingered on her.

"Why drones?" he said, turning away from her. "It's such an antiquated attack tool. If their purpose was to push everyone underground, then they were very successful.

"As far as we know, after Elimination Day or E Day six months ago the Hans and their Machinas are a thing of the past. There is no credible threat arising from that party. We're sure of that. But something's afoot, and I'm guessing there's going to be another attack soon. Another Drone Attack? We just can't see where their next target is. There's no signature that we could see. I'll toss the baton to Deputy Defense Minister James Henry. Henry, please continue…"

The screen flashed and a picture of a man appeared.

"This man is Hari Salim, the son of General Dio Salim. Father and son were leaders of the underground Defiance forces who battled the Hans in the Philippines. Hari is also a former Colony agent. But is it really their group that unleashed the First Drone War launched twenty-one days ago? Or another group?" Henry asked the crowd.

"Lee Jae Seung, another former Colony agent," he continued. Her gaze settled on Lee's image. It was a young Lee, when he first stepped in Concordia as a Han captain, with a topknot of hair on his head. Her memory of the day she first met him was seared in her brain. Lee looked like a young samurai warrior, he didn't have the Bushido swords, nor the multi-layered vests of the ancient warriors, but seeing him in uniform as a Han officer was a very intimidating sight.

"Agent Brice? Any comments from your end?" Her uncle's voice was sharp, and she stood up straighter.

"No, sir," she said. A picture of Hari appeared next. She had a sudden feeling that her breath was trapped and about to explode inside her chest.

Avila stood up and approached the screen, then turned to address the assemblage. "We thought that by battling the Hans, our problems were finally solved. But another group is battling for supremacy. Is it to take over the last remaining viable resources of Earth? The mastermind, whoever he is, is brilliant. We're facing a take-over soon as well as a possible second drone attack, if we don't find who's behind it."

President Mallard then stood and spoke up.

"The question is, where can we find these people?" he finally said. "I've been apprised by the Colony, and they have looked far and wide for Lee and Salim. The last time we saw Salim was Suvarnadvipa. Unfortunately, he escaped when the AQs assisted him, killing two Echoes, and wounding eight." Mallard glanced at her, a question in his eyes. But he turned back to the screen.

"We've recently received some new information," Mallard continued. "Sources have pinpointed Salim's location to one particular London office. Why London?" he asked the group. "What's in London to generate their interest? I don't know, and that's why we need additional eyes and ears. I'm quite desperate to solve this problem. If we don't, we have to come up with plans to evacuate the central government again, this time to an undisclosed location. Something's definitely brewing, but we don't know what."

The room went quiet.

Mallard spoke again, this time with force. "I want four teams assigned to the United Kingdom's Thames River Coalition. Brice, you're part of one of them," he said. "I need everyone there yesterday. Bridge 6 will coordinate. They're worried Thames might be the next target."

Bridge 6 was the Intelligence arm of the Thames River Coalition, the Colony's crack-shot partner in many operations around the world. But she knew she wasn't really being commissioned to Thames to help their work.

"Permission to speak, sir." The room quieted as everyone turned to look at her.

"I object to being a part of this team," she said. Her voice was trembling, but she stood her ground.

"Objection noted, Agent O'Rourke," Avila answered.

"But it doesn't change anything. You know it's a great risk that you're even allowed to be any part of the Colony Intelligence team."

"I object to your plan to use me as bait to lure said suspects, sir." She was shaking now.

"You're a good agent and the best damn chance we have for finding these people," President Mallard replied. "And you know it. Besides, we were successful in Suvarnadvipa, right? It means they wanted to get you, Brice. You go where I say you'll go." His voice was cool and unperturbed. Gone was the idealistic supervisor agent she had met in Concordia. Gone was the person who visited them at their home in Singapore when they were young. This person who tried to woo her mother in the past years, was gone. She looked at her uncle and he nodded.

"It's cruel and inhuman, sir. I object to it." She stood up, and stepped closer to her uncle. Henry caught her arm.

"Why don't you assign another agent, President Mallard?" Henry asked. "It doesn't have to be Brice. I can go, sir," Henry volunteered.

"Objection noted on this, Agent O'Rourke, Deputy Director Keyon We are understaffed, and we need every available agent in the field," Avila answered, then faced Henry. "Salim was unsuccessful in retrieving you in Suvarnadvipa, and that is why Quinn Mathews will be assigned to you."

"But he hasn't passed the Colony test," she argued.

"Quinn will be there as your security. No more arguments," her uncle said in a firm tone.

President Mallard took off his glasses, wiped the lenses and put them back on. He focused his gaze on the other people around the table, then returned his gaze to her.

"You know how Salim and Lee think. Try to find out what their plans are, if you can. Gabriel Patrick from Bridge 6 is waiting for you. Now go. Good luck." President Mallard stood up, and without so much as a goodbye, left the room.

The four men stood as President Mallard left.

When the highest officer had left the premises, the noise level would ratchet up as those left would continue to hash their plans openly. But there was a palpable awkward silence felt around the room. She knew they didn't want to discuss their plans in front of her.

She stared right back at them, then raised her middle finger in a brief salute, and left the room.

"C'mon Brice," Henry said as he grabbed her elbow, and led her back toward the trains. "Let's have a coffee break. You need to eat."

When she passed the hive of Colony agents in their cocoons, their screens went dark again and they let her pass by in silence. But again, there were sounds of thumping on the floor, but she felt too heartsick to acknowledge the sound of faint, rebellious support for her.

They walked in silence as they approached the train tracks leading to the Colony.

She knew Henry was probably thinking too of their former comrades in arms in the Colony.

The train arrived, and Brice slumped in a seat, exhausted by the Colony experience. Even her security Bee stayed quiet on top of her head, as if asleep.

As the train pulled away, she thought of Hari and Jae. Why were their movements tracked in the Thames River Coalition?

She also thought of Quinn. Would they work well together? So many questions needed be answered. She felt exhausted, and looked outside the window. There was no view to see as the train passed through twisting, subterranean tunnels. Just darkness.

Chapter

Denver Congressional Hall

Colorado River Coalition

United States of America

American River Coalitions

08 January 2064

7 years, 6 months, 24 days before the Drone Strike

Mallard

The congressional hearings were now conducted via image streaming so that government agencies could save time traveling to Denver to testify.

He scanned the crowd again and this time, took a hard look at the lawmakers in front of him. Most of them had aged from the first time he saw them at their initial congressional hearing six years ago.

He touched his hair and wondered if he had aged as

everyone had in this room. He glanced at Avila, and his hair had greyed too. They were aging minute by minute, the stress compounding when they faced this group of very demanding legislative leaders.

"Defense Minister George Mallard, welcome back to the Congressional halls. And congratulations on the new position as Defense Minister," Senator Blair said. He stood up and the other senators did the same. He was surprised at the unexpected gesture from the lawmakers, who had always been tough on him with their questioning.

"Let's also give a big hand of applause to the new Deputy Defense Minister Avila O'Rourke." A burst of applause sounded out around the hall, and he and Avila stood up amidst the cheers.

"And now..." Senator Blair banged the gavel, "you know how we hate wasting everyone's time here. What's the latest on the situation in the United States, and the world around us, Minister Mallard?" he asked as he sat down, impatient as always, his arms akimbo while he glared at the panel below him.

He turned to Avila and nodded to him as Avila stood up to give the latest count. "I'll give the floor to my deputy, Senator Blair. He's the point person going around and checking the Machina status around the world."

"Senator Blair, it's been six years since the Great Migration of the Hans to different lands. Some are more successful in getting back their territory – Paris and Berlin were the more successful cities," Avila said. There were sudden whoops and cheers from the crowd behind them.

"Cheers to our French, German, South Korean and Chinese allies. We know all this from the recent news. But tell me, what's the main reason this has happened, Minister

O'Rourke?" Senator Blair demanded.

"We've noticed more deaths from the Han human population all over the world. Paris, Berlin, and Shanghai have recorded the burning of human corpses in their camps. The deaths have a direct connection to the vulnerability in their defenses. After all, the Machina soldiers are just machines controlled by their human counterparts," Avila said.

"Is there a way for the Machinas to be obliterated completely?" Blair asked. "Minister Mallard, I want to hear your opinion," another senator piped in, and all of the senators were looking at him.

"The Defense master control is in Pyongyang in North Korea, and the Hans have protected their country deep, deep into the sea. They took advantage of the chaos after the Polar Shift. That was the window when they created the Machinas and unleashed them all over the world. But after that, Pyongyang is impenetrable deep in the sea," he stood up to answer this, and Blair turned to him and pointed a finger at him.

"I've told you six years ago. Get rid of the Machinas. And we have some successes, and also a lot of failures. How's the Sollus program, Minister Mallard? It seems to be a success, but it's too slow for us." Blair waved impatiently and scowled at him.

"The Sollus children are all doing well, Senator Blair. They are now sixteen years old, and they have integrated well into human society," he answered. There were a number of boos from the crowd. "If you expect some Sollus children to fight the Machinas, I don't think it will happen."

"So we're doomed then!" Senator Blair answered and a group of people clapped and jeered at the back. "Order in the halls, please! Security, please escort everyone out. This will be a private discussion, and the public will be requested to leave." The senator turned to the cameras while the congressional guards stood up to walk toward the unruly crowd. Once they were escorted out, the senators spoke again.

"You spoke about a program six years ago that you had plans of using the captured Machinas. It wasn't approved by this committee, you know. We'd be as immoral as the Hans. Any alternative solution?" Blair asked.

"Minister Mallard, please continue," another member of the panel acknowledged his presence and leaned forward, eager to hear what he had to say. "I'm Senator Hillel, please continue what you were about to say. The Hans have declared the cities they've occupied as Open Metropolises. They intend to open the cities as showcases of Han culture, thumbing their noses at us."

"We have another program in the works, but it needs congressional approval, Senator Blair. Whereas the Sollus program is for AIPs created from two-sourced parents, Project Aequilavum is the creation of another Homo Roboticus genus with DNA from robotic chromosomes. They will have no parent chromosome from two sets of parents, just artificial chromosomes from a robotic genome," he explained.

"So explain it simply, it's a Sollus AIP, but how do they look, how about their personalities? How do they integrate with the Homo Sapiens like us?" Senator Blair asked bluntly.

"Based on Mendel's inheritance laws, the AQ, for shorter purposes, will look like the Sollus, it's just that there will be no camps where parents wait for their offspring to grow from infancy to fifteen years old. Reformation takes a month to build the Aequilavum," he answered.

He watched the expressions of the congressional panel. This time, it felt different than six years ago. They were eager, and salivating for victory, no matter the cost. Everyone was interested in a sentient droid who could beat the Machinas.

Were they creating monsters?

"Thank you for taking the time to clarify this to us, Minister Mallard. You can be reassured we will explore this with vigor, and if we get a majority, a new law will pass for this program. That is all." Blair banged the gavel, and the senators conferred with each other, forgetting about the people in front of them, people who were in the field making sure that the nation's defense systems were up to par, and that the Machinas would be a thing of the past.

Would the creation of this other program finally defeat the Machinas?

He turned to Avila, and seeing the exhaustion at his face, he knew it reflected his own sentiments.

He was tired of it all, and longed for a simpler life before the robots appeared. Perhaps this was not the life he wanted. He wanted something more; what it was, he wasn't sure. But the life he was seeing in front of him was not the life he wanted.

Sollus Compound

Yang Bioresearch Institute
Kallang River Coalition
Singapore
Asian River Coalitions
08 January 2064
7 years, 6 months, 24 days before the Drone Strike

While Brice was at school, an envelope had arrived for her. She sat in the kitchen of the Sollus compound apartment she shared with her mother, Ira, and Eilish, and just stared at it. She wanted to wait for her mother to arrive before she opened it.

Ira held an envelope near her, and jumped up and down with one foot. Eilish, who was beside her, copied Ira, but fell. Ira picked her up in one swoop. She kissed Eilish and giggled, before turning to her. "Hey Brice, it has finally arrived. Shall we open it, or wait for Mother?"

She smiled at her two sisters. Ira was now twelve years old, and she had the same green eyes as her own, but her hair was reddish brown, a striking combination that made many people stop and stare at her.

"Wait for Mother," she said. "Wait for her, Brice," Eilish piped up.

She reached toward Eilish and kissed her glassinex cheek. Eilish had remained a Simplex, with the mind of a six-year-old, and most parts of her body were now older than her age. She hugged her closer. She didn't know what she'd do if anything happened to Ira or Eilish.

She had applied at all the universities in the US, even Harvard, as Uncle Avila had pressured her to go there since it was her father's alma mater.

School was a breeze for her. She had skipped grades twice in her school years, and high school wasn't intellectually stimulating for her. The guidance counselors all advised that she was ready for university.

A small red dot on the wall blinked. The red indicated that there were no new messages.

When will it turn green?

"Still no messages from Hari?" Ira whispered to her.

"None. I'm worried about him. Damn," she said.

"Brice, no cuss words, Mom said." Eilish looked at her, while Ira giggled by the side. "You sound like Mom, Eilish."

"What's so funny? And why are there no messages from Hari? Where are they, Brice?" Eilish demanded so many questions to be answered.

"Hey Eilish, why don't I play Snakes and Ladders with you, huh?" Ira motioned an OK sign toward her. It meant that she was going to take care of Eilish while she could check her messages in peace.

She reached toward the wall toward Videoton, a device that showed images of the news and a way to receive all one's messages, play games, talk to each other, an all-in-one ubiquitous device in every home. She touched a button to check her messages, but it showed an egg dancing around the screen.

There were no messages from Hari. The Salims had gone back to Manila for a vacation. It was publicized that things had changed for the better in the Han-occupied countries. In the Philippines, the Hans had declared Pasig River and Palawan as Open Metropolises. As long as there was no fighting involved between the citizens and the Hans, citizens were invited back to their former homes.

Uncle Avila and her mom had cautioned the Salims against returning to Manila, but Tio Dio wanted to see what changes six years had wrought in Concordia and promised just a short vacation. Her mom had begged Tia Noor to let Amil stay with them, so that he could continue his university studies in Singapore. Hari had finished his studies and he wanted to take up medicine in the National University of Singapore. And yet, they still left for the Philippines.

For weeks, Hari had given her constant updates through voice links. A week before, the messages had slowed to a trickle, and for the past two days, she had received none at all.

She stood up. She decided she couldn't wait another minute to open the letter from Harvard. She read the enclosed document twice. And then she screamed. Ira and Eilish appeared and when they saw her jumping up and down, they did the same movement.

"What happened, Brice? What's in the envelope?" Eilish asked.

"Oh, just some news about my new school," Brice said.

"What new school? Will you be gone for long hours at a time again?" Eilish said, and her glassine eyes blinked, uncomprehending.

How would she explain that she'd be traveling thousands of miles away from her to Boston and attending Harvard University?

Perhaps it would be possible that her mother, Ira, and Eilish could relocate to Boston while she was there? She couldn't bear the thought of leaving the three most important people in her life for the next four years for college.

Her gaze shifted to the wall, where a news item of some kind showed an explosion somewhere, people running... And then the location was announced. Manila. Where the Salims were.

Her happiness at her acceptance to Harvard was forgotten. Everything had slowed down, and she felt she was falling, falling to the ground.

She heard Ira's screams. "Brice, Brice, are you all right?"

She felt nauseated and she curled up on the floor. Ira ran and cradled her tightly and rocked her, just as everyone was taught in her family to do.

"Brice, stay with me, listen to my voice." She felt Ira's warm touch and her rocking motions. She stared up the ceiling, trying to remain calm.

She tried to remember the last time she'd seen Hari before his departure a few weeks ago.

He had stood her up twice for the movies, and she had gone to their home to see him.

Tia Noor had answered the door, and it was obvious that she'd been crying. Hari was not pleased to see her when she came knocking at their front door.

She was quiet, sitting on his bed, observing as he packed his clothes in a suitcase.

Gone was the tentative, awkward teenager. In front of her stood a young man who was determined not to show emotion to her.

Hari had grown to the height of his father, just below six feet. He had been a swimmer all his life, and he had continued his love for the sport by being part of the swimming team in NUS. His ripped chest and sinewy arms were well-displayed by the plain black shirt he was wearing.

She thought of all the things she wanted to say to him before he left. But then, she thought of her father and grandfather and the things that were left unsaid.

"Hey Hari, I love you," she told him matter-of-factly.

The shock in his face made Brice laugh. "Got your attention, Hari Salim."

"Gosh, O'Rourke. What a bomb to deliver right before I leave."

Hari stood facing her, his hands full of unpacked clothes, and she saw that he had a question in his eyes. Was she pulling his leg, or was she serious?

"I've loved you ever since I first saw you in Concordia. I know you're too distracted with what I told you now, and you're going to Manila, and all. I'm too young, and maybe too stupid. And you don't have to do anything with the info I told you. But I love you, Hari." Hari blinked and smiled.

"O'Rourke," he said, "I love you as a sister. But who knows. That may turn to love and lust when your body changes, and your foul mouth disappears into the ether world..."

A fat pillow landed on his head, interrupting him.

"Promise to answer me whenever I send you a message," she said. "Otherwise I'll go to Manila and find out what's what!" Instead of answering, he dropped the clothes, lunged at her, and caught her arm.

She surprised him by catching both his arms, pinning them to his sides and kissing him quickly on the cheek. Then she released him.

"Where'd you get those moves, O'Rourke?" he asked

as he massaged his arms.

"Jujitsu," she grinned as they smiled at one another.

"Come here," he beckoned. She moved toward him tentatively. He pulled her in his arms, and kissed her on the lips. "Oh, I'll miss you, Brice. I've graduated from university, and I don't know where my career path will go. I'll keep in touch. Promise you won't take unnecessary risks, hear?"

She embraced him back. "You promise not to take unnecessary risks? Promise me, Hari."

There was no answer from Hari.

Instead, they stood together silently, embracing. No words could explain how deeply the bonds of their shared history held them together. And in the end, they were survivors. They'd do their best to find a way to survive, no matter what.

"Brice, Brice! Uncle Avila wants to talk to you," Ira's voice summoned her back to the present. She stuffed the acceptance letter from Harvard back in its envelope.

There was a slight warming sensation from the communication device that hung like a necklace from her neck. She picked it up. Uncle Avila had been the one calling her name.

"So good to hear from you," she said. "I just heard from Harva..." But her uncle interrupted her.

"When was the last time you communicated with Hari?" he demanded.

"Two days ago. Why, what's wrong?" her worried voice made Ira and Eilish turn toward her.

"Manila was declared a Closed City because of an explosion. There's been absolutely no communication with our sources in the country."

"What?" Words couldn't come out from her mouth. It was too painful to speak, to think.

"Let me know if you get hold of Hari. Did you hear me, Brice? As soon as possible!" Then the line went blank, and her attention was caught by a bloody scene displayed on the wall. Machinus soldiers were tumbled in a pile, their body parts torn like toys.

Brice tried to message Hari again and again; there was no answer. A feeling of gloom suddenly filled the room.

What if the Salims were trapped in Manila? What if they weren't allowed to return to Singapore?

Brice could not comprehend the enormity of it all.

At that moment, she felt like she was watching herself from a distance. The images around her seemed frozen - the letter from Harvard hovering beside her, juxtaposed with the images of explosions and Ira embracing her.

Brice pressed her hands on her chest. She suddenly couldn't breathe.

In moments of distress, flashes of memories often raced through her mind: her family's flight from Antarctica, the moment her mother dragged her inside the Concordia caves with Eilish, not certain about the fate of her father.

She was having an anxiety attack, and she held on to Ira, who continued to rock her, until her anxiety level dropped.

"Thanks, Ira, I could feel my anxiety level decreasing. No, no need to call Mom. I can handle this." She patted Ira's arm.

She closed her eyes and focused on her breathing. Through the years, she had worked long and hard with psychologists to handle these panic attacks, learning tension and trauma release exercises to return her body to a state of balance after stressful events. She was determined not to let the traumatic past bedevil her present.

Ira laid her on the floor and wrapped her tightly in something warm. She closed her eyes.

She willed her brain to focus on what was currently happening to her instead of things that had occurred in the past. She focused on her intake of breath. Inhale, steady one, steady two, steady three. Then exhale, steady out one, steady out two, steady out three.

And then she remembered the envelope.

It held promise, possibilities. A happy future.

There was nothing she could do about the situation in Manila. She could not go there to help Hari or his family, if help was indeed needed. How long would she survive in an occupied country? She would serve no use to the Salims at this time.

"Focus on the sounds coming from the window, Brice," Ira said. She focused on the sounds of bird song outside the house, when another story flashed on the video news wall with a burst of harsh noise.

She thought of their last encounter. She now tried to remember the details in that encounter she hadn't thought of. Why was she so careless with those memories? Hasn't she learned from the deaths of her grandfather and father that every moment spent with someone one loves had to be savored?

No, she never learned the lessons from the past, and this was why these events kept happening to her.

She curled in a fetal position and cried bitter tears. Lessons... lessons she never learned. Regrets...

She promised that if she found some information that

Hari was alive, she would shake off her PTSD and seize life by the throat. From this moment on. She would change, she promised. It would be a new Brice.

Mallard Corporation

Arakawa River Coalition

Shinjuku, Japan

Asian River Coalitions

05 June 2064

7 years, 1 month, 28 days before the Drone Strike

Mallard

He always loved passing through the Shinjuku-Gyoen gardens before arriving at the Mallard Corporation. The cherry blossoms had bloomed a month ago, but as the private ferry passed through the streets, the trees still had a semblance of some of the remaining flowers in the branches. He was half-expecting that he would see the trees anchored on land, but like many of the places he'd visited, waters of the rivers had flooded many parts of the city.

"Fucking droids!!"

"Banish droids from Planet Earth!"

"Eliminate robots!"

His attention was diverted to the streets leading to the nearby Ministry of Biorobotics where people jammed their placards at all passing ferries.

What was new? People all over the world were weary of all kinds of sentient droids. He thought of his own feelings and until now, couldn't shake off the feeling of dread when he thought of his first Machina encounter six years ago.

The ferry made its way away from the flash of people and headed straight to the looming Mallard Corporation.

They stopped at a building and he thought of the origins of the company. His great grandfather West Mallard was a young soldier during the Vietnam War, ninety years ago. He had criticized to superiors about the firearms given to him, and had thought of ways to modernize the equipment.

After an injury fighting in the tunnels at Ho Chi Minh City, West did not go back to the fighting fields. Instead he founded a company specializing in weaponry. West Mallard benefitted greatly from the Gulf War and the wars in Afghanistan since 2001.

Despite his many faults, his father Horatio did not rest on the laurels of his father and expanded the company to other countries. Horatio Mallard became a billionaire many times over, his wealth unstoppable as the company grew to what it was now.

His father had written a proviso in his will that he would get a chance to run the company as he turned 34 years old. The CEO, Ami Kapoor, and the Board of Mallard Corporation had summoned him to Shinjuku and he was curious about what they had to say. He had resigned from the Defense Ministry last week, handing the reins to Avila, and he wanted to explore other areas in his life now.

As he stepped into the austere, elegant lobby of the Mallard Corporation, he thought of the last day he saw his father.

The sun was setting over the buildings surrounding Central Park that day. As he stood on the balcony of his parents' lavish and ornate 44th floor apartment, he felt like he was floating on air.

Behind him, he heard rhythmic clinking and shuffling sounds made by the service staff who were readying for dinner, setting out a perfect arrangement of plates, glasses, and cutlery on a long white table.

He was due to leave for his assignment the next day as a Lieutenant in the army, but the party was sprung as a surprise for him for his West Point graduation. He had no interest in the formal celebrations. Everyone knew his father hated the thought of him entering the military. His father always served himself best.

He could see his parents standing near a window in the library, and eyed his father, who was more distracted than usual. Problems with his companies?

He next gauged the state of prescriptive toxicity of his mother, Patricia Clements Mallard. She was such a sweet mother when he was young, and she was still sweet, but totally cowed by the oppressive personality of his father. She had drowned her sorrows in alcohol, drugs? Who knew?

As the guests arrived, he observed that the men were in suits but with no ties, while the women were bedecked in the finest jewelry and clothing money could buy.

He was about to run to the kitchen when a commanding voice addressed him.

"Dearest George! I thought for a second I was seeing West Mallard in the flesh!"

He cringed. Dreadful Aunt Zoei, the sister of his father. "You are the image of your grandfather!" she continued. He turned away as his aunt reached for him, and returned with a glass of champagne which he placed in her outstretched hand.

His father caught his eye, and frowned. He was about to admonish him when a gigantic tremor shook the apartment's walls. Screams erupted as tables overturned, crashing silverware and glasses to the floor. The screams turned to pandemonium when the movement became a steady swaying.

"Look, look!" one man screamed. "Central Park has disappeared!!"

He rushed to the balcony, and peered down.

Giant waves had engulfed half of the city. The guests standing next to him watched in horror as water continued to roll toward their building.

Many guests screamed and headed to the doorway, and he sprang into action. "It's safer here. Don't go out," he shouted. But no one was listening.

The rest of the guests were screaming and crying and moaning all at once. And then the lights went out. The sun had set, and the room was dark. The room swayed again, and this time, he heard prayers springing from his father's lips. His father was not a religious man, and hearing him pray meant that they were all doomed.

How did he survive that day? He defied his parents by refusing to stay in the apartment and helping the National Guards who were deployed to help the survivors.

They were transferred to a safe point in Bennett Park in Washington Heights, the highest point of land in the city. Many of the survivors thrived in the tragic conditions they were in, while others simply gave up.

His father could not take the shock of New York City submerged in water, and died two months after the Polar Shift.

That was six years ago, and yet it was still very fresh in his mind. Everything had changed when the Polar Shift happened. He inherited the company, which was based in 24 other countries around the world. In his father's will, he could be elected to the board if he so wished when he turned 34. Today.

He had visited this city since he was three years old, and Tokyo had not ceased to fascinate him.

"Welcome, George!" He was ushered into the sleek corporate headquarters in the 20th floor, and some of the Board members who were from Japan bowed to him.

After pleasantries, the Board settled down to reports from subsidiaries around the world. There were reports of factories closing down, many of the older weaponry laid to waste when newer inventions were created.

"We had to phase out many of the factories and make it fully robotized. No wonder many are displaced and without jobs. Hence, the demonstrations all over the city." Kapoor faced him and said brightly, "Any thoughts on this, George?"

He stood up as a round of applause was heard around the room. "Thank you, oh, what a welcome, indeed! The problems of Mallard Corporation are not just experienced here, but it is a global phenomenon. As the current human population ages, technology advances non-stop replacing old weaponry, old machines, and sadly, robotics will replace workers. Do we modernize till humans are replaced or do we scale down, balancing the needs of society?"

As he spoke, his thoughts turned to the corporation he was poised to inherit. There was a hunger for more than profits. He wanted to change the conversation on robotics. Not by expanding his father's business to the 22nd century. He wanted to explore politics and change the current laws of the country. Why not do both? He can be part of this company and still explore running for the US Presidency, right? He can step down when the formalization process of the nominations begin.

He couldn't see years of his life drained away as a Defense Minister, when he could not defend its laws.

He couldn't also see years of his life being drained away, staying in this company, obsessed with profit and margin, year after year.

Once he left the Defense Department, he had been more vocal about his beliefs in returning to a simpler life pre-machines. He had been giving more and more speeches and the public had clamored for these as he traveled around the country to visit his father's vast company.

It felt right that this was the path where he felt fulfilled and he felt it was his mission to be more vocal about it.

He made a decision.

When the Board Meeting ended, he tapped a communication device which was attached to his ear and called Mira. But she had not been answering his calls in the past days. It was ten p.m. and most likely she was still not asleep. It was best to visit her and fly back to New York the next morning.

He felt fear and exhilaration at the same time. Was he making a mistake? He needed to talk to Mira. It was time.

New York City

United States of America

American River Coalitions

05 June 2064

7 years, 1 month, 28 days before the Drone Strike

Mallard

His private seacraft landed at JFK International Airport, and he was in a hurry to clear Immigration to meet up with Mira.

From the first time he had seen her in Concordia, he had been drawn to her. But she was married to Esteban at that time. When Esteban died, he was inexplicably pulled toward her very brainy, scientific self and the side of her that had thrown caution to the wind and dived headlong into the emotional cauldron of raising a family without a husband, being a mother to a Sollus, a Simplex, and a very complicated Homo Sapiens.

The watercraft passed by the streets of Harlem and he marveled at how New York City had rallied after the Polar

Shift eight years ago. The city was in a state of shock for a few months, but then the general population accepted their fate and moved on. Such resilient people.

With defiance, the city did not go underground, but stayed above ground, closing the floors that were flooded and erecting steel barriers to raise the streets.

Watercraft replaced cars. Central Park was a water park for the first few years, but then people missed the grass and the bike lanes. So the city council tried to recreate every last bit of the park; it was just five floors higher than what it was before.

He passed 110th Street, and often wondered why Mira loved to stay in this neighborhood.

She had tried staying at one of the old townhouses built in Harlem in the 1900s, but after a few restless months, she decided to stay in one of the houseboats along the Hudson River.

Mira was waiting for him as his private watercraft landed. Eilish was there too to greet him.

Ira was in her last year of high school and also greeted him warmly, but quietly left the conversation and stayed in her room till dinner.

He was still uneasy with AIPs, and he realized he had to learn to live with them if he wanted a future with Mira.

Wine and cheese were prepared by the deck, and they sat down, gazing at the water of Hudson Bay.

The reflection of the light on Mira's hair heightened her gold-burnished highlights. The wrinkles at the side of her eyes had deepened, but her smile was as warm as always.

"How was Shinjuku?" she asked.

"I accepted the role as member of the Board. At the same

time, I'll also be setting up the machinery to run for the Presidency of the United States," he said.

Mira was surprised. " I've heard your speeches, but you never mentioned a run for the Presidency as one of your end goals."

"There seemed to be deeper problems in the world and I want to solve them," he said and reached out to her as he saw confusion on her face. "I don't want my end game to be running the Defense Ministry. I'd like you to be beside me when I run the country, Mira."

"But what really is your platform, George? I've heard your speeches. You want to return to a simpler, less mechanized world. What does that mean when I have two Roboticus daughters in my care?"

"It doesn't mean a family can't have divergent values, Mira. It reflects the divide of most families in America. We've been so divided in this country by different opinions," his voice rose a fraction, sensing the tension between them.

"But it's precisely this stance that infuriates me, George. You can't espouse these beliefs when they fundamentally threaten the existence of my children." Her eyes flashed, and a side of Mira he had not seen was now evident in them.

"I love you, Mira." He held her hand and kissed it. But she took her hand away.

"Do you really love me, George? Do you really understand me? I believe that Ira and Eilish have the right to exist. Your belief of a limited role for them is a fantasy. They are here to stay. They will rule the world someday," she said with certainty.

He could not believe her words. The Roboticus genus

would not lead the world one day. Only the Homo Sapiens had the right to dominion on Earth. It was the only way.

Was it love that he felt that moment for her? Or was it hatred?

It dawned on him that he could not abandon his beliefs. And she could not abandon her daughters.

She stood up.

The wine and the cheese on the table were forgotten. It was time to go.

He wanted to touch her one more time, and embrace her. He reached out to embrace her.

But she had moved near the door of the houseboat.

"Goodbye, George." She kissed him at the side of the lips. She turned away and walked toward Ira's room. She reached out to Eilish and carried her toward the room.

Then he heard the lock click.

He turned his back and walked towards the jetty. He moved liked an automaton as he entered his watercraft, sat at the driver's seat and turned on the ignition. Tears clouded his eyes as he sped away, far away from Mira's houseboat.

She was gone from his life.

The machines have no place on Earth. His heart hardened. He was going to win the Presidency of the land and he will change the laws. He will prove her wrong.

Central Park Stadium

New York City

East River Coalition

United States of America

American River Coalitions

12 June 2064

7 years, 1 month, 21 days before the Drone Strike

Avila

People were clapping and cheering, many were jumping up and down their seats.

He tried to look for an empty seat, but all the seats were filled in the Stadium, forcing him to go to the back row where he was forced to stand up.

His focus was on the stage and the speakers. Turning to look around the stadium, there were streamers with crude depictions of AIPs on a noose or sentient droids burning on fire.

"Ladies and gentlemen, it is our pleasure to welcome the United States Presidential contender, George Mallard..." the emcee had not finished his spiel, but the crowd rose up and started cheering.

George Mallard was beaming, his hands raised up, his salt and pepper hair distinguishable from far away, his megawatt smile so distinct and charming that the crowd howled as he stood there before his speech.

He thought of the frantic call he received from Mira a

week ago. She was incoherent at first, but he calmed her down by asking a few questions at first.

"So you broke off with him, but he didn't take it well?" he asked.

"George has been sending me flowers and chocolates and the kids love it, but I'm firm on my decision, Avila," Mira said with no hesitation. "Am I crazy?"

"What made you decide to break it off, Mira?" he asked.

"Haven't you listened to his speeches? Ever since he resigned and threw his hat in the Presidential race, his rhetoric has become inflamed. This is the real George we never knew. Read it online, my God," his sister-in-law's voice was rising again.

"All right, what do you want me to do, Mira?"

"I don't know if it's the right decision for me to break off, but can you see what he's up to, please?"

"Mira, he's my former boss," he said with hesitation.

"This is for me and the children, Avila. For some reason, I've never felt at ease with him when the kids are around."

"Alright, don't worry about it. I'll get back to you in a few days," his soothing voice calmed Mira enough for her to say goodbye in her usual voice.

He flew in from Denver to New York City to set up the surveillance himself. He couldn't trust anyone with this delicate task.

For the past few days, he'd been following George and observed him around the city as he met up with donors and different anti-robotist groups around the country.

This was his first major speech and wondered what he would share to the crowd.

He was surprised that Mallard's voice was conversant like he was talking to a group of friends, not thousands of people.

"No one should ever experience dealing with a Machina. It is the most unnatural thing in the world. When I first set eyes on one ten years ago, it was terrifying."

"Artificially Intelligent Persons should not be allowed to live forever, they should have an expiration date like the rest of humanity." The crowd erupted when they heard this line, and Malllard bowed when he heard this.

"They should not hold a sensitive positions of power in the government...

"They should not take the jobs needed by the American people due to automation. Those jobs belong to us," his speech was interrupted many times and people were climbing up on top of their chairs cheering him on.

"I'd like to apologize to the public that I was in charge setting up the Roboticus programs in the United States. We need to return to our natural roots, before the machines. And as your President, I will introduce legislation eradicating these programs. We need to get rid of these programs. There should only be one species on earth – Homo Sapiens!"

His next words were drowned out by the eruption of applause and shouts of approval. The ground shook as people stomped their feet, and cheered his name.

"Mallard for President! Long live George! Put an end to the Roboticus programs!"

He stood up shakily and turned his back against the adoring crowd of George Mallard.

As he stepped away, his steps faltered and he fell on his knees. It was a relief to get away from that maddening crowd.

What will happen if he wins the Presidency? He thought of his adoring crowd. Will they all turn against the Roboticus? Will they resort to violence to get what they want?

She thought of Mira. Her instincts were correct about this man. Mallard did not deserve to be around Mira and his nieces.

Mallard did not deserve the Presidency of the United States. He was a dangerous, dangerous man and did not deserve to win the highest office of the land.

He had to build a dossier on him, his former boss and mentor. It was a very dangerous task and he could not trust anyone but himself to investigate Mallard. He sighed. Another formidable enemy in this fragile, vulnerable land.

Chapter 11

London,

"Welcome to London!" Gabriel Patrick said as he embraced Brice. He eyed her dark uniform, and her monitoring Bee, then looked over the four men accompanying her. One was Quinn Mathews.

"Wow, you've got a whole phalanx with you. Henry wasn't yanking my chain when he sent word that you and a few others would be visiting our shores. Agents, make yourselves comfortable."

"How are you, Gabriel? How's Amelia?" she asked, and embraced him again. "How're my cute godsons, Sam and

Andre?"

"They're great. The twins about to start nursery," Gabriel said, and chuckled.

"What! Oh boy, time flies!" She shook her head. Gabriel had been a fellow trainee in the Colony training program, the sole exchange recruit from European River Coalitions.

Gabriel directed the arrivals to a boat, and when they were settled, he steered it onto the River Thames. He picked a brisk speed, but the sun beat down on them mercilessly.

"Just cover your face, Brice. You'll get used to the heat," Gabriel shouted. His voice was loud, because he was trying to beat the wind roaring around them.

She took off her jacket and rolled up her shirtsleeves, then untied her sneakers, placed them inside her backpack, and pulled on a pair of flat driving shoes. Finally, she pulled off her pants, revealing short pants.

"Thought I'd pick you up via land, eh, Bricey?" Gabriel said. "You're so sick of all the water, eh?" Gabriel's cheeks were red, but he was clearly enjoying the ride.

"Gabriel, I'd do anything to see land!" she replied. "Where's Hugh?" Hugh was a Scot from Edinburgh, and Gabriel's acerbic investigative partner.

"Absent for the day. He's in charge of interrogating some shitty Brits who helped stoke the great Alpine Fire," Gabriel said.

"Fire in the Swiss Alps. I'm not surprised with this heat," she said and shook her head.

Gabriel nodded toward Quinn, who was seated at the back of the boat. "Who's the hearthrob?" he whispered, his lips pursed.

Brice pulled off the rubber band that held her ponytail

and shook her hair into the wind. "I'm glad you can still gossip, dear friend," she said in a low voice. "Be nice, I was assigned security. He's an Echo and a Sollus." In response, Gabriel's mouth formed a surprised O. And then he grinned and gave a thumbs-up sign.

She turned toward Quinn. "Gabriel, please meet Quinn Mathews, former Echo lieutenant, he just took the exams to enter the Colony, until it was postponed indefinitely."

Gabriel smiled at Quinn and held out his hand. "A pleasure to meet you, Agent Quinn," he said. "Wait till you take part in the Beast exams. What a lucky bastard for you not to take part in that."

"I heard it's a crazy test, Sir," Quinn replied, gripping his hand.

"Welcome, welcome to Thames," Gabriel said cheerfully. "It's as hot as hell for this early hour, but please forgive us for the weather."

"When does night fall in this part of the world, Gabriel?" she shouted from the other side of the boat. The wind was blowing her hair in a frame around her face.

"Hardly ever. It's sunshine, heat, and humidity nearly 24/7." And then he slowed the boat's speed.

"Avila insisted I show you something, Bricey. Do you see that?" Gabriel pointed to his right.

Thousands of houses were lined up by the shore. They appeared to have been built in the river.

"It's beautiful!" she said.

"Many people have shifted to living in the water, Bricey," Gabriel replied. "The flooding is unstoppable, so why not just live in water? If you can't beat 'em, join'em. Makes perfect sense, huh?"

She nodded.

"It's safer too in summer or winter," he continued.

"The summer drought is more tolerable than the winter downpours, I can tell you that."

"Still a beauty," she said, turning to the front of the boat. The Tower of London loomed in front of them. Well, half of it loomed. The other half was submerged. Around it stood charred buildings. Though they were half-submerged as well, wisps of smoke could be seen rising from them.

"I thought there were plans to build new edifices around the Tower?" she asked, turning to Gabriel, but he shrugged. "I don't know what the blokes in Parliament are planning, but I think they want the buildings to keep smoldering there to remind the citizens about the Han occupation."

She stared at the still-burning buildings. "They came to Concordia in boats. We had to run to the caves to escape them," she said softly.

"Yes, I heard the story myself from Avila. I saw the bombing run they made in the Thames in '58, but we were ready for them. Unfortunately, Belfast and Edinburgh weren't fast enough for the Han invaders." Gabriel's voice had gone low and husky. The devastation in Belfast and Edinburgh had been immense. "You were lucky you were able to escape. There was no Plan B for us. Some arrogant blokes thought these jerks from the other side of the world would never have the audacity to invade us. They were terribly wrong."

In fact, the United Kingdom had had a year to prepare for invasion after the Pasig, Concordia, Tokyo, Hanoi and other cities were invaded.

But the Han attacks on top of fast-rising waters in

Northern Ireland and Scotland proved too much for the local population. There was resistance in the first month of occupation, but the Machinas were too strong. In just 58 days, Belfast and Edinburgh were completely overcome by the Hans. Well-warned by this example, London and other large European cities fortified as best they could. The formidable Brit resiliency was shown in the outright defiance of leaving burned buildings standing for everyone to see.

"The Machinas are still roaming around those lands?" she asked.

"Yup. But you didn't hear it from me, Agent Brice. And because of that and the ongoing possibility of future destruction, I think it's time to encase the Tower of London and bring her underground."

She sighed. They were passing under London Bridge, which seemed sturdy even though the waters had devoured most of the buildings surrounding it. The effects of the Polar Shift were frustratingly random. Many cities were submerged, and though some stood steadfast in the encroaching waters, the effects were devastating. She didn't know which was worse – watching landmarks subsumed by water and seeing cities sink entirely beneath the mire because of a natural phenomenon, or an invasion by occupying forces.

"The government's been spending billions to shore up Thames from the flood-surge."

"Good to hear," she said. "I can swim, but I'm terrified of your storms!" Gabriel laughed and turned to Quinn.

"How about you?" he said. "Where are you from, and how did it fare after the Polar Shift?"

"My hometown in Maui is gone, Agent Patrick," Quinn

said. "Honolulu fared better, but barely. We still have our volcanoes, though. They're seething beneath the waters. Quite spectacular when they erupt!" Quinn said.

"How interesting," Gabriel said. And he shot her a smile, and tilted his head to the right, a shorthand language which meant he approved of the new agent from the Colony. "Call me Gabriel, Agent Quinn," he said, and offered him a mock salute.

"Quinn here, Gabriel," Quinn said, and smiled. "How're the storms in this part of the world, Sir? I heard they've gotten fierce!"

"They come once or twice a month, but better that than a flood," Gabriel said, and shook his head.

"You're such a baby, Gabriel," she teased.

"And it doesn't help that the Intelligence community is all atwitter about another invading force. We all know something's afoot, damn it!" he replied. "We're prepared for natural and supernatural disasters, but I don't know how we'll survive another Drone attack. Lakes Michigan, the Potomac and San Francisco Bay suffered huge casualties from the Han invasion fifteen years ago. Are they trying to force us to capitulate without a fight?"

She shrugged. His words reminded her of the meeting at Colony HQ the day before, and she didn't want to think about that.

"What's your suspicion, another Han resurrection, this time against London?" Gabriel said, but she shook her head.

"The Hans are not a threat, that's what HQ is saying. I'm sure they won't be able to rise again, Gabriel. Reports are saying they've been affected by the nuclear blast from the South and E Day was devastating to the North Korean army."

Gabriel nodded. "Mallard and O'Rourke still suspect Jae and Hari, and you in particular, Bricey. That's the truth of it. You won't get any horseshit from this English fella," he said.

"The Colony would be happy if I just led everyone straight to those two," she said, "although they aren't sure if they're the actual culprits. I'll do everything to help you, you know that, Gabriel."

Gabriel was a newly-married agent with a wife and two-year old twins when he arrived at the Colony three years ago.

The recruits took turns baby-sitting the overwhelmed young family. But Gabriel bonded with his American counterparts, since he was the only inter-agency recruit from the European River Coalitions.

"I haven't thanked you enough for providing back-up support to us, meaning baby-sitting duties three years ago, Brice. Thanks to many people, we survived the terrible two's. I'll save you any day, Bricey," Gabriel said, and glanced back at Quinn. "Remember that, Agent Quinn. Agents help one another, in good and bad times."

The boat slowed and approached a dock. On the pier, two men were standing at attention, and a third was waving at her.

"Gabriel!" she said. "Three men just to escort me this early in the morning?"

"In case Hari and Jae try a jail break for you again, Agent O'Rourke," Gabriel replied.

Away from the water, the heat was even more searing. She followed Gabriel toward three Windstream vehicles waiting for them.

"Whew, relief from the heat," she said, settling into

a cushioned seat. She pulled out her scarf and wrapped it around her shoulders, temporarily disturbing her monitoring Bee. The driverless Windstream was Gabriel's vehicle of choice. A British invention, it was part workhorse and part race car, capable of reaching 220 miles per hour, but steady enough for Bridge 6 operations. The car was soon speeding along in the land lane, whizzing next to other driverless cars.

"You used to love driving, Gabriel," she said. "Too tired to steer?"

"Too wired and distracted with the intel," he said. He pushed a button and the view from each window was replaced with a screen.

The screens divided into four and then two of them filled with a live feed of Diego's and Henry's faces from Denver Colony HQ.

"Gabriel, a sight for sore eyes!" Diego said. "You're looking good, man. How's Amelia and the twins?"

"Good, good," Gabriel said. "But it's not looking good here, Diego. Too much negative space, if I may put it that way. Too quiet. Better to have shadows. So we've looked into your suspicions about Hari, but there was no evidence he's here, until yesterday." And Gabriel gave an exasperated sigh.

"Your dirty fingers were all over that drama in Danube, Gabriel," Diego piped in. "Naughty, naughty... talk about shadows..." Gabriel's expression was neutral. He was a good spy. But she'd heard the barely concealed snickers about this all around the Colony.

The Danube River Coalition in Germany fared better than their other European counterparts in battling the Hans. For one, very little land submerged during the Polar

Shift, and the country was able to mobilize quicker to defend their territory from the encroaching Hans coming from the North Sea.

Some of the needed help came from their British counterparts to eliminate their Machina problem. It was heard that the Hans were losing their robot soldiers. They just didn't know why they were disappearing.

"Did they disappear under the Thames, Gabriel? Naughty, naughty!" Diego smirked, then chuckled. "What did you do with all those robots, huh?"

"I don't know what you're talking about, Diego," Gabriel deadpanned and changed the subject. "So Hari, our boy. What's he up to, dear Brice? Why is he here in the Thames? From Suvarnadvipa to Thames is a big jump."

She didn't answer.

"You know," Gabriel continued, "this is quite a peculiar case, and that's why we couldn't wait for Bricey's arrival. We raided the offices you told us about last night, Diego."

"I expected as much. How did it go?" Diego's voice was matter of fact, which meant that the situation was important enough that Bridge 6 took the lead in the investigation.

"The raid at the Memory Banks was brilliant, Diego! But everything looked perfect, just as I had surmised. We found traces of Hari and Jae Goo Loo's DNA, but it was minute. We're analyzing to see if it was planted evidence. Unless they're ghosts, it looks very well-planned and executed."

"But Hari and Jae, they were part of us at one point in time. And if this is their operation, what do you expect but perfection? And why are they here in London? I can't think of a reason."

Brice was monitoring the constant stream of information

that was scrolling on the screen in front of her.

Quinn was also scrutinizing the images and data.

"Back office, huh?" she said to Gabriel. "Anything interesting in the files?"

"It looked like any back office, too clean," Gabriel said, and Diego nodded. "Why are they at the Memory Banks? What do you think are they interested in?" Gabriel said. Diego scanned the images in front of him.

"What is it for? Why would they need the banked memories of two billion people?" Gabriel wondered. "But those are private companies, and getting in would be a bitch."

It was inevitable that with the installation of security cameras around the world, some entrepreneur would harvest their data, and collect and organize it in a way that made it marketable to the people recorded there, offering storage as retrievable, viewable memory from birth to death.

"They can't steal from them, Sir," Quinn interjected. "Memory banks are encrypted to a particular person's DNA."

"Any security footage from the memory banks in the last 24 hours?" Quinn asked, and thousands of faces appeared on the screen. "Here they are," Diego said. And then he cleared his throat gruffly.

"I'm sorry to have to ask this, Brice," he said, "but they're monitoring your vitals in the Barracks and your pupils are dilating when you look at the man in the left-hand corner of the screen. Do you know him?"

She closed her eyes, and pressed her fingers on her forehead.

"Headache?" Quinn said as he turned toward Brice.

"No, it's just the heat," she whispered.

Brice felt her heart beating fast.

Alarm chimes sounded in the machines in front of them and it zoomed in on two faces. It was Hari and Jae.

Before she could react, a piercing sound came from the sky. Everyone on the street looked up. A formation that looked like a cluster of bees had appeared above them. They were weaponized drones, she realized. In seconds, there came the sounds of bombs whistling down. Trails of light and fire streaked across the city. The air was filled with the sounds of screams as people ran to take cover.

The Second Drone Attack had begun.

Chapter 12

Harvard University

Boston,

Charles River Coalition,

United States of America

American River Coalitions

23 April 2068

3 years, 3 months, 10 days before Drone Strike

Brice looked at her watch. She was late.

She imagined her mother waiting for her, staring at the clock, patient with her tardiness, as always.

The sun was shining down brightly on this warm Boston day, and the sidewalk held throngs of people.

She glanced at the video walls and frowned when she saw the ubiquitous face of George Mallard, US President now running for re-election. The news was all over the university that he was going to be present today for the unveiling of the Roboticus Sollus program in its third year anniversary. The campus guides were all Sollus to mark the occasion.

There was a distant flash of red which she recognized immediately as Ira's scarf.

"Ira, over here," she shouted. Her sister's deep burgundy tresses and green eyes gave her away.

"Brice! Have you seen Mother? She's late, and I have classes to go to," Ira fretted.

"Oh, come on, Ira. Is Professor Leroy giving you a hard time again? Just stand your ground, and you'll be okay." She tried to calm her sister to no avail.

"He hates me," her eyes were downcast.

"The professor hates that you paint, and he does not. Those who can't, teach, you know that," she shook a finger at her. "Just concentrate on your painting and he can go fuck himself," she said as her sister chuckled.

An Art History major, Ira had shifted to painting in oil and she had encouraged this passion.

Ira then shouted with glee, "There's Mom and Eilish, thank God." Her steps slowed down. "Uh oh, Mom got distracted with the guides again."

The Robotics program had been a success, and a commercial renaissance on all things robotic had been one of its results. Human beings were now clamoring for the same rights as the robots, to push the boundaries and live forever.

Her mother was listening raptly to a student tour guide, as intent as the parents with children about to enter the freshman class.

"Brice, Ira," Eilish screeched when she saw them.

She picked her up and Eilish's feet bounced against her knees. "How are you, sister?"

"Good as ever! I brought Lulu," Eilish brought out the doll she was clutching and showed it to Ira. "Thanks for Lulu, Ira," she said, and then gave her a kiss.

"Let's go near the guides, shall we?" her mother said. "Please pretend to listen," Mira whispered. "It's discourteous, for God's sake. George and Avila invited me today for the third year anniversary of the Sollus program! Isn't it fantastic? And look, there's your uncle!"

Uncle Avila and Mallard were standing by the boat landing. She tried to catch their attention, but they were busy talking to the crowd gathering in front of them.

Her mother gushed on and on, but Brice barely glanced at the Sollus guide.

"Mom, let's go," she nudged. Instead she was surprised when her mother raised her voice.

"Why are you in such a hurry, Brice? It's still two days, and you haven't graduated yet and you're on to the next item in your checklist. Slow down," her mom admonished.

"Mom, I'm graduating in two days and I have a gazillion things to do. I don't need to pretend to listen to the guided groups, Sollus or not. C'mon, let's get out of here. I'm tired of seeing the faces of those two, too. We don't need to be here and stand at attention."

But her mother wouldn't budge. "Your dad and I used to run around here, many years ago. I want to tour the campus again." Her tone was wistful. The wind picked up, and the boat bobbed a bit, and when it reached the Cooperative Dock, the guide stopped speaking, and without breaking a beat, turned to the students and parents and declared a coffee break. She and Eilish stepped back, and let the younger students and their parents go ahead.

"Seeing those cheery guides... it makes me miss you all the more, Eilish," she said. "How are you, my dearest?"

"I'm good, Brice," Eilish beamed. "I love Boston!"

"She's good!" her mom said. "As loving as ever. Perky, friendly. The children in our neighborhood love her," her mother said this with a smile on her face, but her eyes told a different story.

Avila had offered to let Mira stay at the O'Rourke family home in Boston, but her mother decided to strike out on her own, accepting a role in the WRC as Director for Environmental Changes. Her mother, Ira, and Eilish settled in Harlem, near the Hudson River. In a year, Ira joined her at Harvard, and both of them had expressed countless times that it was time to move to Boston.

"Is it the first time you've seen George after four years?" she asked. She wanted to see her mother's reaction to his name. Mira had always been reticent to discuss her relationship with the man she had known since she was six years old.

"It didn't work out. We tried, you know?" Her candid words were a surprise. It was the first time her mother acknowledged that anything personal had happened between the two of them. "You're eighteen and Ira's seventeen," her mother said. " All of you can hear these things from me now," she said.

She was still stunned by the admission, and Ira signaled to continue the questioning.

"What happened?" she asked. "After going through so much together in Concordia and Singapore, I'd thought you two could have found common ground."

"I don't believe in his philosophies for a simpler

existence prior to the Polar Shift. It's quixotic and absurd. And so I've decided…" her mother shook her head and brought their hands to her lips and kissed them. "You three are my priority, you know. How about some coffee?"

They all walked hand in hand to the Harvard Coop.

Though one of the oldest buildings in Harvard, the building was air-conditioned cool inside, and bursting at the seams with people. She led her mother toward the elevator.

"So many floors to choose from! Which way?"

"Twenty, Mum."

"Twenty floors underground? So much has changed." One hand went to her eyes, and she knew she was brushing away tears. Memories of her father always overtook her when she visited Boston.

The elevator took them soundlessly to the 20th floor.

"Thank God, at least this bookstore still exists. Their coffee's amazing! At least that hasn't changed!" And her mother laughed.

"Nothing has changed since a hundred years ago. It will go the way of the cockroaches till the end of time," she said as she approached the barista and ordered a double espresso, her mother's caffeine of choice.

"Let this be my treat! You go look for a place to sit, Ira." Her mother shooed her away, and she directed Ira and Eilish to her favorite spot in the library.

"The Asian History section?" Mira said ten minutes later, dropping two coffee cups and a Danish on the table as she sat beside her.

"I've always been interested in it, Mom," Ira said.

The look on her mother's face told her that she was working up the courage to say something important. And she was.

"I saw the application to Gesu, Brice," she said in a quiet voice. "Harvard Red Cross sent me an advisory."

"Oh, that was fast," she replied. And she took a deep breath. "Let me explain. I was thinking that before I start going to grad school, I'd like to go back to the Manila in the Pasig River Coalitions. In the Philippines, if that's okay with you, Mom."

"Occupied Philippines, Brice," her mother in anger. "Or what's left of it. For heaven's sake, why go back there?"

She tried to touch her mother's hand but she pulled away.

"Aren't you happy here? You've been here four years and I haven't heard any complaints. If you want time off, why don't you just go to European River Coalitions before it sinks completely? Anywhere but the Philippines!"

"You know," she started, then hesitated. "After all these years, I still remember the heat, and the taste of salt water on my tongue. I miss the feel of sand on my feet. I miss the warm smiles of the people."

"I know where you'd go, Brice. But we've had no communication from the Salim family in four years. You couldn't find what you're looking for, even if you returned to Concordia, Brice. You're searching for a place that does not exist anymore."

She pondered the words of her mother. "Aren't you curious about what happened to the Salims?"

Her mother slammed her hand down the table and got to her feet.

"Why do you have to open up this topic? Your Uncle Avila obviously blames himself for allowing them to go back to Manila. And don't be naïve! Manila might have been declared an Open City, but the Hans are still in charge, don't forget that. And let's not forget the fact that you're from the United States, which might raise a few eyebrows at Immigration. It's too risky, Brice. Please," she said, "don't go," her mother pleaded.

It was the first time that she heard her mother plead to her. But it did not change her intention to visit the Philippines. When her expression was non-committal, her mother sighed. "Let's see what Avila thinks of your foolish idea."

"I don't need permission," she said. "I'm eighteen, beyond the age of consent. No one could stop me, even if you or Uncle Avila bring the police in to try."

Her mother turned toward her, her eyes searching, and then she glanced at Ira who was caught between the two of them. Eilish, who was seated at the other side of the table playing with her doll, noticed the lull in the conversation and glanced at them.

"Yes, now I've just realized you truly are an adult, Brice. And Ira, you will be independent soon. Life was definitely simpler when you were kids," and then her mother chuckled.

"What's so funny, Mum?" Eilish asked.

"Brice is funny, as usual," Mira patted her hand.

"I don't get it," Eilish said, and clucking her tongue, went back to playing with her dolls.

"Do you still have nightmares about Concordia?" her mother asked.

She picked up her coffee and took a long, slow sip. "I always dream of Concordia," she finally said. "At least once a week. How about you? Have the dreams improved?"

Mira shook her head. "Memories of the terrible things we witness never go away. I don't know why you'd want to revisit the Philippines, where so many of them happened."

Her mother teared up, and Ira stood up and embraced her. "It's okay, Mum. It's okay."

Instead of offering more fighting words, she stayed quiet, allowing her mother a chance to speak.

"I've thought of the Salims every day since they left," she said. "Especially Noor. She told me she didn't really want to accompany her husband and son to Concordia, and this still haunts me. Could I have done more to stop her? Stop all of them? Avila tells me that communication between the Pasig and American River Coalitions are improving, but so far, there's no response to our inquiries about the Salims."

Mira rested her head in her hands and rubbed her temples hard. "Brice, you know they only allow volunteers to come that work for non-governmental organizations like the Red Cross. The Han government might not let you come if they discover your visit to Manila has a hidden agenda." She shook her head. "Things changed after the occupation of the Pasig and Concordia River Coalition. The islands as you've imagined them are gone."

"I just want to know what happened to them, Mum," she whispered.

"Brice, it's an Open City, but that doesn't mean it's safe. The Han government is finally allowing communication to open, but we still don't have access to the general population. Your Uncle Avila's main line of work is to annihilate the Hans. They'll find out you're his niece, and they'll imprison you. Worse, they'll kill you!"

But she shook her head. "The Hans are too preoccupied with their own problems of survival to worry about someone like me. And besides, I know the language, since Hari only spoke Tagalog to me since childhood, so I can talk like a native. I'll use another name if you want. I'll be Brice Daelan. Look, I just want to see the islands one more time before--"

"Before what, Manila forever sinks into the Pasig River?"

"I've been working very hard, Mom. After I graduate, I want to have a break before graduate school. Like father. Why can't I do the same?"

"Why don't you just let it go?" her mother asked.

"How about if I go to the Philippines for just a summer? The Red Cross chapter in Boston called for volunteers there, and they told me they have a two-month Disaster Response outreach program in Gesu."

Her mother dropped her head.

"Please, Mum..." she said.

"Obsessions are corrosive, Brice. Oh, honey. I guess I have to give up! I could get a court order to try and stop you, but you're of age and it wouldn't work." She reached toward her. "Hari might have changed. You know it's been four years. He's 23 years old now. An adult."

"I know, Mum," she said. "I just want to know how he is. Then I'll come home. I promise."

Her mother cupped her face then kissed her cheeks.

"You have the O'Rourke determination, Brice. As long as you promise to take care of yourself, then yes, I'm allowing you to go to the Philippines."

She couldn't believe what her mother said. She scooped up Eilish and twirled her round and round. Eilish shrieked. It was the same sound Brice had heard when they jumped off the cliffs in Concordia. Carefree, childlike mirth. The kind she'd lost when she lost her island home.

Ira joined their dance. The three of them twirled around. Then her mother stopped them and joined the dance.

Several students stopped and observed the twirling dancers. Many clapped, and others cheered.

There was no music. They danced to music only they could hear.

The Hannese International Airport

Manila Bay

Philippines

Federation Han Asia

22 August 2069

3 years before the Drone Strike

The humidity was always a shock, hitting her like a body slap. She felt her clothes drenched in sweat as soon as she stepped off the seaplane.

The tall Han guards were standing at attention all over the seaport. She walked near one of them, and stared at one soldier from head to foot. The last time she had seen one was as a child in Concordia.

Their Korean features were intact, white creamy skin, almond-shaped brown eyes, aquiline noses; her gaze swept toward the uniform they wore, bright-red jackets with meticulously-embossed patches signifying their brigade number. She looked closely and saw the black-ribbed jackets were slightly frayed.

"Hey you, what are you looking at?" One soldier walked toward her, but she turned away and ran toward a crowd. She took off her jacket, and loosened a shirt from her pants.

Due to Avila's sensitive position in the American River Coalitions, the US Defense Ministry had recommended that she be given a new passport with a different name. She was asked for name suggestions and had chosen Brice Isabel, her second name taken from her Filipino grandmother. She had colored her hair to a darker brownish-black and used permeable dark brown lenses to cover her green eyes. She was correct. The guards barely glanced at her and she was rapidly cleared.

Rain started to pour as she stepped outside the airport. She smiled. As a child, she'd always enjoyed the sensations of rain and dampness. She lined up for a water taxi the size of a city bus. The operator haggled about the fee in Hannor till she spoke to them in Tagalog. Dejected, the operator agreed to charge her like a local.

As soon as she sat down, she felt a slight tug at the back of her head. She dismissed it. Then she felt someone pulling hard on her hair. Brice stood up and faced her tormentors.

"Gago! You Fools!" She was about to get angry but saw two sheepish schoolgirls looking at her with alarm.

"Oooops, we're sorry!!" one said. "You don't have those almond-shaped Korean Han eyes. We thought you were one of them!"

"Go!" She shooed them away and the two petrified girls fled from her death stare.

The ride to Quezon City was disconcerting. She hadn't

seen the city since she and her family had first landed in the Philippines after the Polar Shift. Her family had stayed in the capital city for a few days before transferring to Concordia Island. She looked around in wonder at the busy megalopolis, now full of tall buildings changing the city's landscape. The water bus took them to an area of smaller streets. Here, colorful graffiti streaked across walls and buildings, most of it cuss words against the Han soldiers.

A variety of boats clogged the river, and when the traffic sign turned green, faster boats whizzed past, splashing nearby boats carelessly.

The driver was a talkative fellow, but as they entered Gesu, she couldn't listen to him anymore. Her thoughts were a hundred miles away, back in childhood memories of the time her father had brought the family there to show them around the school where he'd spent a year as a Red Cross volunteer. It was here where he learned Tagalog, the language his mother Isabel had spoken.

The Gesu was the oldest Jesuit University in Asia and the most prestigious Jesuit campus in the country. It consisted of a variety of modern buildings scattered between well-tended gardens and sports complexes. She got off the boat there and walked into the heart of the campus.

The Red Cross building was easy to spot; it was a modern five-story structure set on a bluff, emblazoned with its large namesake insignia. As Brice looked over the place where she would live and work for the next two months, a water ambulance stopped in front of her, its sirens blaring loudly. A group of patients emerged from it, many limping or walking with the help of a cane.

She hurried to the reception room to get her keys. After bringing her bags to her room, she set out to explore the grounds.

She felt suddenly self-conscious about the way she was dressed. Her jeans were faded and her t-shirt was clean but plain. Some of the students were dressed more formally, but then she noticed a group wearing the same kind of attire and felt reassured. She followed a staircase toward the main campus on the lower level, slowing her pace when she came to a planting of flowers. She hadn't seen these kinds of flowers since she'd left her old home in Concordia, and she fingered the vibrant petals and inhaled deeply their tropical scents.

Her thoughts were interrupted when a boat sped by and its splash barely missed a group of students who were waiting for a ride on the nearby dock.

"Assholes, slow down!" one shouted, and several raised their fists to show their displeasure. Boat after boat stopped, unloading group after group of students who all began to head toward the center of campus. Curious, she followed them.

She had an hour to herself before she had to report to the Red Cross offices for the House Rules Orientation. As she approached a gymnasium, she heard the beat of the drums and felt the ground shaking. She followed the sound to a pathway lined with fluttering banners covered with "Welcome Freshmen!" signs. The entrance door of the gymnasium was awash with a rainbow of colors. Every student was wearing a different-colored t-shirt.

She was pushed inside by a throng of people. At the center of the room several students were standing atop chairs performing some sort of cheer dance.

The cheerers had dyed their hair blond, perhaps to distinguish them from the incoming freshmen. There was a burst of applause as a tall boy jumped onto a chair.

Her breath stopped when she saw his face. Was it Hari? It couldn't be! Or could it?

But those intense brown eyes, the wavy hair, his grin. She hadn't seen him in four years, but it was him, Hari, handsome, brash, confident as he danced.

She realized she was blushing and instinctively hid behind one of the freshmen. Over the years, she'd had a recurring dream of Hari. They were children again and he was holding her hand as they jumped off the cliff in Concordia. She'd hoped and prayed for this moment, but seeing him in the flesh was powerfully unreal.

But was he just a freshman? He was older than she was, and she had just graduated. It didn't add up.

Apparently, she'd arrived in the middle of freshman orientation, and welcoming speeches were being given. Now that she'd found him, she seemed suddenly incapable of reaching out to speak to him. What if he'd forgotten her? What if he remembered her, but wished he didn't?

She slipped through the crowd to the back of the hall, and tried to open the door that led outside. But her quick, stealthy exit was foiled as it seemed to be stuck shut. And then she heard a voice behind her.

"So, the red-brown locks from childhood have turned black as midnight," she heard a man's voice say through the noise of the cheering crowd.

She was shaking so hard it was a struggle to find her voice.

"And you've turned blond. I'm disappointed," she

managed to reply. And then she turned to face him.

Some of his blond cohorts were gathering around them. "Hari, stop pestering the freshies," one said as two blond boys high-fived each other.

She felt confused and flustered. This wasn't the meeting she'd imagined for so many years. Clearly, he remembered her. But was he mocking her? And why was he surrounded by this immature dyed-blond throng?

"Fancy meeting you here at Gesu. Aren't you a little old to be a freshman?" she said, and Hari's posse burst into laughter.

She yanked so hard on the door handle that it finally opened. "See you around," she said, and ran toward the Red Cross building. There were jeers and cheers behind her, and also Hari's voice. "I'll see you again, Brice!"

She walked slowly across the campus, her mind whirling. The sight of Hari had flustered her. She'd felt as if her breath had stopped when she saw him, and she hadn't fully exhaled since. She went into a bathroom to splash her face, and when she looked at it in the mirror, discovered it was bright red. She turned the cold water on full blast and splashed at herself until the redness disappeared. She glanced at her watch. It was time to go.

The lobby of the Red Cross building had filled with volunteers registering for that night's orientation. The students appeared to be from across a wide range of backgrounds; some well past their teens, others who didn't look like they could carry a sick person five steps.

When the crowd was ushered into the auditorium, she stood at the back of the room. She was still trying to clear her mind from running into Hari.

A man stepped up to the podium and spoke into the

microphone. "Good evening," he said, "my name is Dr. Hernando, and I'm the Red Cross Director for Gesu." His next words were interrupted by the sound of a loud explosion.

She stood rooted for a second. What the hell was that? she thought frantically.

And then she saw the Red Cross Director running toward her. He ran past her, toward the general direction of the blast sound, and for a reason she couldn't name, she followed him.

Outside the front door of the building, smoke was billowing, and with it came the smell of burning acid. When the smoke cleared a little, she saw a dozen bodies sprawled in the courtyard in various poses of distress. Some of them didn't have arms, and one or two had missing legs. The blast had done horrific damage.

By instinct, she ran toward a person in white who seemed to be a doctor. A stretcher appeared beside her, and she opened it and squatted to lift one of the injured onto it.

At that moment, Dr. Hernando clapped his hands.

"All right, that's enough."

The student volunteers looked at each other in confusion. "As I mentioned before the blast, I am Dr. Hernando, Red Cross Director for Gesu. Let me congratulate the people who chose to go inside the disaster perimeter fence. I count eight first responders here from the new batch of volunteers. For the next two months, they will be the leaders of the volunteer teams."

And then he clapped his hands and said, "Injured people, you can leave now."

Slowly, the people on the ground began to stand

up. Minuscule wires and metallic parts were clearly protruding from the sites of some of the injuries.

She was stunned. These Machinas knew how to obey orders from their masters, but lacked the personality programmed into Eilish, her sister.

The droids shuffled past her into the building. They seemed to be avoiding looking at the humans. One, a sizable male, wore his hair in a topknot. She had a feeling she'd seen him somewhere before, but as she pushed through the crowd to get a better look at his face, he disappeared inside the Red Cross building.

The Red Cross director's voice came again.

"Each of the eight teams will have a mentor who will be a medical resident who's agreed to help me out for the summer. Mentor number one is Hari Salim." Before she could register surprise at this information, he looked right at her and pointed. "You, what's your name?" he said.

All eyes were on her, and she felt an urge to run. She didn't know if she wanted to escape Hari or the crowd. "Brice Isabel, Dr. Hernando," she croaked.

"Very well, Brice. You'll be the Team Leader for Team Palawan, since Hari's from Palawan."

The Director continued to separate the other volunteers into teams.

"To those who fled the scene of the crime, or were frozen by fear, I do hope in a real disaster I will not see you cowering in a corner," he said. "Teams will be called Leyte, Cebu, Bohol, Boracay, Palawan, Batanes, Sulu and Samar. Now off you go to a short introductory class with your team leaders, before retiring for the night. I'll see you bright and early at 7:30 a.m. You are hereby dismissed."

Suddenly, Hari was standing in front of her.

"I guess you can't run away from me forever," he said, not hiding the fact that he was looking her over from head to toe. "Brice Isabel?"

"It's as fake as my hair. For security purposes, I had to change my name and my hair color," she said. "So you're a doctor?" she said with a shaky smile.

"Yes, when I left Singapore, I had just graduated from university. When I arrived here, there's always a need for a doctor, and that's what I am now. And you?"

"I just graduated from Boston, and I'm here for the summer. Why didn't you answer my message, Hari?" She looked him over. His hair was now blond, but his eyes were still the kind eyes she had known since childhood. His swimmer's physique was still intact, but the muscles had hardened, like he was lifting a ton of rocks as a work-out or something else.

"All our messages are monitored, Brice. It would be risky. I'll talk about it later," he whispered.

He raised his voice, and said sarcastically, "And God, Dr. Hernando is quite heartless, naming teams after islands that have almost disappeared off the face of the earth!"

There were a few jeers and laughter when he said that, and he acknowledged most of it, but then turned again to face her.

"How's Tia Noor?" she asked. "I've missed her every day since you left," she said as she relaxed, feeling again the level of ease they always had when they were ribbing each other. "If not for her calm voice and leadership, we wouldn't have survived the crossing to Vietnam."

"My mom is back in Concordia, awaiting my dad's return. He's in prison," he said. He waited for her reaction.

She was so shocked that she was speechless for a few seconds.

"No one knew that, Hari."

His skeptical expression befuddled her.

"As I've said, we can talk later. Now, go to your first class. I'm teaching it, and boy, you're going to learn a lot." Hari's patronizing tone irked her. But then he whispered, "Any questions you have, I'll answer." And he turned and walked away.

In the classroom, she found a group of older, mostly bored-looking Gesu students who stared at her with the curiosity she'd been used to as a green-eyed foreign-born child. She was designated the team leader, so she thought it would be good form to introduce herself.

It would also be fun to upset their expectations. "Kamusta, ako si Brice," she introduced her name with a casual wave of her hand. Hearing her speak Tagalog made several of them more attentive, so she kept going. Making her voice deeper, miming Dr. Hernando, she said, "Tignan natin kung sinong duwag! Let's see who the cowards are." They all laughed and some of them cheered. "C'mon team. Let's do this!"

When Hari entered, she took a seat. He introduced himself again, and proceeded to lecture.

She noticed that the top-knotted Machina was now seated in the classroom, right behind her. It was obvious from the faded olive green shirt with a Red Cross heart he was wearing that he was a helper for the class. The robot's face was expressionless. So was the robot sitting beside him, a woman who had a scar on the side of her jaw.

"Kamusta? I'm Brice, and you are?" she extended her hand but the two robots did not shake her extended hand.

"Lee Jae Seung," the male robot answered. That name. She'd heard it before. And then she knew where.

"I remember you..." she started to say. But he interrupted her.

"I'm sorry but we are not allowed to talk to you, ma'am. I am here to assist you in any way."

"Don't call me ma'am," she said. "Call me Brice."

Lee was staring at her blankly. But the female robot was now reaching for her hand.

"I'm Chin-sun," she said, but stopped talking when Hari approached.

"We're not allowed to talk to the helpers. North Han orders. Something you want to share with the group that's interesting?" he asked in front of the class.

"Nothing to share, Hari. I mean Dr. Salim. Sorry for distracting you." Hari nodded, and walked away.

She noticed that there was a small folded piece of paper on top of her desk. She opened it, and saw that Hari had scrawled something there.

"Change of plans. I have no time today. But any questions you have, I'll answer tomorrow after classes."

She pretended to listen to his lecture, and as soon as they were dismissed, she fled back to her room.

There, she threw herself on the bed. She knew she had to calm herself before an anxiety attack overwhelmed her.

She tried closing her eyes again, and then got up and did her shaking and dancing exercises. She had to concentrate on the here and now, she kept telling herself. She had to remind herself that there were no threatening circumstances surrounding her, and that she was in a safe place.

She'd missed dinner, she realized, but wasn't really hungry. The tiny clock at her bedside table read ten p.m. She had so many questions to ask him, and she couldn't wait for time to move forward to tomorrow.

She felt so exhausted from the day's activities and seeing Hari, that her eyelids weighed heavy. She didn't try to fight off sleep.

Gesu Red Cross Building

Philippines

Federation Han Asia

August 23, 2068

2 years, 11 months, 9 days before the Drone Strike

She was up early and headed to the common hall, as she had been told to do the day before. Dr Hernando was in the middle of the room and he was screaming at the top of his lungs.

Another bomb drill? Many of the volunteers covered their ears in anticipation of the blast. But this was no drill.

"Listen up, people!" he yelled. "There's a big fire at the Veterans' Hospital in Quezon City, and we are needed as ancillary help for the hospital staff. You're there to bring the medical supplies and to observe. Are we clear? Now, move it!"

She ran to find her team, which had gathered by the door. They looked at each other with alarm. "I can't believe this is happening," one of the team members said, her eyes wide with fear.

"Shhhh...Dr. Hernando's still talking." She placed a finger to her lips, but her group was distracted and worried.

"I just need this to pass requirements for college. I never expected to participate in a real emergency," one girl moaned.

Dr. Hernando finished his talk and walked away. She turned to her volunteers.

"We all signed up. None of you were pushed into doing this. So, if you don't feel like joining this exercise, please stand aside. All right?" About half the team raised their hands.

"Stay here and restock emergency supplies, then meet us in half an hour at Veterans' Hospital, and bring water and food for our team. And make sure Dr. No there doesn't see you, or else I'll say this never happened. Do you hear?" They nodded, then scampered away as they heard the sirens of the ambulance arriving in front of the building.

She ran toward the vehicle, feeling adrenaline pumping in her veins. She felt incredibly energized by this emergency, but as she looked at the grim expressions around her, forced herself to stop smiling.

The hospital was nearby and when they arrived, Dr. Hernando and the other doctors had already created a perimeter tent and established a command center. A group of other tents were set up around the hospital as well.

Hari appeared when she was preparing medical supplies. He looked dazed and disheveled, as if he'd been hit by a truck. When he left the tent, she followed him. He seemed to be in a hurry.

"Hari, where are you going?" she said, and ran to catch up to him.

He looked around first to make sure no one was

listening. "Father's here, confined in this hospital for the last three years. I have to check on him."

"Tio Dio is here?" She brought one hand to her heart. She felt faint. "Wait, Hari, Dr. H. might find out that you're missing!"

"I don't care. I have to see that my father is safe."

"I'll go with you," she said.

"You can't," he replied. "He's not allowed to talk to anyone."

She kept walking. "I'm still coming," she said. She couldn't imagine not seeing Tio Dio when she had an opportunity to do so.

"How is he?" she said. She felt her emotions oscillating between anger and curiosity. She longed for answers about what had happened to the Salims when they returned to the Pasig River Coalitions.

Hari was walking faster. "He was imprisoned in Muntinglupa after he was captured three years ago, but due to ill health the past year, he was brought here and confined in the hospital." Hari hesitated, then continued. "What the hell," he finally said, and his steps slowed. "He's been asking a lot about you."

She was shocked. "Really?" she said.

Instead of answering, Hari started to run. Finally, he reached a row of tents that had been hastily erected to hold evacuated patients. He looked inside them, one by one, until he reached a tent that had a guard posted outside. "He's got to be here," he said. "I'll ask if we're allowed in, and if I can bring a visitor."

Hari disappeared into the tent, and quickly returned. "We have five minutes. Let's not waste it. Don't open your mouth. I don't want to get into trouble. Don't ask any questions the Hans could record. I don't want them to know you visited Father."

Hari fished something from the backpack he was carrying. It was a pair of dark sunglasses. "Here, wear this," he said, "and cover your head with this." He produced a scarf. "Now, as I said, not a word."

Inside the tent guards were posted at every corner. They were stopped by them in an anteroom where they had pictures taken of their faces. And then the lone woman guard frisked her before she was allowed to enter.

She instantly recognized the handsome man in the bed. He looked frail, but the curly hair was still abundant, although now it was all white. And the eyes that looked at her were as intense as they always were. With a nod from Hari, she briefly lowered her sunglasses so he could recognize her. His shock was visible.

"I can't believe I'm seeing you," Tio Dio said. "You've grown up so much!"

"Hello Tio Dio..." she said, unsure about her next steps. Would she be allowed to approach his bedside?

"Come here, nearer," he said, and he reached out to take her hand.

They were silent for a long moment. She remembered the last time she had seen him, the night before he'd left for the Philippines. He was very happy that he was returning to his native country. Did he have any inkling of his fate?

"How's your mother?" he finally said.

"Struggling, but fine, Tio Dio. She accepted a post in the WRC four years ago, right after you left for the Pasig River Coalitions," she replied.

A soldier shouted something at them, and Hari held

his father's hand. "It's time to go, Father. The guards are giving us three minutes."

There was a gleam in Dio Salim's eyes. "Brice..." he said, and his grasp tightened. And then he whispered, "Hari is working in the Defiance movement against the Hans. Please help him."

"Not here, Father. You're endangering her," Hari hissed as two soldiers approached.

"It's time to go," one said. As she turned to Dio, he had a smile for her.

"Give my love to your mother."

"I will, Tio Dio. I will." She turned and walked from the tent as though she was in a trance.

Hari whispered, "Act normal. Don't give them any hint that my father told you any important information."

"I wish you could have warned me that he was going to try to recruit me." It was a serious situation, but she couldn't help it. She chuckled.

"Let's find a quiet place to talk," Hari nodded toward a cluster of narra trees a good distance from the tents. The hospital tent had been cool, but the air outside was so humid her entire body had been drenched in sweat within seconds of going outside, and she was eager for shade.

She settled onto the grass, took off the rubber band tying her hair, and let her hair loose. The fire must have been contained, because the fire trucks had pulled away from the hospital building, and people were milling about in a confused state. Hari dropped onto the grass beside her.

Jae walked past them, following a few steps behind another volunteer. They were carrying medical supplies to the Gesu Red Cross tent.

"Looking for us, I bet," she said as she held up a hand to catch Jae's attention, but he just kept walking. "What happened to him?" she said. "I bet no one here knows his history."

Hari nodded. "He saved our fathers. He refused to follow the orders of that evil officer in Concordia."

"Uncle Avila told me about that. But no one wants to talk about that part of our lives in Concordia." She shifted her gaze back to the robots, then asked, "They move like zombies. Was Jae incarcerated?"

"The Han Army dumped discarded Machinas in Manila, in the Pasig River. They were decommissioned and kept in a warehouse, and after a few years, were permitted to be used by the Red Cross as helpers."

"Everything Tio Dio said about you helping the Defiance is true, right?" she said, and Hari nodded.

"After we landed in Manila, Father was approached by them to work against the Hans. When they colonized Concordia in 2058, the Hans stripped the locals of almost all their rights. No freedom of movement, no right to elect our own officials, no free press. High taxation! And it's so obvious they just needed the land for their people. They didn't care about the welfare of the people they'd colonized."

She sighed. Deep in her gut, she knew everything made sense.

Jae appeared again, holding bottles of water and corn on the cob.

"He was imprisoned like our fathers when he disobeyed orders," he said as he glanced at Lee.

"First among the Machinas to disobey orders?" She turned to look at the AIP. Again, she marveled at his blank face. "Will he remain like this forever? It seems like a fate worse than death."

Hari didn't answer.

A family passed by, two children laughing as they chased butterflies.

The sight made her smile. She turned to Hari. "Don't you find it bizarre that after a horrific accident happens in Palawan, a small crowd gathers, and one inevitably sees vendors selling fresh corn. It's very true here now..."

"Or dirty ice cream, fried banana fritters," he said. "I'm just waiting for balloons to make their appearance, and we're in fiesta mode." And they both laughed.

As fire cleanup commenced, a squadron of stone-faced Machina guards marched around the grounds of the hospital.

They marched toward them, and whistled at them. It meant they had to stand up and go back to their proper places in the tent.

"By the way, how's Ira? She was 12 when I left four years ago. She must be...?" Hari started counting with his fingers, but she didn't let him finish his sentence.

"She's now eighteen years old, the same age I am right now. She's a junior in Harvard."

His voice was incredulous. "What? That's great."

"She is adorable. So sweet, and so kind. She's the glue of the family. What?" She saw Hari grinning.

"I bet the fire in your belly keeps Tia Mira on her toes," he wagged his finger at her. "Like you always did when we were kids."

"Well, the Sollus are just like us. Some are adorable, and many are something else. It really depends on how the parents brought them up, and how the schools they attended molded them. I'm sure a benevolent one will rule us one day, and his nemesis will be an evil criminal, perhaps an AIP too. Who knows?"

"No rebellion about rules foisted by humans?" Hari asked.

His question reminded her that for the last four years, he had lived under the thumb of a foreign conqueror, while she had lived with freedom in a place ruled by the American River Coalitions.

"The anti-robotist fervor is gaining momentum. Humans want nothing from them," she said with weariness.

"I'm sure some robot firebrand will rebel and start a movement to disregard rules created by humans," Hari said. "But who wants to live beyond 200 years? Would you like to live forever? I wouldn't. But 200 sounds pretty good." Hari propped his chin on his knee.

"Were they cruel to Tio Dio?" she asked, and she saw that his mood darkened.

"You remember how ruthless the Hans were the first day they appeared in Concordia? They have remained exactly the same."

She paused before asking the next question.

"Was Tio Dio tortured?"

Hari nodded. "Every day for a month. It only stopped when he began a hunger strike. Word of this spread, and the torture stopped, but only because the North Han Army didn't want a revolution on their hands. Their main goal was to find a safe place to live when their land was decimated. If they faced a revolution and couldn't control it, there would be no land for the Hans to live in.

"Talking about bravery, tell me, how did you persuade

Tia Mira to allow you to visit here?"

"Pure pig-headedness. She finally caved when I promised to come back home after two months," she answered, but Hari had one eyebrow raised.

"She believed that, knowing you? Did you hypnotize your own mother, tie her up a tree?" Hari chortled saying this. But then he turned serious.

"Brice, I know what Father said to you, but I won't allow you to join the Defiance movement. Father has his flaws, you know, even though he can be very persuasive." Hari shook his head. "Your mother will never recover if something happens to you. Think about her."

"But..." she started.

"No, nothing you say can change my mind," Hari said with certainty.

She glanced at Hari and he was defiant. She knew that look, nothing could change his mind at this point.

"Did you hear anything about the blaze?" she asked. "Was anyone injured?"

He looked around and stepped closer to her. "You know, all this was staged," he said in a very quiet voice. "It was just a trick. Dr. Hernando works with the rebel movement too. The leaders wanted to know how they were treating Father. There were reports he wasn't doing well. So, Dr. Hernando planned this with me. He isn't as bad as you think."

Then he stood up. "Time to go. People will notice that we're not in the Red Cross tent. Hurry back to your place. I'll follow after ten minutes," he said, as he shook off the dirt from his pants. Without much of a wave, he walked to the side, whistled to Jae, and disappeared.

In a blink of an eye, he was gone.

She tried to remember everything that had transpired in the past hours – the sudden announcement of a fire, the rush to the hospital, the setting up of a medical triage, seeing Tio Dio after four years. The images swirled around her, but the only distinct memory was Hari, the way he looked, the way he acted in front of her, from her vantage point. If only she could gather her memories and just replay all the memories with him, she'd die a thousand deaths to relive it.

She had confirmed it seeing him. She was hopelessly in love, and he had no idea about how she felt.

But she didn't feel hopeless. This was her childhood friend, surely he would feel what she was feeling?

Or not. But she was curious about the Defiance movement. Even if Hari did not allow her to join the movement, she wanted to know all about it. The invitation from Tio Dio was extended to her, and it had nothing to do with Hari.

She had an idea. She was caught once when she was following him to the caves in Concordia when they were children. It was the same thing now, but with higher stakes. She wanted to find out about the Defiance movement. And this time, she wouldn't be caught following him.

Hari was waiting for someone at the base of the library steps. He nodded to someone who approached him. She was surprised to see that Jae had accompanied him.

He hailed a water taxi, and she saw that it was colored

light blue. Was he going toward the Pasig River?

She motioned toward the driver and his taxi that she had hired for the day, and they followed Hari's water taxi.

After thirty minutes, the water taxi stopped in front of them. Hari and Jae stepped off, and she told her driver to stop too. She fished for something inside her purse and reached for her wallet. She counted the bills and handed them to the driver.

"You don't have to wait for me. I'll stay here the whole day. You can go now," she said in Tagalog, all the while making sure that Hari and Jae were still within sight.

She followed them till they reached the ancient and historic Quiapo Church.

If the Defiance headquarters were here, why choose a place that was so public with thousands of devotees visiting the church every day?

The streets behind the church were lit with bright lights, and she continued following them at a distance. The coffee shops lining the sidewalks were bursting with people. Sleek and sophisticated office workers jostled with the fishermen peddling their catch to the people near the waterways. One would never think this was a Han-occupied nation.

When Hari stopped in front of the church, he paused and made a sign of the cross. He paused briefly and waited. Was it a signal for someone, a warning? He continued walking again.

She walked slowly in front of the church and instead of praying, she just stared in awe at the edifice of Quiapo Church. There was a long line in front of it, and she knew the people were there to visit the statue of Nuestro Señor Jesus Nazareno, a figure of a dark Christ in black wood that was deemed miraculous. From memory, she remembered that the church originated in the mid 1500s and was originally made of bamboo and nipa leaves but had been transformed through the centuries into a magnificent Renaissance structure. Since the Polar Shift, water had reached the top of the pews, but still devotees lined up for a glimpse of the statue.

The general cacophony of vendors selling candles and flowers for the hourly Mass drowned out the sounds of bells ringing atop the church.

She continued to walk, brushing past old ladies selling candles or herbs for all kinds of ailments. Craning her neck, she jumped when she realized she had lost sight of Hari and Jae.

Where did they go? She ran past a dark alley and two men were turning toward another corner.

"Halt!" Five men stood in front of her including Hari.

"Brice, are you following me?"

She raised both her hands. "Yes, guilty."

"She's Brice Isabel, I can vouch for her, though I'd rather wring her neck now." Hari faced her. "What the hell?" he asked in a very angry tone.

The four other men disappeared into the darkness and all she could see was Hari's angry face.

She reached out to touch his face, but he swatted her hand away. "Your father invited me. It's out of your control, Hari. It's my decision and no one else's. Now, let me go and join you, wherever you're going."

Hari was silent for a time and she let him observe her. She was not backing down.

"Okay," he answered in a soft tone. "You can observe, but you can never talk about what you've seen. The Hans will imprison and torture you for this info. Come on. Just follow me," he reached for her hand.

She asked, "Where's Jae?" But Hari shrugged and didn't answer her question.

He walked ahead of her and motioned for her to follow him. Another dark alleyway? She had lost her directional bearing as he kept turning corners to reach his destination. A deliberate attempt to mislead her? He need not worry. She didn't know where she was, up, down, turn-around. She was lost.

Then he stopped, took out a flashlight and beamed it around a wall, as if searching for something. And then he pushed away some dirt from a hidden panel and pushed a lever.

A door popped open. He hoisted himself, then motioned for her to follow him.

"Down here," Hari was crouched down, at the opening to a manhole on the ground. "There's a ladder going down. Just follow me."

The journey into the dark hole felt like a drop to the bottom of the earth. All Brice could see in the flashlight's beam was a stairway that seemed bottomless.

"Close up the manhole, Brice."

"How? I can't." She gripped the ladder, holding on for dear life.

"There's a rope to your side. Just pull the rope with one hand, and the manhole will close."

She reached out to her right, and felt a rope. She tugged it and miraculously, the manhole closed.

"Thank God," she exclaimed with nervousness.

"You can do it, O'Rourke. Focus and relax your grip on the ladder," Hari said in a stern voice.

"Easy for you to say, Salim," copying the tone of his voice.

"O'Rourke, you're such a pain. I give up," he sighed, then chuckled.

Suddenly, their old back-and-forth banter was present again.

"Hey, remember. This place we're going to is classified, Brice. I'm letting you in because I trust you to keep a secret."

"Lead the way, Hari. Yeah, I'll soon be on to the Han headquarters to spill my secrets," she joked.

"Ah, huh? Really? Hang a noose around your neck if that's the case. Ooops okay, here we are. Watch your step," Hari cautioned.

She focused her eyes downward and Hari was now on flat ground. He reached out to help her from the ladder.

"Let's wait for our eyes to adjust to the darkness. Ready?"

"Ready, steady," she said with anticipation.

"Welcome to Defiance." Hari moved to a stone wall, and pushed it. Amazingly, it gave way.

The first face she saw on the other side of the wall was Chin-sun. Her bright smile was welcoming, but she turned to Hari, confused.

"Is she part of all this?" she asked.

He just nodded and kept walking.

They were in a tunnel lit by intermittent lights. It was lined with doorways, and though she wanted to peek into some of the rooms, Hari didn't allow her to stop until they reached a door that led to a room filled with men and women hunched over rows of glass terminals.

"Monitor Station. We don't know when the Hans will

attack us. It's better to be prepared." He pointed to the monitors. "They have sensors for everything that moves outside."

They continued to walk and stopped in one passageway, and a man guarding the door glanced at her, but Hari stopped him from further questions.

"She's the niece of Minister Avila O'Rourke, Suhan. She's with me and I vouch for her." Hari brought his arms around her.

"Hair check for both of you then." The man reached out with a small tool which he held over Hari's head. It nipped a bit of hair which was then analyzed in an instant.

"DNA test," Hari whispered.

"Next," Suhan motioned to her, and her hair was subjected to the same test as Hari's.

"99.9 % genetically related to Minister Avila. As I said multiple times, Hari Salim, this is a highly unreliable tool. She can be related to the Minister, but she can still be a traitor…"

"All right, Suhan, that's enough speculation," Hari cut his conversation mid-way. "I will take note of the objections and bring it up with the powers-that-be."

A loud sound interrupted their conversation, and Hari pulled her inside the portal.

"Let's go, Brice," Hari pulled hard and closed the door.

The passageway on the other side of the door was even more dimly lit. It opened into a room that held a group of people gathered around an oblong table. The assemblage was listening with rapt attention to a man wearing a plain white t-shirt and very faded jeans. He looked like any of the countless locals going about their business near Quiapo Church. But there was a singular way he paused to listen to a question, as if a bird caught mid-flight.

She turned to him with a question in her eyes and he nodded.

"Uncle Avila..." she said his name out loud, and stepped forward to greet him, but Hari stopped her.

"Let's wait for him to finish his meeting. He won't be happy to see you here. In fact, I may be excommunicated from the group when he does," he said nervously.

Her uncle must have sensed her presence and turned toward them. And then he stood up and stepped toward them.

"God damn it, Hari! How can you bring her here?" Avila hissed at him.

"Father cajoled her into joining Defiance, Avila," he started. He wasn't finished explaining when Avila uttered innumerable expletives.

"Damn Dio! I knew it was futile to hope that you'd stay in the Red Cross, Brice. You're in trouble with me, Hari." His voice was sharp and his arms were tense, as if he was about to hit Hari.

"Coming here was my own decision, Uncle Avila," she said as calmly as possible. Her comment was greeted by silence.

"She followed me from Gesu, Tio Avila. I'm really, really sorry for that. But I thought since Brice is here, she would want to see this process, the last step of Jae's transformation," he said.

"I'll talk to you two later," Avila said. "For now, Hari, bring her up to speed. We're wasting time arguing, when this day should be a special day for Jae." And he turned away from them dismissively.

"Come on, Brice. I'll show you around," Hari said,

grabbing her elbow and leading her out of the room.

But she stopped walking when she saw a familiar face in the hallway. "Brice!" a man said. His tone was effusive.

"Amil! I'd know you anywhere." She ran to her childhood friend and embraced him. Amil still looked a lot like Hari, but whereas Hari's features had hardened into angles and planes, Amil's were softer, and all curves. He had round brown eyes, cherubic cheeks, and a large, robust belly.

"He just got married," Hari said, "and it took just a couple of months to turn pudgy." His tone was teasing.

"Guess what, Amil?" he continued. "She's here for the summer to volunteer for the Red Cross, but today, Father shamelessly recruited her."

"Hay, Tio Dio. He'll never change. I'd guess he'd recruit all the nurses and doctors in the hospital if he could," Amil chortled with glee. "We heard about the fire, Hari. We have to thank Dr. H for that feat. How's Tio Dio?"

"He could be a snake charmer in his prison bed," he said and sighed. Nothing ever seemed to make his father feel defeated.

"Don't worry, Brice. Tio Dio recruited me too," Amil said, and grinned. "Anything to bring the Hans to their knees is fine with me. So what do you think? Can Brice join the group?" Amil asked.

She turned to Hari, a question in her eyes.

"I don't know. It's complicated. If she's caught, she could become a bargaining chip. Avila's already furious that she's here." And he turned in the direction of her uncle.

"I can make my own decision, guys," she said. "I don't need anyone's permission."

"If her aim is as good now as it was as a child throwing

mangoes, then I vouch for her," Amil said and raised a thumb.

"Why don't you try me?" she said and Amil laughed.

"We can talk about all the serious stuff later," he said. "Jae's Reformation is happening right now. Let's go see him," Amil said.

"She's not allowed to see his Reformation, Amil," Hari said. "Go ahead. We'll find a spot where we can talk." He tried to lead her away, but she stopped him and turned to Amil.

"Hey Amil, hope to see you later. I want to know everything about your unlucky bride." She blew a kiss to Hari's cousin.

"As naughty as ever. Let's catch up later, Brice," Amil waved back at her.

Hari was walking ahead, and she ran to catch up with him. He opened a door to a small room with no windows.

"So, what's happening, Hari?" She blurted out a question as soon as they entered the room. She noticed a tiny blackboard with chalk on one side of the room.

"The Jae that you've seen a while ago will be gone today," Hari said.

She gasped in surprise. "What do you mean?"

"The River Coalitions are preparing for Elimination Day of the Hans, Brice," Hari started. "I can talk, you can interrupt me anytime."

"Okay," she stammered. She had a lot of questions, but she bit her lips to stop herself from asking them.

"Remember the Sollus program with Ira? It took five years for the infants to turn fifteen years old. The US government has recently passed laws to create another Homo Roboticus genus – Aequilavum. It takes one month to create one AQ. And it's an AIP to specifically fight the Hans. The River Coalitions have banded together to create these AIPs to battle the Hans."

"What? They have no reason to exist except to battle the Hans? That's quite a questionable move," she exclaimed.

"The Defiance movement is helping all these countries allied with the US to create the AQs. It's a great risk for us for this experiment to happen, right under the noses of the Han government, but plans are still need-to-know. We've heard about the final Elimination Day against the Han government, but that's it, we're under orders not to talk about it," Hari said.

"So the Jae who was a helper in the Red Cross will be gone forever?"

"Yes," Hari nodded. "He'll be replaced with a Jae that's an AQ."

"With flesh and bone like Ira?" she asked.

"Yes, flesh and bone like Ira. But still looks like Jae." Hari stood up and started to pace in front of her.

She pondered this answer, then asked, "How is that possible? Will he have DNA from human parents like Ira?"

"No. No DNA from human parents. His DNA is from robotic chromosomes. Jong Hwan-Kim pioneered this research 60 years ago. The skin is a perfect terroir for creating organs, tissue, muscle, almost anything in an Artificially Intelligent Person." Hari walked to the blackboard and started drawing a Machina figure.

She stood up too. The details of the origins of an AQ sentient droid were too much for her to digest, and she stared at his drawing. "But where does he come from, what family, what lineage?"

"Every Machina soldier is distinctly different from every other, like the terracotta warriors of Xian in China. There were eight thousand soldiers created for Qin Shi Huang, the first Emperor in China, but every soldier was unique. They will use the concurrent biological Mendel signature of Jae that's embedded in him by the Machinas."

"But what about his memories? What memories will he remember?" she asked.

"His memories are embedded in him," Hari said in an impatient tone.

"From where?"

"I don't really know the details, but the US has devised a way for Jae to have memories. I heard everything can be sold on the black market. Fifty years ago, donors could sell their sperm samples, but now you can sell memories from birth. Where've you been? How come you don't know such things?" he asked in an exasperated tone.

"I was just under the Harvard rock, very busy trying to meet all requirements to graduate," she said in a defensive tone.

"Anyway, memories are nothing if they aren't hinged on specific people to ground them on. So, Jae has adoptive human parents with the same memory markers as he has. Every day, when he regains consciousness after the Reformation process, for a month, his parents talk with him about their past, an interesting mélange of memories – Antarctica, Washington, D.C..." Hari rattled off a number of places that she realized she was familiar with.

"Huh? Who are the adoptive parents, may I ask?" she was asking the question without a hint of emotion, but her heart started beating fast.

"The Moores. Do you know them? They've been here

for a month working with AQ Jae, weaving their histories so he's integrated well into the human system." Hari's eyes widened. "Good God! Were they your neighbors in Buckminster City? How's that for coincidence? They're here to meet Jae as an AQ. Wait, I'll ask Tio Avila if you can meet with them. Wait here," and he was gone in a flash.

There was a knock and Hari entered. Behind him were a man and a woman, and even without introduction, she let out a whoop.

"Dr. Philip! Mrs. Simone! It's me, Brice O'Rourke!" she said. In a few seconds, the three became a closely entwined knot.

"Brice, after all these years! My goodness! You're a young woman now," Mrs. Moore was openly crying as she embraced her.

"This is absolutely joyful," Dr. Moore said. "But how did you get here? From Avila's previous messages, we thought you were in Boston. How are you, my dear?" He embraced her and brought both hands to her face. "Of all places to meet you."

"Mrs. Moore, Dr. Moore," she started to ask something but was interrupted...

"Call me Simone, and call him Philip," her childhood friend's mother insisted on calling them by their first names.

"Simone, Philip, how is Julia?" she asked awkwardly. Their daughter had been her and Eilish's closest friend in Antarctica, and she had wondered about her all these years. But their smiles vanished.

"Julia died in the Polar Shift," Simone said in a soft tone. "How ironic that we abandoned your grandfather in Antarctica for safer climes in Washington, D.C., only for that city to disappear in one day. Unfortunately, we weren't with her, and that's the only reason we're alive. We'd left the day before to attend a scientific conference in Chicago."

This was terrible news, and she felt herself tensing up.

Hari went near her. "Brice, Brice..." he embraced her, and rocked her for a minute to calm her down. She was grateful that Hari knew she had PTSD, but she had mastered the lessons of grief, and after a minute, she patted Hari's hand, and sobbed.

Crying was a release from the tension built up, and she had learned that she could take bad news faster if she could harness its positive energy.

"We're so sorry we brought you such devastating news, Brice," Simone walked to her and embraced her.

"Julia was a wonderful friend. But that's the past, and there's nothing I can do about what happened ten years ago. I'm eager to hear what Reformation means for you and Jae, that is, if I'm allowed to learn what it is," and she directed her statement to Hari.

"Simone, Philip, I'm glad you met my niece, Brice."

Her uncle appeared at the door. It was high time he started explaining what was happening here in the Defiance movement.

Avila

The ghosts of his past were assembled in this room, alive, and right in front of him.

He tried to calm his breathing and remind himself

that the Moores abandoned Antarctica out of a sense of desperation. And in the end, they lost their daughter even if they escaped the Polar Shift.

He was touched that when he'd reached out to them about needing American adoptive parents for Jae, they jumped at the opportunity, even though it meant risking their personal safety by going to Manila, a Han-occupied territory.

But he had banked on the adventurous spirits of this couple. It took a certain amount of craziness and derring-do to inhabit a land like Antarctica, and the Moores had this quality in spades.

"We jumped at the chance to make things right with the past," Simone Moore was telling Brice. "We are forever sorry we abandoned Antarctica in its hour of need." And she took Brice's hand and squeezed it.

Avila's eyes rested on Brice. He sighed. He had underestimated his niece's resolve to see the Salims in the Philippines. Was it good for her? He observed his niece. Years of therapy had erased the symptoms of some of the worst post-traumatic stress syndrome he had seen in all his years as an agent in the Colony. Maybe there was nothing to worry about. Maybe she could handle herself.

"Hari, please accompany the Moores back to the common room so they can have dinner as they wait for Lee Jae Seung's Reformation process to end," Hari said, and the three left, leaving Brice alone with him.

"Why did you not tell me in person that you were leaving Boston, Brice?" His voice was calm, knowing that reprimanding her would elicit a rebellious stance. "I had to hear about your plans from Mira and Analie. I do hope you're back in Boston by the time of the wedding next month," he admonished her. Perhaps, guilt would compel her to return to the States.

"I wouldn't miss it for the world, Uncle Avila. Auntie Analie will never forgive me if I miss that family event," Brice said in a contrite voice.

"Yup, she'll wring your neck," he warned her.

"Before I say anything else, thank you for changing my documents, Uncle Avila. It's a great help," she said.

"You have to be very careful. We engaged our own security team for the Moores. But you're a sitting duck for the Hans. Giving you your own security will raise suspicions," he said.

"I'm with Hari, Uncle Avila. And I'll be careful. Don't forget that your legal rights as guardian ended when I turned eighteen," she said.

"How can I forget? You remind me of that fact every time you see me!" he said.

"So what is this mad experiment with the AQs, Uncle Avila?" Brice asked.

"C'mon, I'll show you something." Avila led her outside. Then he entered another room with a bigger window. He tapped it and motioned with his hands that he was allowing Brice to see the whole process.

Jae was lying on a hospital bed. What looked like an entire arsenal of machinery was attached to his body.

"Why didn't you just use the discarded Machina soldiers, Uncle Avila?" she asked.

"In Jae's case, the AQs will be returned to the Red Cross and await instructions from the US Defense Department."

"For the great Elimination Day against the Hans," Brice said.

"Where did you get that info? I told Hari to bring you

up to speed about Jae, and nothing else," he said in anger.

Brice continued her questioning, ignoring his previous statement. "How long has this been going on?"

"It's been going on since Congress passed the bill creating the Aequilavum," he answered.

"Isn't that Machiavellian? Does the end to eliminate the Hans justify the need to create the AQs? What happens when the Hans are defeated? Will they be executed?"

"It's war, Brice. When the Hans are eliminated, they'll be reprogrammed to live as private citizens."

"But only after the mission is completed?" she asked.

"The AQs have free will, don't get me wrong. We are not complete monsters. Their memories are programmed from birth – they've lived, schooled in the United States or other Coalition countries, from pre-school to military school. They're sleeper agents, but to those who have experience with these kinds of agents, it's complicated."

"Uncle Avila, I'd like to join the Defiance movement. The AQs as you've said have free will. Why can't I exercise my free will to help Hari, Amil, and the movement? Let me help." She reached out to his hand, and intertwined her fingers with his.

She then embraced him. And her head rested on his shoulders.

"Please?" Her uncle was very tense from the moment she saw him inside the Defiance headquarters. Slowly, she felt him relax.

"Ah Brice," he kissed the top of her head. "I've done everything to protect you. I can't ask you to go back to Boston, can I?"

"No, Uncle Avila. I'd like to help Hari. Just give this time to me," she pleaded in a beseeching tone.

He thought about his choices. If he stopped Brice, he knew she would never forgive him till his last breath. And he'd regret this decision one day.

"Brice, promise me that you'll use your head, you have to be careful. The Hans are ruthless enemies."

"I will, Uncle Avila. You have to trust me."

"Okay then, help Hari. He'll be transporting Lee back to the Red Cross so as not to arouse suspicion. But this time Jae is no longer a Machina. He'll be an AQ under Hari's mentorship..." Brice didn't let him finish his next words, drowned out by her whoops and cheers.

The question remained still to be answered. Would he ever forgive himself if anything happened to Brice? No, he knew he could never forgive himself if anything happened to her. But Brice made the decision herself. It was time to respect that.

He walked toward the door and opened it. Hari was outside.

"Hari, bring her into the Mentorship program with Jae," he said as Hari's eyes widened in understanding.

"Yes, Sir," Hari saluted.

"What is the Mentorship program, Hari?" Brice asked.

"We'll be the first people he'll meet after his parents. We are not his handlers. But we can help him navigate the world that's opened to him. You can help him see the world through your eyes."

"Have you been doing this a long time?" she asked

"Yes, I've mentored many AQs. So does Amil. It's highly risky, but highly rewarding, you'll see."

She turned to look at the inert body on the stretcher. And suddenly the gravity of her decision to join the Defiance movement dawned on her. She had a role and a mission.

"We don't have a lot of time," Hari said. "I need you to help me bring Jae back to Gesu tonight, as soon as he's ready. So, Brice. Are you ready?"

"I'm ready," she said with no hesitation.

By midnight, the day's Reformation process was complete. She watched as Jae regained consciousness.

The Moores were there to greet him and they were given privacy together before Jae was brought back to Gesu.

Then it was their turn to meet Jae.

"Jae, I'm Hari. I'll be guiding you and bringing you back to Gesu. This is Brice, your other mentor."

Jae smiled back and shook both their hands.

"Oh, we have to get Jae's old clothes," Hari said in embarrassment.

"Yes, I know the mission. I have to dress the part," Jae reassured both of them. He turned around and disappeared to dress again. When he reappeared, Jae was wearing ripped, stained clothes looking like the assistant of Hari at the Red Cross.

"Great!" Hari bantered to him.

She observed the interaction of both men and realized that Hari had been doing his mentorship role for quite some time. He did not coddle Jae, expecting him to know his own role too in the Defiance movement.

Hari held Jae's arm to steady him as they walked back

through the labyrinthian passageway to go together toward Quiapo Church. A Red Cross waterboat was waiting for them.

The evening air was damp and the warm water felt heavy under the oars.

"Are you okay, Jae?" she said. When he nodded, she scanned the Pasig River for boats one more time, then looked at her watch. Twelve more minutes before they reached the Gesu campus.

Jae lay quietly in the back of the water ambulance, hidden under blankets and Red Cross paraphernalia. Hari manned the driver's seat, wary of every boat that passed them.

"I'm okay, Ms. O'Rourke," Jae said, and smiled at her.

"Call me Brice, Jae," she said, returning his smile.

"Yes, Ms. Brice O'Rourke, I mean Brice," he said, and Brice chuckled.

"So how do you feel about sleeping in the cupboard in Gesu again?" Hari asked.

"Oh, I definitely need an upgrade, Dr Hari. I might begin to smell like camphor," Jae said.

Hari laughed.

"May I try a joke on you?" Jae said. "Humor is a gift my adoptive father and I share."

"Very unusual, Jae," Hari said. "But hit it. Let's hear your jokes."

"So, why are robots shy?" Jae asked.

"Why?" Hari gamely answered.

"It's because they have hardware and software, but no underware," Jae grinned as she and Hari tittered over the joke, surprised at Jae's sense of humor.

"Why did the droid cross the road?" Jae was trying

another joke.

"Why?" she asked.

"Because the droid was programmed by a chicken," Jae said with no expression on his face. Then he broke out in laughter.

She giggled, realizing that even Ira didn't have this kind of bantering. Jae's voice kept changing from monotone robotic to the tones and textures of a human voice. Brice laughed and laughed, but it was a laughter that verged on grateful tears. It was clear that the experiment was going to be a success. Jae was becoming more than just a collection of electronic parts. He was feeling, sharing, growing; becoming human.

After this first successful transfer of Jae back to Gesu, her life quickly settled into an interesting routine. She'd attend Red Cross classes by day, and then, after five p.m, meet up with Hari and they would set off together to bring Jae to the Defiance headquarters for further observation. They would wait for him and return him back again to Gesu.

As the three of them worked together, the awkwardness she had felt toward Jae began to dissipate.

She found herself reminiscing with him about his days spent in the Antarctic. She found out that he had lived as a child two blocks away from her in Buckminster, but he had moved out when most of the families fled as the ground shifted around them.

She wondered how it felt to live on borrowed memories of another person's private life. Were some memories expunged to delete personal interactions with other people? Were memories extracted just of places where the donor stayed?

One day, she couldn't stop herself and asked, "Do you

remember specific people you've known?"

"Many specific memories of people are hazy. The first significant memories I have are of my adoptive parents, the community here and the number of people I've met in Gesu," Jae said with no trace of bitterness. "I am grateful for what I have. Truly grateful," he smiled.

His memories originated from four or five different people, and so there were a number of places he'd been and places he was familiar with.

She questioned him about little details in Antarctica, and Jae would answer correctly.

Hari would often ask Jae about his training as an American officer in the army. He could remember voices, but not faces. It was all hazy after the Reformation.

She loved the trips to Gesu because she was able to fill in the gaps of information she had with Hari. The boat trips gave them time to catch up with each other. It also gave Brice time to really observe her childhood friend.

When there was a lull in conversation with Jae, she turned and asked Hari, "Why did you stop sending messages to me?"

"All our communication was monitored," he told her. "Even if I sent you a message, the Hans would have read it. We just refused to ensnare anyone in our old life."

Gone was the awkwardness of youth, the self-consciousness of teenage years.

Here was a man who was sure of himself, not to the point of arrogance. But his convictions were ironclad. He believed in the obliteration of all Han entities in the Philippines, the restoration of government institutions, the return of all basic human rights that were taken away by the Hans when they took over the Philippines after the Great Migration.

"One of the worst parts of the Hans' invasion is that they imposed their Constitution on us. We had a system of government that was working when they arrived. Why did they not just appoint a governor that they approved of?" Hari asked in frustration.

"Perhaps it's because they have no land to call their own any more," she surmised. "Catastrophic events wiped out all their history; the nuclear attack on North Korea, the Polar Shift, the Great Migration..." But Hari cut her off.

"It's cruel to force one culture onto another."

Their conversations were lively, and disagreements were few. The years might have separated them, but their views and opinions were still in sync.

As the weeks went on, she liked the trips back and forth from Gesu more and more. She liked watching Hari navigate the Red Cross boat, expertly maneuvering the complicated water byways of the metropolis.

He was always kind to Jae, never impatient with him as he slowly learned the ways of being human, always laughing at Jae's stories and jokes.

One day, she noticed Hari seemed to be watching her as the boat motored slowly toward Gesu.

"Do you remember the last day before we left for Manila?" Hari said, and chuckled.

"Yup, I lunged at you and stole a kiss from you," she said. "So much for raging teenage hormones. I was loco!"

She was surprised when Hari leaned toward her, caught a hand and held it firmly.

"You've done so well, Brice. You've grown so much, and I'm proud of you," and he held her gaze.

"Thank you very much for the diagnosis, Dr. Salim. I'm

still so embarrassed till now. I couldn't believe I forced a kiss on you," she said. Hari pulled her toward him and in an instant, kissed her.

"I wonder what's Jae doing?" she said, quickly changing the subject, and turned toward the back of the boat to check on him.

Jae seemed comfortable under his blanket. But a big smile covered his face.

"I can keep a secret. Please forgive me as I've overheard your conversation." Jae's face was flushed, as if he was caught with his hand in the proverbial cookie jar.

She laughed, and patted his arm. "Does being an AIP make things easier or hard now, Jae?"

"It's extremely hard, Ms. Brice. I see a lot, I hear everything, and understand many things. It is overwhelming," Jae said this, then laughed. "C'est la vie!"

She smiled at him. "C'est la vie, Jae. But so you won't be overwhelmed, you just have to learn to focus, and obliterate everything else. One task at a time," she took off her seat belt and climbed over to the back to be beside Jae.

Jae was lying on his back. She moved beside him and looked upwards. A million stars were twinkling back at them.

"What a nice view, huh?" she said, enthralled by the view.

" Looking at this view every night before I get back to Gesu makes it tolerable, staying in the closet. Brice..." Jae paused, "what if my nature is to multi-task? I have so many things processing in my head. So many memories, yet I couldn't focus on one."

"Just think of this view when everything seems overwhelming, Jae. Just be still. What is most important to you will come up. Be the best you can be, Jae. There are no limits for you. Deal?" And they shook hands.

As they neared the Gesu entrance, Hari leaned forward, suddenly tense. "The Gesu gates seem to be blocked," he said. "What's happening here?" A group of men were on the dock, as if waiting for them. Their uniforms showed them to be Han officers.

"Looks like trouble... Let me do the talking," Hari said.

He gave the men a friendly wave.

"Any problem, officer? We need to go inside Gesu. Red Cross business."

"IDs, please!" the officer replied.

"I'm a doctor and we're just going to return the ambulance to the Red Cross building," Hari said.

"No exemptions, Sir. You too, Miss."

"Hand over your ID, and don't say anything," Hari whispered to her. The soldiers examined their IDs, then motioned for them to get out of the boat. They were searching for something else, and found Jae hiding at the back.

And then the first soldier addressed them again. "Hari Salim, and Brice O'Rourke, you are under arrest."

Quickly, they were handcuffed and put in the back of a troop ship. They were positioned side by side, turned away from each other.

She started to shake. What was happening? Where did they take Jae?

Chapter  13

Victoria Station, London

Thames River Coalition

United Kingdom

European River Coalitions

22 August 2071

22 days after Drone Strike

People were running madly in all directions. She started to run with them to escape. There were women looking for their children, and children looking for their parents, and shoes and bags were all abandoned as people fled. She took the stairs up toward Victoria Street, but Gabriel and other agents grabbed her, pulled out handcuffs, and snapped them on her wrists. She didn't want to look at Quinn's face.

Gabriel was fuming as he tightened the cuffs on her wrists.

" We have confirmed that it's Hari Salim and Lee Jae Seung who were seen at the Memory Banks, Brice. And I can see by your face you know it too. If they are responsible for second Drone Strike and they're doing it as a way for their leader to save you, thanks to you, we will hunt them down. Agent Lt. Quinn, you stay behind us." Gabriel's voice was shaking, as he made sure the cuffs holding Brice were secure.

"Come with me!" he said, jerking Brice by the cuffs. "You move when I move, and no phony tricks to distract me." Her security Bee emitted a red glow, and she knew that her situation was now considered to be at the highest levels of danger.

Gabriel dragged her toward the Underground where a thousand other people were also heading, many of them covering their ears.

"This is not a drill. This is not a drill. Evacuate to the Underground," Gabriel shouted to passersby. He led them to the underground railway tracks and opened a door that led to a long, steep stairway. People were jostling through the passageway, in spite of the presence of policemen encouraging the crowd to stay calm and proceed in an orderly fashion.

"I'm just praying to God my wife and children were able to evacuate in time," Gabriel muttered, and gave her hands an extra hard yank.

The European River Coalitions had prepared for the inevitability of overwhelming flooding by building fully functional underground cities. They'd hoped to never have to use them, but the drone bombings meant this last hope had been dashed.

The sounds of sobbing filled the darkened hallways of

Victoria Station.

News images were beamed onto display terminals, and people gazed transfixed as images of the bombing run were replayed again.

Exhausted, she just wanted to close her eyes and rest for a minute, but an angry voice jolted her into alertness.

"Brice and Quinn, the Colony has been apprised of your situation. The WRC's Submersible 250 is waiting for you at Dock 42. Follow me," Gabriel turned and he took her to a long passageway that led to an underwater dock, where a submersible aircraft was floating.

"You'll be taken to the 10X class submarine. Diego and Defense Minister O'Rourke will communicate with you in this vessel," Gabriel said, and with these words, turned and left.

She was not surprised, but still saddened that he didn't even say goodbye to her.

"Let's go. It's time to leave Thames," Quinn said. He took her elbow in a gentle manner and led her to the Submersible 250. Though his face was stony, his voice was calm.

The vessel was filled with both European and US soldiers. All were regarding her with the same wary expressions. Did they blame her for the bombing run?

She was led to a corner seat, where she pulled her knees to her forehead.

From the corner of her eye she saw three soldiers standing near her. They were carrying weapons. Soon she realized they were guarding her every move.

Mayet Ligad Yuhico

Chapter 14

Han Prison

Pasig River

Philippines

Federation Han Asia

September 22, 2068

2 years, 10 months, 10 days before the Drone Strike

Brice was slapped a hundredth time. Someone grabbed her hair and pulled her head back, which pulled her eyes open as well. In the room, she saw three people in full military uniform, staring at her. They vanished as her head was pushed into a bucket of water. She couldn't breathe. "Ang ganda nito, pare!" someone said, and the soldiers laughed. He was speaking Tagalog. Were these the soldiers collaborators of the Han government? Finally, her head was released and she sputtered, water streaming from her face.

The soldiers were human. She recognized one as a human Han officer with a distinctly pale face. When the atomic bombs were unleashed in the Koreas, they sent tons of dust, ash and debris into the atmosphere, reducing the amount of sunshine available. Temperatures dropped, causing an "atomic autumn." Unfortunately, the Koreas were separated by a geographic border, and the effects meant for one country were inevitably felt in another.

There was laughter again, and a new group of soldiers entered.

They were handsomer and had a more erect posture, obviously one of the officer Machina. She had not seen them up close up since that day in Concordia when the villagers fled to the caves, but she'd hosted them in her nightmares. She felt a sudden cold sweat cover her body. What had they done with Hari?

"How many in all, Lieutenant?" The bulbous-nosed Filipino officer asked. "Kunin mo itong puti at ilipat mo sa kabilang kwarto."

And then she was unshackled and dragged for ten seconds. Was she brought to another room?

She felt someone untying the cloth around her eyes.

"You know what we do with girls like you?" one soldier asked, again in Tagalog.

"Subukan lang ninyo," she replied, and there was deathly silence in response. She felt another slap. They were not expecting that she could speak the local tongue.

"As I've said, do you know what we do with girls like you? We've been following you since you arrived. Now, tell us why you were seen in Salim's hospital tent."

When she didn't answer, another soldier approached. She peered closely into his brown-black eyes, trying to determine if he was human or a Machina.

And then she remembered Jae.

Where was he? Was the Defiance secret finally out?

"I'm human. Isn't that what you want to know?" the soldier said, and spat on the floor.

She spotted a body lying next to her, as lifeless as a bag of garbage thrown by the side of the road. Her throat tightened. Was it Hari? She willed herself not to show her feelings.

But she was sure it was him. The curly hair gave him away.

She felt blood thickening around her lip, but her hands were tied, and she couldn't wipe it off. A handkerchief was peeking from one of her pants pockets. The handkerchief had been a gift from her mother.

What would her mother think if she knew she was in a dirty prison, Hari lying probably dead, beside her? She knew exactly what they did to women in a place like this. She would be raped, and there was nothing she could do about it.

The soldiers were now whispering and nodding toward her. Her time was up. She started reciting prayers her father taught her when she was a child.

"St. Michael, the Archangel, defend us in battle, be our protection against the wickedness and ..."

And then, a soldier went to Hari's body and dragged it over to her.

"Hari..." she said. When there was no response, she nudged his foot with her own.

"Hari, please wake up," she begged the inert form.

"Is he your boyfriend?" one of the human Han soldiers said and the rest started laughing.

She shook her head.

"Why are you with the Salim boy?" another one asked.

"He's one of the doctors of the Red Cross team. I'm a volunteer for the Red Cross. I came here only for the summer."

"A doctor? What is he doing with a discarded Han soldier?" The soldier shook his head in disgust. "From North America. Junk. Piss off!" And he pulled down his pants and urinated on her leg as the other soldiers jeered.

"You better tell us what you've been up to, or your friend will die." The soldier said and pointed to Hari.

She turned away from him.

"So you don't want to answer?" the first soldier said. "Maybe this one can!" And he pointed into a shadowed corner of the room.

There, chained to the wall, was another man. She recognized Jae and gasped.

"Looks like this robot is your boyfriend too, huh? Think you can talk now?" And he kicked Jae. His eyes were closed, but when he felt the kick, he opened them. He gave Brice a wink the soldiers couldn't see, and threw her a grin. But the smile disappeared when the soldier undid his chains and dragged him next to her.

"No, no, no!" she cried. "He's just one of the discarded Machinas. He's helping the Red Cross. He helped us carry medical paraphernalia. He knows nothing…"

The force of his slap made Jae's body shake.

"We know what you've been up to," the soldier said and pushed Jae to a standing position against the wall. The soldier unzipped his pants, then turned him to face the wall. As he thrust his penis against him, Brice turned away.

"He's just a machine, he knows nothing, please…" she cried.

"If he underwent Reformation, imagine the memories I'm giving him!" the soldier laughed.

"I bet he'll remember your small dick, Fool!" one soldier said.

The molesting soldier zipped his fly.

"You better have an answer tomorrow," he said, "otherwise you three are dead. And we'll just throw your bodies in the Pasig River."

The soldiers blindfolded her. The last thing she saw before the blindfold took her vision was Hari's body, still limp on the floor.

And then someone untied her hands, pulled off the blindfold, and without saying a word, pushed her inside a room that seemed to be a cell. She lost her balance and fell. When she heard the door shut, she started to cry. But even as she sobbed she was flooded with relief. She'd survived the interrogation. She was alive.

The floor was rough but at least it was dry. She got up, felt the walls till she found the door and tried to listen for voices, but her ear had barely touched the doorway when she was abruptly lifted into the air. She'd been caught in some kind of net.

The more she struggled, the tighter the ropes around her became. Keeping still was her only option.

Pinned in the net, she finally fell into an exhausted sleep. When she woke, she was back on the floor, and the net was gone.

She closed her eyes, and fell back to sleep. After an hour, she woke with a start. There was no illumination of any kind. The cell was as dark as the inside of the blindfold.

She stood up and tried to measure the cell with her feet. She measured eight by eight feet across, and when she turned to measure the width, her foot kicked against a toilet bowl. There was no bed, no kind of bedding, not even any newspapers to cushion the floor for sleeping.

So she sat on the floor. She could hear her rapid breathing, and willed herself to calm down.

There was a slight illumination at the top of a wall. Was it a window up there too high to reach? If she was going to survive, she decided, she had to use her brain. She could not use her emotions or feel sadness or despair. She had to find a way to survive and help Hari and Jae out of this hellhole.

She patted her pockets until she found a ball of cloth. Her mother's handkerchief, the one she gave Brice before she left Harvard. That day felt like a hundred years ago. She used it to clean the grime from her face, wipe her sweaty forehead, and then tie her hair up. The handkerchief still smelled like her mother's perfume. Was it only a month ago when they were all in Boston? That memory of their day together was enough to make tears well in her eyes. She sobbed but stifled the sound. If the room was bugged, she was not going to give the soldiers the satisfaction of letting them hear her cry.

She stood up and started walking around the room again and decided she was going to walk till she felt sleepy. Even if it took a thousand steps, a million steps. She was not going to cry anymore, either. The Hans were not going to break her down.

The next day, the sliver of light Brice could see through the small window disappeared and she heard the sound of falling rain. Because she could not distinguish night and day, she decided to befriend darkness like she had as a young child in Concordia, where electricity was sparse.

Life in prison quickly fell into a rhythm. In the mornings, the sounds of a soldier approaching meant that food was about to be delivered. A tray was thrust into a small opening in the middle of the door, which meant she had to run to catch it or it would fall onto the floor. She had to eat the food quickly, as it disintegrated five minutes after arrival.

She was never allowed out of her cell. She couldn't stop wondering how Hari and Jae were faring, but there was no way to find out. But she knew she was being monitored, and in a way, taken care of. At seven in the morning, like clockwork, powerful air gusts from vents embedded in the walls forced her body into the air, and then dropped her down again. An exercise contraption appeared on one wall. She didn't want her muscles to atrophy, so she used it to do yoga positions, stretching her legs around the rubber bands hanging from it. And then she jumped as high as she could for a hundred counts, did a hundred push-ups and ran in place. Her regimen kept her fit and moved the monotonous days forward.

Bath time was every two days. A vent opened and sucked her clothes away and water for showering appeared from a tube in the wall. It was hot and plentiful, but always brief. After a few minutes, the room was filled with hot gusts of air that dried her off, and then clothes were dropped from another tube in the ceiling.

But other than that, silence. Solitude. And though she worked hard against it, despair.

In an effort to get out from the deep funk she was under, she devised a game to amuse herself. She lay on the floor, out of view of the door, so she could listen to prisoners in other cells. She was happy with the slightest sounds, even cries and whimpers.

Who did the voices belong to? she wondered. Were they coming from Hari or Jae?

But she couldn't tell if the voices belonged to them. After a few days, Brice reached the conclusion that Hari was dead. She was certain that the son of a leader of the Defiance Army would be the first execution by the Han Army. She just hoped they hadn't tortured him.

She obsessed over what the Han Army would do with Hari's body. Would he be thrown into the Pasig River, like slimy garbage? Would he be kept in some kind of a morgue?

And how about Jae? Would he have been dismantled piece by piece, parts of him strewn like shells on a beach, or displayed somewhere as a warning to the other Reformatted soldiers?

And then she realized they weren't the only ones in dire circumstances. Were the Hans interrogating Tio Dio? Were they torturing him again? And what about the Moores?

The noise of the rain continued for days and days. But eventually it became less, and then a faint glimmer of sunshine appeared once again in the small window near the ceiling.

She'd do anything to see the sun again, feel its sticky warmth.

And Hari. She would do anything to talk to him one more time.

Without a warning, her prison door opened. A pair of soldiers marched in, and dragged her out from the cell. Her knees scraped the floor but the soldiers didn't care. She kept her head down and willed herself not to cry.

She was not going to succumb to fear, but in the end, she retched, vomiting whatever food was in her stomach.

Han Prison

Pasig River

Philippines

Federation Han Asia

October 1, 2068

2 years, 10 months before the Drone Strike

Colonel Kang Chul-Moo

So this was Brice O'Rourke, the niece of Avila, the Defense Minister of the United States. She was very young, and even if she was brought to the room on her knees, she didn't scream like almost all the prisoners interrogated here.

Her father was a prisoner in Concordia, his first Station Command in the Great Migration in 2058. Was it a coincidence that she was here? What were the odds?

"Untie her blindfold," he ordered.

The eyes that were revealed showed fear at first, then it was a familiar reaction when she turned away, repulsed by his face.

It was the reason why he reached toward his belt and

unfurled it and hit her arms. The rage he felt toward people who looked at him was indescribable.

When South Korea detonated its own nuclear weapon against the North in Kyushimo in 2052, he was stationed at the North Korean military base ten kilometers away. He remembered that day. It was an ordinary day. He was preparing for a meeting for his boss at JQ Command when a brilliant, white-blue streak of color flashed in the nearby window. Then he heard a freakish roar that shook the whole building. The shards of glass from the window hit him covering his face in blood.

At that instant 160,000 people from the city died. He crawled through bodies buried in debris, down twisted staircases, past screaming people. He made it to the front of the building only to be puzzled at the sight in front of him. The bustling military complex was gone, replaced with a burning inferno. He sat down in shock as people ran past him.

Time stood still. He didn't know if hours or minutes had passed. A medical triage area was set a few hundred feet from where he stood, and he could hear people shouting and giving out orders. But he could not move. It was as if his muscles had stiffened from the shock of it all. Blood continued to drip from his face, but he couldn't touch it, afraid that half of his face had blown off.

A kind stranger, an old man whose hair was singed and who had cuts and bruises on his face gently touched him on the side of his arm. The unexpected human touch brought him out of his stupor, and he stood up. Together, they walked towards the triage area.

Another doctor took pity on him and did his best to staunch the flow of blood. He needed to go to the hospital for further reconstructive surgery. One eye was gone, his nose was blown off, the skin of his face was burned beyond recognition.

The hospital where he landed was overwhelmed with the severely injured and dying. But he was alive, right? In the days after, he'd had six surgeries and countless consultations with plastic surgery doctors, but he was forever disfigured, his face eliciting hatred and ridicule.

Mostly pitiful looks, like the look he received from the girl in front of him now.

He whipped his belt.

When O'Rourke fell, he turned toward the local soldiers and whipped them too, his rage apparent at the Filipino soldiers, who helped the Han Army man the prisons. They were still collaborators in his eyes, pieces of shit who turned against their countrymen to help the dwindling human Han officers who were sick and dying.

"Why did you go to Quiapo Church with Hari Salim?" he asked.

"Hindi ko po alam," she cried in Tagalog.

He whipped her again with his belt and then felt excruciating pain at his side as he did so.

"Truss her up," he hissed at the soldiers. He glanced sideways and looked for the Machinas. The droids were good at maintaining security, marching along the perimeter of an area, running after prisoners, but their fine motor skills were inadequate and lacking. They couldn't even hold this prisoner and tie her up, and he was frustrated that he needed the human soldiers to do this job. He spat in disgust.

His sputum fell on the side, and he recoiled at the dirty floor. He hated this hell hole, and was sick and tired of this prison. He longed for home in the North Korean Penninsula.

But then he almost laughed, where was home?

Ever since the poles shifted and his homeland was inundated by waters, his people dug deeper toward the tunnels prepared decades beforehand, in case the government's calculation was correct and waters rose to cover the land.

The labyrinth of thousand-mile tunnels was dug deep fifty floors below; the general population of people was subjugated to slave labor to help in the manufacture of Machina soldiers. They were promised land in exchange for these labors and, for the most part, the Great Migration of 2058 was a success, their occupation of countries too easy since many of the occupied countries were too distressed about the disappearance of their land and people in the cruel event of the Polar Shift.

Living in the toxic tunnels for years took its toll on many of his countrymen, including him. The effects were just becoming apparent years after being exposed to metallic fumes and chemicals.

Was it all worth it? He was grateful to see land here in the Philippines. Seeing Concordia Island after a tumultuous journey was heaven on earth. To see land again, to see the sun!

Just gazing at the smiles of his wife Hae-Eun, his two children, Ae-Cha and Kyung-Mi, as they settled in land they could call their own was enough, he reasoned, to stay in this prison for long stretches of time.

He walked across to the prisoner. How stupid was she to even think that she could come to a Han-occupied country and get away impersonating a Filipina?

Her round-shaped eyes and light skin could pass her off as mestiza, people of mixed-blood parentage he had seen walking around the city, showing their country's Spanish, Chinese, and American heritage. But she could not hide her identity forever.

Why were the Americans here? Was she a spy? Was there an imminent invasion?

He whipped his belt again, this time aiming for her feet. She winced when he aimed at the ankles.

"What is the name of the other person who accompanied you and Salim?" he asked.

Her crying stopped. Was she surprised that he knew the other prisoner's name?

It was unfortunate that the other prisoner in the Gesu Red Cross watercraft who had Korean features escaped in the first hours of his captivity. No one was able to take his name, his DNA...

There was a flash and lightning struck outside the high windows. Everyone winced at the sound, including him.

He was still pondering the imminent invasion of the Americans. Would they try invading North Korea it should be again? should be in one line They tried many times, but could not penetrate the bunkers of Central Command.

There was another lightning strike, and then the lights went out. That's when he saw a figure who had Korean features stride into the room. He was surprised when he was shot in the chest and the Filipino soldiers beside him toppled over with their mouths open. He felt blood gushing out from him. He suddenly remembered the pigs his father used to butcher in his native town of Dae-Ki.

He could not believe he was going to die in this hell hole.

Oh, to see the sun again, to see another day with his wife and two children.

At least he gave them the chance to experience a little bit of happiness in a cruel, cruel world. It was all worth it. And he would do it all over again.

Brice's limbs were aching from being trussed up in a make-shift pole beam and she tried to relax her shoulders, but winced.

At first the blows to her arms and feet had hurt but her attention was on the face of her tormentor. She could not help but pity him. Parts of his face were like shredded paper, layers of skin in varying degrees of color from dark brown to pale white, a mish-mash of layers that were entwined haphazardly.

Many of the local Hans kept to themselves in villages, but many of them had flash burns and injuries from the blast that South Korea detonated on their land fourteen years ago.

She heard the loud crack of a lightning strike and the people beside her jumped, even the soldiers guarding her.

Suddenly, she felt the whole building shake. A burst of blinding light flashed at the window. A loud boom sounded again and again. But this time it was more like a cannon shot than thunder.

The lights went out then a man entered the room, his face in shadow. Without hesitation he shot Kang Chul-Moo and then the other soldiers near her.

"Jae," she cried. He was wearing dark clothing, and his face was blackened with soot.

There was another explosion that crashed against the wall opposite the door. She watched the wall crumble, and the beam of light suddenly shining through the hole where the wall had been blinded her. A man whose features were not visible entered the room in a vest and protective headgear and was standing in the rubble. When he pulled off his mask, she shouted, "Uncle Avila!" and started to cry.

"What did you get yourself into?" he said and hugged her close.

"Where's Hari?" she asked as Jae hugged her.

"Jae was able to escape two days ago, and he led us back here, to you. They've been looking for me for a few days. If I wasn't captured, they will use you so that I could surrender to the North Korean Army. Come on, let's go. "

Avila pulled a small jug from the backpack he was wearing and gave it to her. The water inside was clean and refreshing, and her uncle's gentle touch made her weep harder.

There came sounds of commotion from outside. Another man appeared in the hole in the wall. It was Hari. He wore a bandage on one eye and an arm was hanging limply. She ran to him, her eyes blinded by tears.

"It's okay, Brice," he said, embracing her. "Jae saved us."

Avila cleared his throat, and she realized that it must have been a shock for her uncle to see her embracing Hari.

"Let's go," Avila said. "Further enemy reinforcements might be arriving in a few minutes, and I don't want to be caught in the middle of a firefight."

She took a step and stumbled. Despite her attempts at exercise, imprisonment had made her weak. Avila held one arm and Hari took the other and together they helped her through the hole.

Outside, they passed the Filipino military who worked for the Hans. "Do not fucking look up or glare at them. They're with us," Avila whispered. "They're double agents.

The Han Army isn't the only one with collaborators."

When they reached the water's edge, a battered boat sped toward them. When the boat docked, Jae went ahead to help her and Hari.

"Time to get out of here!" Avila's clipped tone brooked no argument.

Thirty minutes later, they were docking at a broken-down pier next to an old house. It was a hodge-podge of clashing architectural details, a remnant from the Philippines' Spanish and American colonizers. They entered through its back door, Jae serving as rear guard, making sure that they were not followed.

The house was dark, but Avila led them to a room that looked like a busy emergency room in a hospital. It was filled with doctors and nurses running around transporting patients on gurneys. Among the staff were familiar faces from the Red Cross, and one or two looked up and smiled at her.

She recognized one doctor in white as Dr. Hernando, the Red Cross Director. He quickly assessed Hari's arm as broken, and sent him into another room for a cast. Then he took her pulse, held her chin, and checked her eyes. "Your injuries don't look serious," he said, "but let's see if anything's broken." He brought a small implement to her ear, which discharged a tiny pellet that checked for internal injuries. A nearby machine seemed to offer diagnostic results. After studying them for a few minutes, he turned to Avila and announced, "She's clear!"

"Good," Avila replied. "After they're cleaned up, I need to talk to you, Hari, and Jae."

Dr. Hernandez nodded. "Very good. Some warm food will taste good, right, Ms. O'Rourke?" he said. "And the nurses will give you their famous hyperbaric bath, yes?" Avila left the room and Dr. Hernandez followed him. And then Hari came back, fresh plaster encasing his injured arm. As they realized they were alone, she and Hari embraced again.

"I thought I lost you," Hari said and kissed her cheek gently, as if kissing a child.

"How long were we gone?" she asked. She felt cold, and rubbed her arms. Hari pulled her close.

"Seven days. Are you okay?" he asked.

"Are you?" she replied, gently touching the bandage on his eye.

"Where's Jae?" she asked.

"He'll be joining us after the nurse's visit," Hari said. "We meet Avila in an hour. Let's just rest for now." And with his good arm, he pulled her even closer.

"I love you, Brice O'Rourke. I thought I'd never see you again. I regretted not saying those words earlier." And he kissed her on the lips.

"I've loved you all these years, Hari," she said.

"Yes, you made that very clear when you were fifteen, O'Rourke," Hari said, and grinned.

She laid her head on his chest. She closed her eyes. She was enormously relieved to have finally confessed her love for Hari. Amazingly, it had been returned. But would they ever be able to be together, or would they always be separated by war and violence?

Dr. Hernando entered inside the room again followed by Avila. Beside him was Jae, with a smile on his face.

As Dr. Hernando and Avila spoke to each other on hushed tones, Brice stood up and walked towards Jae. Brice embraced him. To her surprise, his body was warm. " Thank you for going back for us, Jae. Not a Machina anymore, huh?" she said. "Are you enjoying yourself as a ..." she searched for the words.

"AQ. Aequilavum, Brice. It means balance," Jae grinned. "I was told that it's the spinning of consciousness into memory that makes me warm. More tiny bits of information to process in between processors. I just need recharging every two days, otherwise I'm fine."

She stared at Jae. His face looked different. His expression was animated, his eyes lively. Where does machinery end, she wondered, and when does the soul emerge from robotic DNA spliced into organic material? She could ask the same question about humans, she realized. How did it all connect so that sentient existence was possible?

"Excuse me. May I have your attention?" Avila said.

He was standing with his arms crossed. His expression was angry.

"This is a Colony safe house, but the three of you are not safe here," he said. "What I'm proposing is that you leave tonight. I'm recruiting you two to train with us in in the US Defense Team." Avila turned toward Hari and Jae. "You can think about the offer while en route to Denver. You were all tortured in varying degrees. It will be good not to talk about it before the debriefing. Psychologists will be on hand in the plane."

"What about me?" she asked.

"What about you? You go back to Boston, and determine the future course of your life. I'm not going to recruit you for the Colony. Your mother would kill both of us," Avila said in front of Hari and Jae.

"I'm going to apply to the Colony, Uncle Avila. Whether you like it or not," she said.

Avila shrugged. "Oh, you can apply. But I won't lift a finger to help you." He turned toward Hari and Jae. "There will be a year and a half of training. Once you've become agents, you will receive a salary from the Colony, and Hari, you can continue your medical residency in the US. Your parents are in the custody of the US forces and are being taken to safety."

Everything was turning out much better than she'd hoped, as she saw the enormous sense of relief in Hari's face.

"Regarding your place in the Colony," Avila said to Jae, "this will be the first time we'll accept AQs as agent-trainees. We've realized it's a whole new world out there. We can't fight without your help. Please, let's help one another."

Jae shook his head. "I have vague memories of my soldier days," he said in a low voice. "I'm useless in the Colony."

"You broke out of the prison and led us back there. Without your help, my niece would have been hurt and possibly killed. Because of this, you have my eternal gratitude. And you saved Hari, another important member of the Defiance team. You are more capable then you think." Avila held out his hand. "You deserve more than a place in the Colony, Lee Jae Seung."

Jae shook his hand gravely. "Thank you, Director Avila. I am grateful that I was able to help. I would be glad to join the Colony to be of service to the United States." He turned to her and Hari. "I did it because I was saving my friends," he said.

"I'm following my gut instincts here," Avila said. "If the Colony plays its cards right, I am looking at the future leaders of the next generation. Hari could even be set up as the next de facto leader of the Philippines, and vanquish the Han Army."

Her uncle eyed her from afar. She noticed that he was looking at Hari embracing holding her hands.

"Your personal life is your own business," Avila said to them. "Just keep your heads straight during training, Hari. If you decide to go into training. That's all I ask."

From outside came the sounds of a water vehicle slowing and stopping. "Let's go," Avila said. "They're waiting for us."

The boat ride took them to farthest reaches of the Pasig River. It was a cloudless night and a starry array of constellations spread across the sky. And then a grey aircraft glided soundlessly toward them.

"At last, the Leviticus is here. Let's go, let's go, let's go." Avila sounded joyful as the airship landed on the water.

The sound of laughter coming from her uncle was so uncharacteristic. She was shocked since she hadn't heard that sound from him in years. It was an alien sound from him, which deeply troubled her. Was life so harsh for her uncle these past years, and was she the major source of his distress?

There were three stop-overs from Manila to Denver. The military seaplane's first stop-over was ten hours to reach Honolulu. Hari was fast asleep beside her. Too wired to rest, she stood up and roamed the corridors. Her uncle was in another part of the plane, and she walked around to look for something to eat.

Jae was sitting in one part of the plane, and his eyes were closed.

Brice knew, from her experiences with Ira, that the Roboticus genus had self-powered mechanisms that replenished when they were asleep.

Jae opened one eye, "You can't sleep too?"

"No," she answered and sat on the empty seat on the other side of the aisle . " How did you escape and were you scared returning for us, Jae?"

"It was scary, but I had to do it, Brice." His eyebrows furrowed and his mouth drooped.

"Were you tortured?" she asked.

"Excuse me, Ms. O'Rourke, it's time for you to rest. You all have to go through a debriefing before you can talk about any of the details that transpired in prison." She followed the voice and saw a lady in her forties, in a dark blue suit. One of the many handlers of the DOD.

"If I don't get a chance to see you again, thank you, Jae," she leaned towards him and kissed his cheek. He beamed at her. "I'm do anything to get you out of that miserable place, Brice. I'd die trying."

I'd do the same for you, my friend. Now go to sleep and rest," she blew him an air kiss as the lady from the DOD scowled at her.

As soon as they arrived at the Denver River Coalition Training Facility, Hari and Jae were separated from her.

Avila was determined not to allow her to work for the Colony, so as far as anyone was concerned, she was a non-combatant and not allowed inside Colony premises. But he couldn't stop her from applying.

She was whisked off to a housing facility used for visitors

and given two days to finish all the necessary paperwork to fulfill requirements in applying to the Colony. The food in the dining hall was exceptional, and she often retreated there to push forward the paperwork and ponder her next move.

Taking a break from answering the millions of questions being asked of her, Brice fiddled with her pen and looked out the window, toward a view of the Colorado Mountains.

She wondered where the Colony HQ was situated. They had told her only that it was relatively nearby. She wondered constantly what Hari and Jae were doing.

A woman entered the dining hall. She was impeccably dressed, but her face was a mask of agony. It was her mother.

She sprinted to her and grabbed her in a hug. So much had happened since they'd last been together. She felt suddenly like a child again, looking for the kind of comfort only a mother could give.

"Why didn't Uncle Avila tell me you were arriving?" she cried.

"I arrived this morning, after speaking to Avila last night. He told me that you had been debriefed about the events that happened in Gesu. And now that you're here and resting, he felt it was time to call me, a lapse of time I feel is nearly unforgivable. How are you, my darling?" she said and stroked her hair. "Your uncle has also postponed the wedding till everything settles down."

"I'm sorry, Mum," she felt a deep sense of regret about the postponement of Avila's wedding, but didn't regret the events that transpired the past month. "How are Ira and Eilish?" she asked in a worried tone.

"Ira's worried to death. She wanted to come here but I persuaded her to continue going to class. Brice, don't blame yourself for what happened. You were all prisoners of war," her mother cradled her like a child..

"For some reason I survived," she said in tears.

"Perhaps it was to see Hari again? " her mother said.

"I love Hari, Mama. You know I have since we were children. He's the only one I'll ever love."

" Brice, I've heard you wanted to apply as an Intelligence agent of the Colony? How about your other dreams?"

"Those dreams are all in the dustbin. I've seen the real world. It's not just about getting rid of the Hans or saving the environment. I want to end this war, Mama. It's all I've ever known since childhood," she stood straighter as she said this.

Her mother pulled away from her. "You are so much like your grandfather. Do you know that?" She gave a deep sigh. "What would Daelan say if he was told that one of his sons would be felled by bullets shot by a Machina? That another son would be heading the Colony, and his only grandchild would join the Intelligence agency as well?"

She cupped Brice's face with her gloved hands. "The world has turned upside down," she said. "Who knew where all this would lead?"

She steeled herself for her mother's protest. She was no longer a child. Her mother couldn't stop her from doing what her heart told her to do. But the words she spoke next surprised her.

"Whatever you're planning, I'll support it. I'll support it one hundred per–" Instead of finishing her sentence, she embraced her mother.

"You don't have to say anything, Brice. I trust you to do the right thing. Even regarding Hari. And I'll always be here for you," her mother said these through her tears.

She was surprised at her mother's answer. It was all she ever wanted to hear from her.

"Don't worry about me or Ira or Eilish. We will be fine. Follow your dreams, Brice."

"I will, Mama. Thank you, thank you. This is an incredible gift."

Chapter 15

Thames River Coalition

United Kingdom

European River Coalitions

August 22, 2071

22 days after the Drone Strike

Quinn stood beside her, as if by standing with her, she could be protected from the hate and fury emanating from the United World Coalition forces.

"Thanks, Agent Quinn," Brice said, and Gabriel and a phalanx of other soldiers stepped toward her, blocking her view of him.

"It's okay," Quinn said, but he edged away from her. "Agent Brice, I'm here if you have questions," he said. "I have orders to assist Agent Brice, Agent Gabriel. Until my orders change, I will stay with her."

"It's your funeral, Agent Quinn. But be forewarned,

you have a highly intelligent, wily suspect in your hands. You better open your eyes wide, soldier," Gabriel warned Quinn. With those final words, Gabriel turned, and without a goodbye, left the Submersible.

The bunk she was assigned in the brig was barely big enough to contain her body.

As she tried to make herself comfortable, she realized something was missing. It was that buzzing sound made by her monitoring Bee. The thing was gone!

The chaos around their escape must have disoriented it somehow.

But it didn't take long for the confined space to trigger her anxiety. She closed her eyes and tried to breathe evenly but it didn't help. The events she'd just lived through this day kept running through her mind.

She brought a hand to her chest and rocked gently. She had perfected this technique. She breathed in for ten seconds, exhaled slowly, then did it again. Please, please, let me be calm, she prayed.

She closed her eyes, and soon she felt her breathing becoming more regular.

She sat up and opened her eyes. Quinn was intently staring at her, but when he realized she was calm now, he smiled.

"Where are they taking me?" she asked.

"That makes two of us who would like to know this. I'm so low in the food chain, I don't know a thing," Quinn said, and shook his head.

"Quinn..." she started.

"Everything's monitored," he whispered. "Just keep your thoughts to yourself, Agent Brice."

Brice slumped back in her bunk. Being inside a

submarine felt like being sucked into the deepest pits of the ocean. The last time she'd felt something like this had been during her family's escape from Antarctica. She had survived that harrowing journey, and she had to cling to that inner core of belief from childhood that she was going to survive, in even the most terrible of conditions. She had to fight, and crawl her way out of this. She had to. It was the only way.

Chapter 16

Denver Colony Training HQ

Colorado River Coalitions

United States of America

American River Coalitions

9 February 2071

5 months, 23 days before the Drone Strike

"Lee Jae Seung, old chap, let's go!" a grinning Henry James said, and pointed to the water. But Jae just shook his head and turned to Hari.

"Salim," Henry said, "try to persuade your all-machine, half-human friend to jump. Or is it the other way around, half-machine, all-human?" The wind made his guffaws reverberate.

The teasing of this embodiment of the AQ was relentless, and she wondered if Jae took it in stride or was so stoic he wasn't showing his true feelings.

"Let's beat the woman and the droid!" Henry teased again, and nervous laughter came from the back of the craft. Though Jae was laughing, he looked as if he was about to throw up.

The Beast craft they were in was a low-flying air pod that hovered in invisible mode. Used for drops near the ground, the Pods had been fashioned after early twenty-first century motorcycles. In a land-scarce world, they'd become the thrill-seeker's way to jump from the sky and race over the surface of the sea.

"You ready?" she asked. Jae was still crouched on the floor of the craft. And now he was clutching his stomach.

"This is crazy," Jae said.

"Just a walk in the park!" Hari shouted as the door opened, and his voice disappeared with a gust of wind.

"Blind in the dark and pushed from this aircraft vehicle is a death drop," Jae said.

"It's the Pod you'll be riding in when we drop, Jae. It's a Colony tradition," she shouted. She was trying to put up a brave front for him, but inside she felt a thrill of fear.

"You thrive on this, Brice. But okay, if you two crazy ones aren't bothered, then it shouldn't bother me." Jae sighed, and began to crawl toward her.

"Twenty-six more hours to go, Jae!" Hari flashed the Victory sign at him. "You're nearly done!"

Diego Rojo was checking their gear before they dropped off. It was a tradition that the Colony Head accompany the recruits to their Beast exams.

"Okay," Diego said. "All good and ready to go. Remember, you fail the test if you don't have your eye drops in place!"

He held a metal device in front of Hari's and Henry's

eyes. When their retinas had been read, Diego placed a drop of liquid in their eyes. The liquid hardened instantly into a transparent portal that offered a means for the Colony to track their movements. As graduates, they would use it as the perfect spy tool.

Hari flashed a V sign again, stepped into the open hatch door, and jumped from their pods.

"Good luck on the mission, Hari!" She threw an air kiss to him as he dropped to the ground.

"Shit!" Jae gasped as he watched Hari's descent from a window. "Are you sure this is the last of the exams?"

"Hey Jae, the Colony was going to give you a passing mark just for having the cleanest mouth of all the recruits!" Henry James was grinning. Diego motioned him toward the door.

"Henry, you're next," Diego said.

Henry hyperventilated.

"I thought you had superpowers, Henry James," she teased.

"Now relax, Henry, for Christ's sake," Diego said. "Just feel the wind, and let your ears do the reconnaissance. If they pop, you're near 10,000 feet."

"Yes, Sir!" Henry saluted Diego, who pulled out a muslin blindfold and tied it over Henry's eyes. "Brice, my love. Kiss me before I jump?"

"All right, Henry." She leaned toward Henry as if to kiss him on the lips, then pushed him out of the plane.

"You're a sly woman, O'Rourke! I'll get my kiss when I land..." Henry's voice trailed off as he disappeared from their sight. "You're a brother from another mother, Henry!" she shouted after him.

She turned to Jae. "Come on. I'll help you," she said.

"How about if we jump together one after the other? Is that allowed, Diego?" Jae's eyes were still closed, and he was now seated, his arms around his knees.

"Sure, you can jump naked for all I care. But the blindfold remains," Diego said.

Jae got to his feet. "You go ahead. I'm just behind you," she said. Diego guided them both toward the hatch door. As they stood in the opening, she embraced Jae. Then she went back to her own Pods . "You can do it. Ready, get steady... go!" She revved the machine, and when Jae dropped from the sky, she revved her own machine and the Pod flew out into the air.

As the altitude fell thousands of feet, she felt her stomach jump to her heart, and her heart jump to her ears. It was terrifying, but the Beast exam was the culmination of the Colony exam.

She'd worked hard to get to this point and she wasn't about to screw it up. Was it only twenty four months ago that she aced the battery of exams for her to enter and join the Colony? She was finally allowed to join Hari's and Jae's batch as agent-trainees. She'd learned to ignore the taunts she heard that the only way she was able to get in that batch was because of nepotism.

The following training period had been the most brutal eighteen months of her life.

Spycraft was a very serious business.

As she and Jae fell, she tried hard not to look at the Pod next to her. Instead, she directed her thoughts back to remembering that with this test, the course would be complete.

The Colony taskmasters had driven them at a relentless pace. Classes included training in hand-to-hand combat skills, weapons, and guerilla survival tactics.For some reason, she actually liked her Krav Maga classes. She felt empowered that she was learning skills that were even better than guns for offsetting an enemy's powers.

The groups of trainees were sometimes tested not on bravery alone, but on how they reacted to extreme levels of stress. Some of these tests included confinement in a dim, unlighted space, and high levels of noise, both triggers for her too-recent imprisonment experience, but she knew her every move was observed, and forced herself to act calmly in all circumstances. The Beast exam was the culmination of these tests, an assessment of physical and emotional prowess in the face of adversity. Those who passed would be the elite of the elite agents.

The earth was zooming closer by the second. Once they landed, they were to find five flags, which were scattered all over the Colony lands. The first to get five flags was the winner.

Beside her, Jae felt stiff as a board. "Relax, and feel the wind," she shouted to him. "Ten seconds before our ears start popping," and Jae made a thumbs-up sign.

She rubbed the rigid hand she was holding.

"Do you feel that, Jae? Open your mouth, we're at about seven thousand feet. We'll be hitting land soon!"

When they reached a hundred feet, their blindfolds detached from their eyes.

"I can see the tops of the trees," he shouted.

"Shut up," she shouted back. "I don't want Hari and Henry to hear us." The trainees would work as teams to recover the flags. For this Beast part of the exams, Hari and Henry were the enemy.

The Pod submerged when it hit the waters of the Green River, a major tributary of the Colorado River, but it bobbed to the surface and floated, and they clung to it, as their eyes adjusted to the darkness.

"Jae, how are you doing?" she said, wiping water from her eyes.

"I'm good, Brice," he answered. "You can count on me." And then he turned away from her, his senses alert. They needed all their skills to win this game.

She signaled that she was swimming toward land she'd spotted to the south. Their first mission was concealment. Jae followed her, her bobbing head faintly visible in the night.

"I know where we are," he whispered.

She ran toward a thick clump of trees. He followed. Once there, she crouched low and pulled out a waterproof fluorescent map she had stashed in her pants leg.

"How does this compare to the map in your head, Jae? Can you recognize any landmarks?" she said.

"Yes," he replied. "That's Sage Mountain, and to the right is Hourglass Mountain."

"We have to find a flag, here," she pointed to her map.

Jae asked, looking at his own map. "Distance?"

"Less than two hundred feet."

"Good. We can crawl there," he said and raised a thumb to her.

The ground was mushy. On their bellies, they explored the perimeter, stopping when they heard the sudden crack of a branch. Was that Hari or Henry, lurking in the dark?

She put a finger on her lips, and pointed to a tree. And then she jumped to her feet and ran toward it. Jae followed.

"Psst...look up." She was hanging from a branch high in the tree. "Come on up," she beckoned to Jae, and in less than a minute he joined her in the branches.

"I could feel my ears pop, Brice. How high is this? Do you see anything?"

"See for yourself," she beckoned.

"Holy shit!" he said. There were faint lights twinkling to the north. There were lights that appeared indicating a safety harbor, but then disappeared to confuse the participants of the Beast exam.

"Maybe five degrees more, right?" And he started climbing down.

"Hey, watch out for the thorny branches," she warned.

"We crawl across the field, then take cover between the trees till we reach the next field. Sounds like a plan?" He raised a hand to high-five her.

But she backed away from him.

"Wait, Jae, it's too obvious. Diego's such a wily creature. This is a trap." She surveyed the field once more and shook her head. "Okay, I have an idea," she said. "What if we start underwater first?"

"In the dark?" Jae's voice broke, a pitch higher than normal. His incredulous expression made her chuckle.

"In the dark, Jae. There's no other way. C'mon."

"You think there are flags planted under water? In the Green River?" he said, his voice still shaking.

"I'm absolutely certain. Diego said explore the whole Colony area, but didn't say anything specifically about the river. Of course, it's included." She turned toward the water where the Pod was waiting.

"Do you have your underwater headgear?" When he nodded, she said, "Pull it on." She donned her own headgear, climbed on top of the Pod and revved the engine. With the click of some buttons, a roof encircled the open spaces of the Pods, encasing both of them inside.

"Let's go!" she said and the Pods lifted high in the air. They hovered above water for a few seconds, then she raised one hand and plunged into the waters of the lake.

The darkness overwhelmed her for the first ten seconds, but slowly her eyes adjusted to the slight light emitted by the Pods. The river was vast but Brice felt sure she could find at least one flag in it.

She readjusted the buttons in her headgear, and lights beamed on, shining far across the lake, defining the hollow outlines of rock formation. She revved the Pod toward it.

When she reached the area, she saw what looked like a long tunnel had been built in the deepest part of the lake. She revved the engine and guided the Pod toward the tunnel. There was a clink of metal on metal.

Examining the area around the tunnel, she saw a series of deep crevices and moved the Pod closer. And there it was, a flash of unexpected color. It was one of the flags!

She turned to Jae and gave a thumbs-up. But how to grab it? The Pod wasn't made for this kind of function. It didn't have grasping attachments, and if she opened the cover, water would subsume her.

But none of these things seemed to be bothering Jae. In a flash, he opened his window, and swam toward the flag. And then he had it in his hand.

He tapped on Brice's window and nodded. He placed the flag inside his jacket, and pointed his finger upwards. Then he got back into his Pod.

When Brice's Pod reached the surface of the water, she opened her window.

"I forgot your lungs could submerge in water, Jae. Good job!" she said.

It took them an hour to find the five flags that had been hidden under the water. Finally back on land, Jae climbed out of his Pod and ran toward her, holding the flags high. They'd found the flags in just five minutes under the allotted time. They embraced, and as he handed her the flags, he disappeared.

"Jae?" Brice said. There was absolutely no trace of him. One second he'd been standing there grinning and the next, he was gone. But then she saw that the sand he'd been standing on had a large divot. She began to claw at it with her hands.

She saw something shining in the hole. After another minute of digging, she uncovered Jae's head. A cage surrounded him.

Jae was grinning.

"Brice, we have no time. Try to find Diego and bring him the flags. One of us should win. Just promise me that I'll be part of your team when Diego's running Ops."

"Oh, Jae, you know I won't abandon you."

"You have less than five minutes, Brice. You can't let Hari and Henry win."

"Okay, but I'm coming right back for you." She ran to her Pod, and gunned it as she headed north.

She had never felt so alive in her life.

She opened the windows of the Pod. She felt the wind on her face, and up above, the sky was spangled with stars.

At last she saw a flicker of light in the distance. She revved the engines harder. It had to be the designated End.

The light was shining near the river's shore. She stopped the Pod, and ran toward it with the flags in hand.

But then she saw a figure sprawled nearby, seemingly lifeless. Her stomach lurched as she recognized it.

"Hari!" she shouted.

She dropped the flags and knelt beside him. He was soaking wet and his body felt cold.

Taking off her jacket and wrapping it over him, she grabbed the small First Aid kit in her pocket, hit it hard on the bottom of her hand, and it expanded into a thin thermal blanket. She pulled it around Hari.

When she touched the tip of his nose, she sighed with relief. Hari was breathing, though faintly. As she cradled his head on her chest, his breath grew more regular.

"I dove underwater in the dark to get the five flags," Hari said wearily.

"Are you crazy? We used the Pods to dive into the river, and Jae took the flags," she explained.

"You don't have to do this, Brice." His voice was a faint whisper.

"We won, you idiot. Where's Henry?"

"I don't know. Last thing I remember, he was running beside me. Good God, where is he?" Hari struggled and tried to sit up.

"Shhh... stop talking. Someone's approaching."

Bright lights flooded them. She covered her eyes.

"Congrats, you two. You made it." Diego was standing in front of them, and he was grinning. Two other people emerged from the shadows, both covered in soil. "Someone else deserves another shot at a Colony operation, since he was able to extricate himself from a trap."

"Jae!" she said. "How did you escape?"

"Sheer robotic ingenuity, Brice. I clawed my way out." He brushed dust from his pants.

"Medics will check you all out and you'll return to HQ for a little R&R. In two hours, you three will receive your assignments."

"Yes, Sir. Ready in two hours, Sir," Jae answered.

"I'll see you back at headquarters. Dismissed." Diego turned away as medics approached them and led them to a tent hidden in camouflage. Inside were individual cubicles with hot showers installed. They all cheered when they saw this.

She was chilled to the bone, and wanted to rush in to be the first to take a shower, but she held back as Hari was examined by a medic.

She approached him and held her hand to his arm.

"You need a hot shower, Hari. Then some hot food, and you're good to go," the medic cleared him.

"Thank God," she said.

Hari stood up and embraced her. "Thanks for helping me out. I was just so exhausted."

"Of course, Hari. Let's have a shower, okay?" She led him inside one cubicle, and stripped off his clothes. She stripped away her own clothes and joined Hari.

Hari opened the shower, and hot steaming water poured on them. They were silent as they enjoyed the hot water.

After a minute, Hari turned off the water. "Brice, we did it. We passed the Beast exam. We passed, we passed," he hollered as he lifted her and kissed her.

The contours of their naked bodies fit seamlessly like one body, and she wrapped her legs around him as he kissed her breasts.

No words were needed as their desire for each other drowned out their surroundings.

Mallard Corporation

London

Thames River Coalition

United Kingdom

European River Coalitions

9 February 2071

5 months, 23 days before the Drone Strike

Mallard

He had spent the whole day watching the participants take part in the Beast exam, while he was in the plush quarters of the London office of the Mallard Corporation.

Even if he had resigned from the Board, he was still accorded privileges as the majority owner of the stocks of his father's company. He had no controlling power over the corporations, but he enjoyed going around the factory floor, meeting the employees, interviewing and befriending the scientists and engineers that were building the new weaponry in the 22nd century.

His attention was drawn back to the images sent to him of the new candidates. He paused when the image of

Lee Jae Seung appeared on screen.

The physical results of the test were not a surprise for him, since he had expected perfection from the AQ. He was surprised at Lee Jae Seung's creative and innovative decision-making, especially when they had to complete the task of the Five Flags. He paused the image of Jae accepting one of the prized medals in the Colony's Agency Recruitment Programs.

Gone was the stiffness of the Machina soldier that had terrified him as a young Supervisor for the Colony HQ.

The number of AQs accepted to the Colony was at an all-time high, and many other government agencies had accepted them as part of the police and military.

The original plan to force them to become sleeper agents against the Hans was funny. Once they were given consciousness, the AQs could not be reined in in any way.

In the United States, the Homo Roboticus program had created a booming industry for anything relating to the Artificially Intelligent Persons. Machines were nearly unbreakable and lived forever.

It wasn't fair that their human bodies would die and end their lives, when technology had created a viable alternative. Memory banking and infusing droids with human or robotic DNA had become a booming growth industry in a crumbling world.

He had won the US Presidential elections in 2064, 2068 and hopefully a third term on 2072, and his speeches had railed against the robotization of the culture. How he wished the world could return to a simpler state, without this mindless, never-ending state of war with the Hans and the proliferation of the Roboticus genus in all the Coalition countries.

But the culture has thrived relentlessly. Was he willing to do more? He was up for re-election in nine months. There was a tiny window to win and set up his plan for total elimination of the robots.

A beeping sound from another screen snagged his attention and brought him back to the present.

He glanced again at the face of Jae in the screen and shivered.

The new recruits needed to be deployed soon for E Day. There was no time to waste.

Denver Colony HQ

Colorado River Coalition

United States of AMerica

American River Coalition

8 February 2071

5 months, 24 days before the Drone Strike

Brice and Hari savored the walk back to the confines of the Colony Headquarters with Hari, with all its creature comforts waiting for both of them.

"Move it, recruits." She was startled when one of the Colony security agents directed them to a conference room. Director Rojo was standing in the middle of it, the group of recruits clustered around him. He was calling names.

"What's happening?" she asked.

"Haven't you heard? There won't be any vacation after the Beast exams. All leaves have been revoked," Henry whispered to her.

"Are you finished updating O'Rourke, Henry? Okay, listen up for those who are late. This is need-to-know. All leaves are revoked. As new agents of the Colony, you are to participate in E Day, Elimination Day for the Hans. It will be a combined multi-country attack on the Hans, a United States attack under the auspices of the World River Coalitions. You will provide intel for the actual E Day, as the army prepares the land for the attack. Consider yourselves lucky you're part of all this."

There were cheers around the room. Then Diego started rattling names off the board.

"Henry James. Report to Smith. You will stay here in the United States. Your assignment is Potomac River." There was a cheer heard around the room as Diego continued the reading of names.

"Troy, Sumosaki, Ng. Please report to the San Francisco Bay." Another cheer.

"Smith, Benetton, Loong, please report to the Florida Keys."

"Frommer, Daelanes, Gabriel. You go to Thames." More cheers, and a whistle.

"O'Rourke, Salim, Lee. You go to the Pasig River Station." Cheers, hooting, and someone loudly stomped the floor. But she was rigid with shock. Why would they ask the three of them to return there?

An abrupt command from Diego startled her.

"Move it, O'Rourke."

"Can I have a word about this assignment?" she stood

as she asked this question to Diego. He was visibly irked, but he waved her to approach.

"Your mission is different, as you may well have guessed," Diego replied. "You three are to assist Asia River Coalitions and provide intelligence about the Machinas in enemy territory. It's an order from Defense Minister O'Rourke."

"What's this, Director Rojo, a suicide mission?" Hari asked.

"You're not there as a field soldier, Agent Salim. You're going to be based in Singapore. Intelligence gathering is done remotely. We are to destroy the Hans in the greatest sea, land, and air invasion. Date and time of invasion is top secret. So unless you're needed in the field, it's need-to-know." Diego paused for everyone to cease conversation.

Diego turned to the three of them. "You all know the terrain and the language, so that's a big help. You will coordinate with the Pasig Defiance team. They've been apprised of the situation. Any more questions?" he asked.

Hari and Brice looked at one another. The Pasig River was the most dangerous place on earth for them. And then she reminded herself of a promise she'd made when she'd entered as an agent trainee: no nepotism, no matter what.

"Intelligence reports tell us the Han officers have dwindled. It's safer than ever for you to return there," Diego reassured them. "Don't worry, we have your backs. You have an hour to collect your things, and it's time to go."

There was no time to say goodbye to their fellow agent trainees. The clock was ticking and they had to leave in an hour.

She was petrified, and yet exhilarated. A real mission that they had trained for in the greatest invasion against the Hans. She hurried to pack her things. It was time to go.

Singapore Military HQ

Kallang River Coalitions

Singapore

Asian River Coalitions

11 February 2071

5 months, 21 days before the Drone Strike

As soon as they landed in Singapore, an army water boat picked them up and with their backpacks, went straight into the headquarters of the Singapore military. The crackle of energy was visible as she entered the door.

Hari and Jae were behind her and they all paused to observe the hubbub of activities around them.

She and Hari used to visit this stadium for world tennis matches, but all that was under water now. The government had built a replica twenty stories under and the stadium was now used for the military.

A soldier approached them and checked their identities using DNA. Once they were verified, they were ushered inside a room filled with images of various field operations happening that day.

"Agents O'Rourke, Salim, and Lee? I'm Rita Shio, Colony HQ liaison here in Singapore. We've been monitoring different highly classified operations for E Day, most of them planned toward disinformation and subterfuge to confuse the enemy."

"When is E Day planned?" she asked, which was the question on top of all their minds.

"Imminent. Providing intelligence to the armies will be our primary role here, and we can only be asked to go to the field when it's needed."

"What's the current status in Pasig?" Hari asked.

"The Machina troops are on high alert," their liaison answered. "Intelligence suggests they know an attack is coming, but they don't know when or how numerous the troops are."

"Walk us through our roles in E Day," Jae said.

"All right, plans could still change, but you will provide back-up to the US forces, and you'll be on air most of the time. Unless there's an extreme emergency and you have to go in, you will not land in Pasig at any time. For now, you can help with the current field operations operating in real time.

" We can have one mission analysis for you since you came from a twelve hour flight. The WRC have been doing a lot of attacks in different parts of Manila to confuse the enemy. Are you ready? You'll have three minutes to run through the area after an attack. You'll be beamed through the Presence."

Ms. Chio led them to a wide area on a raised dais. "There'll be a live operation in two minutes. If the commander asks, your invaluable input will be requested and you will walk virtually through the area for analysis."

"Ready? One minute counting. Okay, ten seconds. Beam the image," Ms. Chio calmly said, and in seconds, the live operations were in front of them.

"Clear!" called the voice of J Company Commander Bruce Warren, from the WRC forces. "US Colony agents, you are cleared to go to the field."

Brice signaled to Hari and Jae Goo Loo, and together, they entered the field of debris. The parts and bolts they were stepping over had once belonged to Machinus robots.

Brice bent over to scrutinize a shredded uniform. It bore the same red hue she had seen the Machinas wearing back in 2056.

"Same uniform," Hari said, as he kneeled near a pile of machine parts.

"Well, some pants don't match the others," she said. Jae and Hari regarded her blankly. "You men don't really notice any difference in clothing?" she said in surprise, then grinned.

Hari shrugged.

"Can't you see the texture of the uniform material? They're so different, it's as if some of the Machina soldiers belonged to different armies, but of course they don't," she bent down. "Commander, can we ask for a sample of their uniforms?"

"Sure, Agent," the Commander answered as he ordered soldiers to snip samples from the uniforms. "We have two minutes to gather evidence and we have to leave. Any more requests?"

"We're good to go, Commander," she said, as Hari and Jae mouthed that they had no need for further analysis.

"Over and out," the Commander said as the whole live

battle scene was gone in seconds.

""It's as if the Hans had a problem procuring material," Jae said.

"Supply chain issues?" Hari said. "The Hans must be undergoing hard times, if they can't even give their soldiers quality clothing. What next? Naked droids?" And he laughed.

"Please, show them some decency, for Christ's sake!" She was surprised at Jae's sharp rebuke to them.

"Are you okay, Jae?" she asked. They had never seen him angry. Brice took hold of his hand.

"Why don't we finish the analysis here and retire to the Rec Room for a few minutes?"

She walked toward the terminals to await the results of the analysis of clothing material.

"I'm going back to get some coffee first," Jae said as he left the room in an abrupt manner.

"What's with him?" Hari wondered. "He seems on edge, not quite himself."

"Maybe all these Han soldiers in various forms of mutilation from attacks from the WRC have distressed him."

Jae returned in a better mood. "Man, I toured the dormitories, and it's a dream. They're like mini-hotels."

"Oooh, the life of an undercover agent," Hari jested. "Hey man, I'm sorry about the droid joke."

"It's so weird, but I could have been that mutilated Machina soldier. I'm a lucky bastard," Jae shook his head.

"It's fate," she said.

"Fate?" Jae asked. She could see that it was the first time that a philosophical concept had flummoxed him.

"I'll read up on it," Jae grinned.

The ride back to their dormitories was quiet as a military vehicle brought them through the labyrinth tunnels of the Singapore military base. Each of the three was lost in their own thoughts as they surveyed the structures the city state had built to house their personnel. It was even possible to host the entire WRC Coalition Countries here in preparation for E Day.

Once inside the cool fortress of the living quarters, they headed to the Recreational Area where a group of fellow US Intelligence agents were gathered. They found seats with a good view of the video walls, which were showing scenes from news coverage of the Presidential debates for the coming elections.

Hari shook his head. "I've known him since I was eleven years old, and I don't understand how his stance against AIPs changed through the years. His anti-robotist stance is unforgiveable."

"Hey, cheers to you, Jae! Presidential reelectionist George Mallard milked the defeat of the Hans as a campaign slogan. You should run and hide now, droid," Jae was so used to the ribbing of his fellow agents that he was immune to their teasing, but his face told another story.

George Mallard appeared, and there were cheers from the crowd inside the Rec Room. He mentioned his successes in defeating the Machina robots, and his dream for the US to return to its pre-machine existence.

"What does that mean?" There were boos from most of the agents in the room. "What a homophobe. I can't stand him." Many of the agents left the room and passed by them.

"Don't worry about Mallard, Jae," one of the agents

shouted to him. "He's a fucking idiot. You're a part of us."

Jae's somber mood did not change the whole night. She and Hari stayed close to him, and encouraged him to talk. But there were no words that came from him the whole night. A troubling sign.

By the end of the night, she was so tired and jetlagged that Hari carried her to their quarters. They'd been sharing a room since entering Colony training two years ago.

Mira and Avila had given their blessing to their living arrangements because they knew it was impossible to talk her out of anything. And Hari was as close to anyone as family.

He helped her pull off her uniform before undressing himself. Then he slipped into bed next to her and embraced her.

"Think about it, very soon, the Hans will be obliterated from the face of the earth. We can have a life of peace together. Think about it, Brice," he smiled at her.

"Where do you want to settle, Hari? Boston? Manila?" she asked.

"Anywhere you want is fine with me. I can practice medicine anywhere." He slid further into bed to sleep.

There came a sudden and jarring sound of an alarm bell ringing.

"Uh-oh. That doesn't sound good," Brice said, and hurriedly they put their clothes back on.

A military escort appeared outside and accompanied them quickly back to the labyrinth tunnels, and back to the stadium headquarters of the Singapore military complex.

They were asked to return to the Intelligence briefing room they had used this morning. On screen were hundreds of planes filling up with soldiers on their way to different destinations for E Day: Potomac River, Florida Key, San Francisco Bay, Seattle, Michigan River, Belfast, and Edinburgh, while cities in Asia included countries like the Philippines, Indonesia, Vietnam, and Cambodia.

The whole stadium erupted in cheers as updates were given in real time.

"Hey, there it is on-screen, Pasig River and its surrounding cities!" Hari and Jae whooped out a loud cheer. Air vehicles swooped in many areas and started attacking the Han defense forces.

Data started to roll in - number of Han soldiers that were caught in the crossfire, and the number of non-combatants hit. The list from the River Coalition force started climbing too, and reality hit in. It was a war with casualties on both sides.

"Team Pasig, be on the look-out for any out-of-the-ordinary conditions on the ground." They were all surprised when Avila appeared on screen.

"Yes, Sir," Hari said.

"I saw this around two minutes ago, Sir," Jae pointed to something on the screen. She and Hari stepped closer to the images.

"Presence, recreate the images on the Raised Panel. That doesn't look like Machinas. It doesn't look human. AQs? Who would do this?" she asked, perplexed by the scene.

"Oh, God," she retched as she felt the bile in her throat.

The Korean features on their faces were visible and most had bodies opened, ripped open by weaponry slashed through the bodies. Their organs jutted out.

"Defense Minister O'Rourke should see this," Hari said as he touched his Communicator. Avila appeared in virtual form in ten seconds.

"You told us to call you when we thought something was important. Permission to visit the site, Sir," Hari pointed to the scene where they were.

"Good God, what happened here?" her uncle's voice rose as he walked around the scene. "Permission granted to visit the site, but it's too dangerous to do it as E Day is happening. Let me see this site too in the Virtual Space, and I'll get back to you. I'll find out who ordered this attack."

Jae stood motionless near the perimeter of the scene, not speaking. What was he thinking about?

Was it an accident? Or was it a deliberate act? A malicious act?

This act could have been done by the Han Army, but they were in retreat. When did they have the time to gather the AQs and kill them with gunfire?

It didn't make sense. Nothing made sense at all.

Denver Colony HQ

Colony River Coalition
United States of America

Avila

Avila regarded the pile of broken commemorative plates and other awards and knick-knacks around the room. It had felt good to smash and hurl that useless stuff across the room.

He ordered that logs be reviewed on this hit on civilian AQs. The intelligence info that Jae shared about a pile of bodies that didn't look like Machinas, and weren't human, incensed him.

Who did this? It could not be the North Korean government since the mounting casualties indicated that they were unprepared for E Day, and were retreating or surrendering.

He pondered the list of anti-robotist suspects. George Mallard as President of the United States with his divisive speeches against the droids made him a suspect.

But would Mallard even dare kill the AQs? If he won the next Presidential election, would he, as the current Defense Minister even raise this subject to the new incoming Cabinet? It would mark him as an outside player. Worse, he could be hauled to jail on trumped-up sedition charges.

Should he raise it to the WRC? Perhaps he could raise it to a few of his trusted colleagues who had become friends through the years.

But he had to ask someone to look into that pile of

bodies and see for themselves if it was indeed AQs who were murdered. He had to ask Amil Salim and all his contacts in the Philippines to verify the identities. But the country was in the midst of war.

If E Day was a success, and the combined WRC troops had successfully infiltrated the Han-occupied countries, there would be a standard intelligence analysis of the operation.

He should ask Brice, Hari, and Jae to look at the site with their own eyes. He trusted them to make their own judgements.

He thought of Mallard, and their years of working together since he was his supervisor agent in the Colony.

At one point he thought Mallard was going to be involved with Mira, but through the years, it was an on-again-off-again affair. Well, Brice never liked him from the beginning.

This spurred him to a quick decision.

He opened the door to his office and peeked to see if his assistant, Miles Robinson, was seated at his usual place. Miles was engrossed with the images of E Day.

"Miles, get me the DM of France and UK. Haul in Singapore too. Right now with the Presence," he commanded.

"Yes, Sir," Miles scrambled to set up the meeting for the Defense Ministers of the three other countries.

He sat back in his chair as the three other Ministers appeared in front of him.

"Avila, my ass, can't this conference wait? I'm busy enjoying E Day," his UK counterpart Ranjit Singh bellowed at him.

"Busy here as well, but I'm always available for you,

dear Avila," Melanie Amady said. Ever since he had become involved with Analie, he noticed that his French counterpart was always helpful to him about defense inquiries.

"Avila, m'chap. Miles said it's urgent. What's the news?" Ng Lee asked. Ng had been a fellow agent in many joint operations over the years. They'd seen a lot in their younger years tracking down the Hans. "It's a glorious day for all of us. Now get on," he urged Avila to start the meeting.

"My Intelligence agents in Pasig saw something of interest. They saw a pile of bodies that look like AQ, not Machinas. Not human," Avila said.

"What? AQs? Send me the images," Melanie's expression was horrified. "I'll be on the lookout for AQ incidents in my own country. That is quite odd news, indeed."

"Same here," the two other ministers' expressions were concerned.

"Guys, I have to seek your advice. I have a suspect and it's the President of the United States, George Mallard," he said. "He's up for re-election and he won't be as nimble if he loses."

"Uhmmm..." Singh sighed. "Why am I not surprised? I've always distrusted Mallard even before. But go on."

"That's a situation I don't want to be in, my friend," Melanie said, her distressed expression giving way to compassion toward him.

"According to the new World River Coalitions by-rules, as Defense Ministers, we can form an investigative panel right now if three or more members agree to it," Ng Lee said. His background as a lawyer was a hat he'd often wear when divisive and thorny issues perplexed them.

"Send a team to secure the crime scene. I'm aware your niece Brice is here with Hari and Jae. Let's see what we can do. If Mallard is the suspect, we have to be extra careful. That guy would have planned everything down to its final detail if he went through and executed his anti-robotist stance."

"He can't get away with murdering AQs. If the people in the US vehemently object to his anti-robotist stand, will he plan Martial Law, jail dissidents, suppress the media? Crazy," Singh said. "But we've seen leaders just like him after the Polar Shift. Something went loco after these events."

"I'd approach Andrew Yamamoto of the WRC and talk about this, is that okay?" Melanie asked.

"Of course, keep Andrew in the loop. I appreciate that, Melanie," he said and smiled. He was starting to relax and his fury was slowly subsiding.

"If we need to let your agents go underground, without Mallard knowing, do it," Singh said.

"Yes, don't worry about it. Singapore can be their base of operations, Avila," Ng Lee said.

"All right, friends. I'll advise you every step of the way. I have to walk on eggshells here," Avila said.

"Good luck, Avila," Singh said and signed off.

"Give my love to Analie, I'll see you soon," Melanie said and signed off.

"Don't worry, Avila. I'll be here and any questions your agents need, they can approach me," Ng Lee said.

"Thanks, old friend. I'll advise you soon." He signed off and said a silent prayer for the friendships that made the difficult tasks ahead possible. Soon, he had to brief his niece, Hari, and Jae about a possible plan.

The AQ bloodbath was a test for him, he was sure of

this. George Mallard knew that the investigating teams would stumble onto the AQs. He and Mallard had worked long and hard on the AQ program. If he said yes to the investigation, it showed he was still loyal to Mallard's policies and this would surely gain him entry to his new administration. Saying no to Mallard's direct orders would do the opposite.

He thought of Mallard. Such a ruggedly handsome man. It seemed his life was the epitome of ease and success, coming from a patrician family in the East. But Mallard had rebelled against his industrialist father. He could have lived a life of privilege and yet was a very complex person, choosing the Intelligence service over politics early in his career.

But politics had ultimately been Mallard's choice.

There was now the possibility of peace, of course, after E Day. Peace after sixteen years of warring against the Hans.

But after peace, what was George Mallard's game plan?

He had to call Brice soon. If any team could find out the truth, they were the ones he trusted the most to do it.

Singapore Military HQ

Kallang River Coalition

Singapore

Asian River Coalitions

12 February 2071

5 months, 19 days before the Drone Strike

The briefing from Avila was clear.

They had to see the evidence and verify that the AQs were decimated in this land. Their deployment was top secret, under the purview of the World River Coalition. It was a tricky situation where other agents did not know their mission.

Ng Lee, the Defense Minister of Singapore personally escorted them to the WRC seaplane and reiterated the mission from Avila.

The walls of the plane shuddered as the wind howled continuously outside.

Lucius Albright, WRC commander in charge of military support, turned away from the window and faced Hari, Brice, and Jae.

"It's risky to enter hostile territory in weather like this," he said, "and yet, it could be an opportunity for the three of you to do your digging around without detection." Albright regarded the Pasig Team members one by one. "Our eyes are on the ground, and if you need help, just holler. We'll have your backs if you need us. We'll be on the ground to engage against the Hans, but your mission is different. Focus on that. You have ten minutes to do it," Albright said.

"We're good to go, Commander Albright. We're grateful for your support," she said.

"Okay, let's do it then. WRC has penetrated deep into Manila, and resistance from the Hans has lessened. From surveillance photos, they're retreating," Albright said. "Ready for the jump?"

Avila and the WRC Commander debated the best way to hide their mission while maintaining their cover, and a jump was the best for their purposes.

"We're ready, Commander," she said as she reached out to Jae who was green at the gills. "There's no Pod, Jae. Just a straight parachute jump. I'll be behind you."

She, Hari, and Jae landed under cover of darkness. As their eyes adjusted, Brice checked the coordinates and verified that the landing was correct.

"It's over here, c'mon. We have less than five minutes to verify the crime scene," she ran and proceeded to the site.

A figure appeared on the scene, shivering and lost.

"Halt!" Hari said, and drew his weapon.

"Dr. Hari? It's me, Chin-Sun," the AQ they had last seen in the Defiance movement two years ago in Quiapo HQ was here in person.

Brice had just arrived, and had barely enough air to exclaim, "Chin-Sun! What are you doing here?"

"Brice? Brice O'Rourke?" Chin-Sun cried, and hugged her. And then she said, "Dr. Hari and Jae, what a joy to see you!" Tears sprang from her eyes.

"All the reformatted AQs were told by a coded US Defense message to assemble here yesterday, and we were told to await further instructions. I was late by an hour and when I arrived, the AQs, my friends, had been killed by a bomb." Chin-Sun was shaking when she said this and broke down. "I had to flee and returned again this morning to verify the sight and mark the graves," she cried.

"We have three minutes to go," Hari cried out. "We need to get samples and disperse. We have a witness, but we have to go. Albright will be here to fetch us."

There was an incoming message and she had to stop speaking to Chin-Sun.

After a minute, the device crackled again. It was her uncle. "Pasig Team, I've told Albright not to get you. It's not secure.

Do not return to Colony HQ. Rendezvous at a safety house I'll call call in later. Repeat. Do not use any Colony communication devices. Go to Plan B. Amil will be there shortly."

"Oh shit, what happened? We're sitting ducks here." She worried that they'd be shot as the sun rose.

"I'm almost done with the samples," Jae said in a nervous tone. "Are they there yet?"

A boat approached and stopped, and a figure emerged.

"Hari! Hari!" came the sound of a familiar male voice.

"Amil? Amil! Thank God!" Hari said.

"Avila called. I'm to bring you to a safe house. No questions asked." Amil turned toward Jae, and a smile appeared on his face.

"Lee Jae Seung! A sight for sore eyes! And who is this with you?" Amil asked.

"It's Chin-Sun, Amil," she said. "They were told to meet here yesterday and then they were bombed. We need to find out more facts."

"C'mon, there's no safe place here. It's a war zone everywhere. We'll be shot in a minute if they see anything moving here," Amil said as he hurried them

Defiance Safe House

Marikina River

Philippines

Avila O' Rourke's image was on the video wall of the safehouse. He'd been waiting impatiently for their arrival.

"Glad you made it safely," he said. "Now rest and hydrate while we weigh our options." He was in Denver Colony HQ and the Rocky Mountains were visible through a window behind him.

Brice sat down and exhaled. The journey had taken thirty minutes, but the images she'd seen to reach this safe house were seared in her brain. There were dead Han soldiers sprawled on the side of the road, mixed with unfortunate locals caught in the crossfire. Seacraft were left all over, blocking the main pathway of the river. Terrified residents were fleeing and there was chaos everywhere.

Elimination Day for the Hans was a success for the Coalition countries.

She was exhausted, but she needed to be alert. Hunger, thirst, these physical sensations were shut down as they were dealing with a crisis that did not have a game plan.

From a simple plan, they were now in Plan B. Was there a Plan C somewhere if this plan didn't work out?

"Whoever is responsible, it was a deliberate act against the AQs," her uncle's voice was furious. "If it is Mallard, how long has he been executing the AQs, may I ask? These are impeachable acts. I need to know what happened. For now, all sentient robots are at risk, you included, Jae. I'm sorry. It's best that in a few minutes you clear out of this place, and disappear. We have to plan where you can go before the WRC can extract you again. The governments of France, UK, and Singapore know what's happening, including the Head of the WRC. Now, I have reached out to Amil Salim and his men at the Philippines Defiance movement. He agreed to house the three of you safely. I will communicate through him and create a plan before you hear from me again."

"When will the extraction be, Minister Avila?" Hari asked the question in their minds.

"Amil, I propose that you stay here first. Perhaps, they can stay in the caves in Palawan until everything's cleared up." He gave a long sigh. "You're in trouble no matter how you look at things. The city's teeming with Hans and their Machina soldiers. And we have no idea what Mallard's up to. When everything's clearer, I'll get back to you. Give me three hours. Over and out." And Avila's voice disappeared.

They all heard a shrill cry. Chin-Sun was still distressed and she started sobbing again.

"I thought it was our last day on earth!" Tears sprang from Chin-sun's eyes.

"Take a breath and tell us what happened, Chin-Sun," she said.

"I've undergone the Reformation process. With the help of the US government, many of the discarded Machinas were turned into an AQ," she said. "We were able to evade the Han soldiers with the help of the Defiance movement. Without them, we'd be dead." Gone was the shy servant who helped Brice carry medicines and bandages at the Gesu Red Cross. Now Chin-Sun looked her in the eye and spoke with confidence.

"We're in no-man's-land here, Brice," Chin-Sun

continued. "The Han Army hunted us like prey, and most of the humans are suspicious of us. But I'm entitled to my memories, even if they're hazy. I have an adopted family now. What about them? Will they be punished too?"

"How many of you are in hiding?" Jae asked.

"Maybe three hundred. We continued the Colony Reformatting program on our own, thanks to the US and other Coalition governments, until the Hans started the scorched-earth regimen. But we're still using our Pasig Resistance headquarters as a base, thanks to Dr. Hernando. I have to leave. I don't want to be recaptured or reprogrammed. Kill me or let me go," Chin-Sun said and stepped away from them.

"Take it easy," Jae said. Then he turned toward her and Hari.

She soothed Chin-Sun and embraced her. "We'll bring you with us, Chin-Sun. Don't worry."

"Team Pasig here, over. This is Commander Albright. There's a US Skyhawk Defense Attack plane hovering on your area. We are three minutes away from you and we cannot afford a firefight with an ally. You better get out of there now."

He wasn't finished speaking when elements of the US Skyhawk forces dropped on the rooftop near them.

Their lights were cut off and darkness surrounded them. She froze as an incredibly bright light hit her eyes. It was blinding, terrifying. Someone was shining a laser-bright light through the boarding-house windows.

A loud voice followed. "It's the Skyhawk contingent. Don't move, any of you."

"Run now," Amil shouted as he grabbed Chin-Sun and dragged her out the door.

Hari and Jae scrambled to the door. She reached out to Hari and pulled him. They were out the door in a second.

They ran to the fields but she felt that the soldiers were catching up with them. It was so dark that she couldn't even see one foot from where she was. She made a decision and slowed her steps and faced them.

Brice knew she had to do something so the others could escape. She brought her hands up. She knew Amil would do everything in his power to save his cousin Hari from rescuing her.

"I'm a field agent for the US Colony HQ. I'm Agent Brice O'Rourke. Stand down!"

All the lights were upon her, as the soldiers from the US Army approached her.

She looked around. There was no other person except her. She had to save Hari, Jae, Amil and Chin-Sun.

Chapter 17

Rendang Island

Malaysia

Asian River Coalitions

13 February 2071

5 months, 18 days before the Drone Strike

Brice was not allowed to go back to Singapore while she was interrogated about the events that had happened two days ago.

The US Colony used Rendang Island as a black ops place, in one of the smaller islands off Malaysia. Blanketed with mangrove trees, there was no sign of activity from the outside, but underneath was a warren of prisons used for interrogating suspects in domestic and international terrorism.

Placed in solitary confinement, she was not allowed to call her family. Her cell was dark and had no sunlight.

But it didn't matter. Hari, Jae, Amil, and Chin-Sun were

able to escape. The endless interrogations by the Colony would not break her, she thought. She was trained for this, and the interrogators knew she would not divulge information.

Defense Minister Avila O'Rourke and Diego Rojo, the Director of the Colony, recused themselves from the investigations, so that questioning could proceed without prejudice to anyone.

After two days, a panel from the US Defense Department was called to Rendang Island to question her about why she was found alone in the middle of the field in Marikina Valley, with both team members gone.

"Agent O'Rourke, I am Special Agent Bing Delaney and this is my supervisor, Agent Mark Victor." Delaney acknowledged her boss and herself and then sat down to face her.

"We would like to determine if disciplinary actions will be given to you. Who ordered you to land in Manila? Everyone knows that Intelligence agents do not land on ground, but conduct support services in the SG homebase. Please answer," the Agent supervisor Victor asked her.

"As Team Leader, we saw some troublesome intelligence about AQs being killed during E Day. These were AQs created by the US Defense Department who remained in the Philippines. We decided to investigate," she said. This was true and she hoped this would disarm them from prying further.

Agent Delaney's voice was full of skepticism. "On your own?"

"Yes," she lied. "Since I knew the operation wasn't sanctioned by the US Colony, I sought help from my contacts in the WRC."

"May I know the name of your contact, Agent Brice," Victor asked.

"Commander Albright," she said with no hesitation in her voice. May God help Commander Albright. She was sure her uncle had found a way to scrub the connection between the two of them.

"We were given five minutes to gather intelligence, but the operation wasn't a success. We were caught in crossfire...."

The interrogator interrupted with a question. "Why did Agents Salim and Lee disappear from the site?"

"E Day happened the day before and chaos reigned in the streets. We were caught in crossfire between the World River Coalitions fighting the Hans, and the local population fleeing from war. I still don't know what happened to them," she cried.

The investigator gauged her answers.

"Why were you there, Agent Brice? To meet someone?"

"We just arrived from the Beast exam from Denver, Agent Delaney, and we didn't know jack-shit about contacts in a foreign land. We have not cultivated any assets. I just wanted to see what was on the field," she said with stubbornness.

"While we conduct investigations, I would recommend that you stay here in Rendang Island until investigations are completed. You can be given tasks by the Colony HQ personnel who are based here. This is a black ops site but we also haul in the Machinas that we can capture. Most of your duties will be tagging them. Is that clear?"

"Yes, Agent, I didn't mean any harm. I'm just as confused as you are," she answered with trepidation.

"That is all, Agent Brice. You will be treated fairly as

an agent of the Colony. Just don't bend the rules here," Agent Victor said with a wary expression on her face.

Was that a warning? She didn't know.

The interrogators left and she was alone in the room. The chair she was sitting on was a welcome relief from the drab surroundings of the prison. She rested her head with her hands on the desk.

She longed for Hari and the comforts of his embrace. She prayed that the others were safe.

"Agent Brice, wake up," the interrogator shook her and she woke up with a start.

"What time is it?" she asked.

"You fell asleep. We need your help in tagging the decommissioned Machinas arriving in the Station. Can you help us?"

"Of course,"she said.

"Come to the Bay Area. But before that, a Bee will be attached to you monitoring you 24/7. We can see and hear everything you do, starting with tagging the Machinas," a security Bee flew to her shoulder, then flew around her.

"Yes of course, I understand," she nodded.

"Let's walk to the Bay Area then," Agent Delaney said.

She was led through the corridors and into a room with security features outside the door. Agent Delaney flattened her palm and the panel turned green. She motioned Brice to do the same, and the tiny mechanism pricked her.

"Ouch," she winced. She was never used to being

pricked for her DNA. The panel turned green.

The doors opened and there were five Machinas lying on a gurney.

"You're familiar with these Machinas as part of your training in the Colony. Tag them, take photos, and then secure them with a special wrapping. By the way, some prisoners from the Han Army will soon be arriving and we will be interrogating them. We might ask for your help interrogating them in the future, but for now, this will be your task. Is that clear?"

"Yes, Agent Delaney," she nodded.

"Your lunch and break time snacks will be brought to you. I need you to tag these droids before lunch. It's needed by the Colony." Agent Delaney's voice softened, and she patted her arm.

"Thank you," she whispered.

"I'll see you at the end of the day, then." Delaney's voice returned to its stern tone and she left the room.

The Bee fluttered around her, a steady companion with its soft buzzing sound.

She walked toward one Machina. Around six feet tall and light, with their plasticine sheathing and metallic internal parts, these AIPs still had the same effect on her as when she saw them the first time in Concordia. She shuddered.

Seeking the opening at the base of the armpit, her fingers sought the inner contours of the Machina. The serial number must be there. As she touched the inner cavity, she touched the inner spine and felt other linguistic symbols. Was it Braille? She had learned to read Braille as a child when she experienced a conversion disorder and she was temporarily blind for a few months after her father's death.

She closed her eyes. The Bee fluttered closely around her.

Was it reading her temperature? Her sense of excitement?

She willed herself to slow her pulse down. Then she felt the letters again.

"This is A. Messages will be sent here inside the cavities. Everyone ok. Await further messages."

Careful not to show any emotion around the Bee, she bent over and silent tears appeared on her cheeks. They were all safe, thank God. She closed her eyes and steadied herself. She was going to work hard and stay here in Rendang Island till the messages said it was time to escape.

Everyone was safe.

Mallard Corporation

Arakawa River Coalition

Shinjuku, Japan

Asian River Coalitions

13 February 2071

5 months, 18 days before the Drone Strike

Hari

The Arakawa was calm today, and their watercraft sliced through the waters of the river, as his eyes focused all the while on the Mallard Corporation's iconic headquarters.

Designed in 1985 by the gifted Spanish architect El Llado, the building looked like an eagle in flight; its striking uneven multi-tiered levels delighted the eye.

He made a signal to Jae who was on the other side of the boat. When they cruised at the nearest point to the building, he released a thousand surveillance dragonflies that formed into a cluster, then descended toward the building in random formation.

The security to the building had been impenetrable, and they considered many other ways to penetrate it. But the dragonflies were the best, they lunged into the unsecured open vents of the building unopposed.

He and Jae had five minutes to take the images before the insects moved out of the building and disintegrated to nothingness. Incinerated was the more accurate word, he thought.

Would they be able to gather intelligence from this method?

He wasn't sure, but they'd die trying.

For two days, he and Jae had been doing the surveillance, crisscrossing the river, trying to find the best way and best time to release the dragonflies. He was bone weary, but he didn't complain since he knew Brice's condition in Malaysia was much, much worse.

Avila called him today and he had just received word that Brice was able to read the messages inserted into the Machina AIP. Thank God for that.

"All right, we got a good auditory and visual record," a voice sounded in his Communicator. "The dragonflies can get out. See you at C."

C was the code word for their meet-up point. They jetted off to the mouth of the Arakawa where a WRC seaplane was waiting to take them on an hour-long ride to Hokkaido.

Under the ruse of a private ski vacation, the Defense Ministers of the US, UK, France, Singapore, and now Japan were in different parts of Hokkaido to have a winter break. In reality, it was a top-level meeting to discuss their findings on what happened to the AQs during E Day.

Snow, snow everywhere, Hari thought. Hokkaido was pretty as a postcard, but deadly for the feet. The streets were icy and he needed sturdy snow boots to successfully put one foot forward.

He held Jae as he nearly slipped again.

"I'm fascinated with the ice, but man, I could skate with my boots," Jae said as he planted his boots into the snow one step at a time so he didn't slip. He stopped again and faced Hari. "Any more news on Brice?" Jae asked in a worried tone. "I'm constantly thinking of her, worried sick."

"She fawns on you," he teased.

"She's the sister I never had. You're my brother," Jae said. He embraced Jae and then they were both silent, there were no words to assuage the pain they felt. Brice's sacrifice made it possible for them to be alive today.

"Brice constantly worries about me – 'Jae, are you cold? Jae, have you eaten? Jae, are you okay?' I hope she's eating well," Jae started.

"I do too. Let's hope this meeting at Hokkaido starts and ends well. It might affect all our lives." He pondered the secret meeting of the Ministers held in Hokkaido. It was a high-risk move to all their reputations if it was divulged prematurely.

Hiketsu was a second-rate ski chalet, a middling, private

inn of less than stellar repute, but it served its purpose as the Ministers settled in one of the log cabin rooms.

He noted the agents posted at all the vulnerable spots, and he kept his eyes down to avoid drawing attention to the high-level security around the chalet.

Inside the room, there were very few people present. He counted, and aside from the ministers, only their aides were present. The meeting started with Avila thanking Hiro Samagatse, Japanese Defense Minister, for the use of the dragonflies to spy on the Mallard Corporation. On the side, Avila acknowledged him from afar, then smiled at Jae. They sat far away from the center table, but near enough to hear the conversation.

Samagatse stood up and welcomed everyone with a deep bow.

"As you can see from the thousands of pictures taken by the dragonflies, there appear to be thousands of drones being manufactured by this company. But it's a very old weapon, circa 2021. It can be weaponized, and can be used as a surveillance tool, but other than those two functions, it's useless." Samagatse completed his report and bowed to his fellow Ministers.

Ranjit Singh, the usually impatient UK minister, stood up and bowed to everyone present. "We thought that we would have peace after E Day. And yet, Mallard is like a dog with a bone. He wants to annihilate all kinds of Homo Roboticus. We've tracked Mallard's communications..." He coughed twice, and then there was some laughter from other Ministers. "You know we all spy on one another, but it appears the newly installed US President is planning the declaration of Martial Law, the suspension of the writ of habeas corpus, and the arrest of media people. The exact date is not determined."

Many gasped when they heard this, but the French Minister turned to Avila and said, "Sadly, we confirmed it. It's true. You really can't keep a secret nowadays, right? It appears President Mallard's stance has hardened, based on a number of messages we have also grabbed from the leaders of the anti-robotist movement. George has been a very naughty boy, I dare say," she chuckled, trying to break the seriousness in the room.

"Thank you for your surveillance, dear Ministers. In my country, my hands will be tied a hundred-fold in legalese before I can indict a sitting President," Avila said, and the room exploded in laughter.

"Now, our next problem is how do we keep our Sollus and AQs situated in our own countries to be out of harm's way. If the murders of the AQs in Marikina are any indication, Mallard will kill them all," Ng Lee said in sober tones. "We need to keep them safe."

"I have an idea. We can host them at our Space Stations in LEO or Low Earth Orbit till we find a permanent settlement for them," the French Minister clapped her hands, waiting for some of her peers to volunteer places for the Homo Roboticus refugees. "Ever since the Polar Shift, the French industrialists have been building these stations at a break-neck speed. There is no government regulation yet about the building of space stations. Space is the next frontier after Earth."

"We will study the matter in confidence," Singh sighed. "I'm not too sure our cash-strapped government can be so generous, but I'll give it a try. But how do we bring them to space?"

"Japan has also started colonies on the Moon since five years ago. The technology is now present to transport thousands of people who do not want to live on Earth anymore," the Japanese Minister said without apologies. "I have a son who is a Sollus. I will personally bring him to LEO to get away from Mallard," Hiragatse said.

"We have to set a date to gather the Roboticus so we can bring them to the moon station. How about August 23, 2071? That's six months from today." Ng Lee, the Singapore Minister, was straight to the point as always.

There were murmurs and nods of assent from some of the Ministers, but in general, nobody disagreed with the date set.

"Which reminds me, you have to retrieve your niece from Rendang Island, Avila. She might be used as a pawn as leverage against you," Melanie warned.

"Plans are on the way to get her. I might ask your help in that. And weaponry that couldn't be detected by the US government," Avila said.

The Japanese Minister bowed. "How about wings to fly your niece away from Rendang? It's new technology we want to try."

"We might try that, Minister Samagatse." He bowed to the elderly Minister. He was touched and surprised by the generosity of the officials gathered here.

"And so, my dear friends, we have the bits and pieces of Mallard's plan, but we don't know when or where he will strike. Will he declare Martial Law, then hit us with a Drone Strike? Or the other way around? We have to be very careful with our own security since he can sniff us all out, since we're very nosy, truculent SOBs," Singh said. "And remember that Mallard's corporation extends to London, Berlin, and Singapore too."

"We've heard that he's been harvesting data from the Memory Banks in Singapore and London. Either he has been paying for the data so it's off the market for the AIPs or for something more sinister," Ng Lee said to everyone. "We'd better investigate all his other branches."

Everyone nodded in a somber manner.

"We will investigate further the images taken today on Mallard Corporation and update you," said Hiro Samagatse. His words were drowned out when most of the Ministers stood up and huddled in private conversation where no one could hear their exact words.

He glanced at Jae and raised a thumbs-up sign. Such were the ways in which the world's affairs were conducted. Lives were at stake, and yet plans were concretized in casual conversations over port and whiskey, in log cabins and snowy resorts.

He was ready to rescue Brice, even if it killed him.

Yoichi River Coalition

Hokkaido, Japan
Asian River Coalition
13 February 2071
5 months, 18 days before the Drone Strike

Lee Jae Seung

The meeting at Hiketsu was a success, and he and Hari

were next set to visit Mallard's London headquarters for further surveillance.

It was nice for Avila to give them a day off to relax around Hokkaido before they jetted off to another mission.

He opted to strike alone and visit the town of Yoichi to visit the Nikka whiskey distillery. He chose to go to this site because he had a lot of memories of going to Otaru, a tiny little town off Yoichi.

He remembered bits and pieces of a long train ride hugging the Sea of Japan, and he wanted to verify if the memories in his brain were still correct.

Snow covered the left side of the elevated tracks, and when he boarded the train and sat near the window, he looked out to the sea, the waves were unbelievably high just like the wooden block prints he had seen at the Met in New York of Hokusai's *Great Wave of Kanagawa*.

It was majestic and eerie at the same time and he loved it. He got off at Otaru, and walked around the quaint town.

He looked for a coffee shop that he had visited before in his memory bank, and continued his wave-gazing.

Even if it was memories bought from another person on the black market, he marveled at visual, auditory, and textural memories embedded in his brain, so he knew how the coffee in this particular town tasted since he had tasted it in a previous time.

People often asked if he was bitter about hazy 'AQ' memories. But he was grateful for them. His memories did not include the people embedded in the donor's life, but it didn't matter. His memories now of Brice and Hari and his adoptive parents, Simone and Philip Moore, made up for all of the gaps of memories in his brain.

Thinking about Brice made him stop drinking coffee in mid-sip. He didn't know what he'd do if she was gone. All the more reason to find a way to get her back.

His training as a soldier lessened the likelihood of mistakes in the field, but handling emotions was still a learning process for him. Pain was still a new, raw emotion for him.

How does one deal with unbearable loss if it happens? Even Hari would have no answer for him.

His interest in visiting the Nikka whiskey distillery was gone completely. He wanted to get back to Sapporo and prepare for his trip to UK so they could find evidence of Mallard's evil intent and deeds.

He stood up and said goodbye to the town of Otaru. He faced the sea and bowed. Till we meet again, dearest ocean. I enjoyed this memory. Thank you very much.

Chapter 18

USS Submersible 250

Somewhere in the Atlantic Ocean

22 August 2041

22 days after the Drone Strike

Brice's eyes were closed, but she heard the hurried, clicking sounds made by soldiers hurriedly marching past her cell. She opened one eye and saw soldiers from the United States Navy gathered in front of her cell. They had not been there when she'd arrived in the Submersible, but it was apparent that a phalanx of other guards had been called in to guard her. She felt alone.

The Submersible stopped, and within minutes, the soldiers appeared once more in the room.

"Agents, we will now transfer you to the USS Wahoo. Please follow us to the Docking Station," said a soldier.

Outside the door, soldiers stood at attention as she and Quinn were led to the USS Wahoo, a naval ship docked in the Atlantic Ocean. Once inside, a squadron of what looked like paper airplanes appeared above them – tiny miniature drones checking their identity. After a while, the objects combined and formed into a wave, their twinkling brightening the darkened hallway. One tiny miniature drone flew above her.

"Are you my new security drone?" she inquired as she reached out to try and touch the tiny drone.

"Affirmative," a female voice said. This was an improvement on the Bee, which had been mute.

"Where to, may I ask?" she said. The walls of the sub were made of clear glass, showcasing the Atlantic Ocean in all its dark, murky glory. "Can we brighten the lights?"

"We're conserving energy, Agent Brice," the voice said. "Sorry if it isn't as bright as you want, but we'll do what we can." She turned to look at Quinn, and he made a thumbs-up sign. As they entered the labyrinth corridors, the lights brightened.

The door opened with a loud swoosh that made her feel as if she'd been sucked into a funnel. She and Quinn were catapulted into a room full of people.

Apparently, the location of the seat of the government had shifted again, the third time since Washington, D.C. slid into the Atlantic. Denver had been deemed too tenuous a location as the center of power. Now, it seems, the heart of power was this ship.

Diego and Henry were staring at a screen, pointing at the fluorescent green corner of the map displayed on it. When she and Quinn appeared, Diego greeted them and led them to an anteroom.

President George Mallard was seated in the center of the room, looking at all the data on the wall.

"Have a seat, you two," President Mallard said. "The AQ forces have made their play. These attacks are clearly Jae's and Hari's handiwork. As you have seen, their drones are flying non-stop over all lands still above sea level. If they see anything above ground, they send drones to hit it, be it a person, a vehicle, or whatever." He shook his head in disgust.

"But the American, Asian, and Europe River Coalitions are safe and intact, as of this moment. I don't know how long we can hold onto them, however. We have to be prepared for another attack," Mallard said.

President Mallard gave a dismissive wave of his hand.

"The general population below ground remains resolute. The edifices above ground can always be rebuilt. The Thamers are stoic, as if this is World War Two all over again, just under the sea. As of this point, it seems the forces of Hari Salim and Lee Jae Seung control the air and land from all the River Coalitions around the world - Shinano, Thames, Danube, Nile... They've used the drones as their eyes and ears."

And then Mallard turned to her. "Do you know anything of their plans, Brice? You know it'd be easier on you if you reveal where Hari and Jae are hiding. Every human in every city in the world is now living below ground because of their attack, afraid of another drone strike at any moment. What do they want?"

Brice bit her tongue so her face would not register any emotion.

It was five days ago when she retrieved one of the the messages from one of the last Machina droids.

"23082071 evacuation of S/A, Sl. Diego will bring you to Bubble."

She didn't understand the last part of the message but she knew the evacuation of the HR was tomorrow.

"If it's world domination, for now, they have it," Mallard said. "But we can fight back, you know. I won't be dictated to by droids," Mallard spewed his words like a madman. "Because of the drone attack, the government has just declared Martial Law. The writ of habeas corpus is suspended. You'll be brought to the USS Wahoo, a military ship. The Colony will interrogate you, and you'd better give us what we need."

"You mean, you declared Martial Law. Not the government," she said evenly. "And if I don't give you what you want, then what?" she asked.

It was as if the oxygen in the room were taken away. Many of the Cabinet members present in the meeting were aghast at her pronouncements. She glanced at Diego and he was looking down but a smile lingered on his face.

She couldn't help herself. "The Second Drone Strike was your plan, President Mallard. Hari and Jae do not have drones that control land and sea. You plan to shutter the Homo Roboticus program and..."

"Enough!" Mallard shouted. "Bring her back to the brig."

She refused to even look at Mallard's eyes. He had been a friend to her family through many struggles and many years. Did Mallard think that he could use these bonds to persuade her to open up?

She turned around. Her uncle was not in the room.

"We have no choice but to have you jailed. Dismissed," Mallard said.

At that moment, words flashed across the Videoton hanging across from Mallard on the wall. *Martial Law declared,* it read. Next came an image of President Mallard signing papers in what appeared to be an underground bunker.

A bout of polite clapping followed around the table,

though some people in the room just crossed their arms.

The next news item on the screen was about suspending both the Senate and Congress and shifting power to the Executive and Judicial Branches of government. The "writ of habeas corpus" was declared suspended, a male reporter said, meaning the President could arrest anyone without a warrant. All Homo Roboticus AIPs were to be arrested, no questions asked.

A pair of US naval soldiers appeared next to Quinn.

"You are under arrest, Quinn Mathews," one of the officers said, and the whole room erupted in chaos. A number of people around the table stood up and shielded Quinn.

There was a loud bang and she realized that it was a weapon fired by Diego. She and Quinn were encased in the Azucar bubble.

"Brice, Quinn, over here. Now go, go to the side. You'll see the Bubble. Hurry and escape," Diego shouted.

Quinn caught her hand as they started running in the direction Diego indicated.

There were two US naval soldiers who were waiting for them at the side of the ship.

What seemed to be a hundred Bubbles were tied onto the side of the boat and they rocked in the waves, making noise as they banged together.

"Hurry, hurry before they catch you. You need to use the Bubble with a blue door," one of the soldiers led them near the Bubble. "We're with Secretary Avila and Director Rojo. Now go," they urged.

"How old is this ship?" she asked as Quinn helped her toward one of the Bubbles. "I used those transport machines more than a decade ago. Surely they're very outdated by now."

"Now close your eyes," Quinn said. "We'll need to make a jump." Together, they leapt off the ship toward the ocean.

The security drones couldn't keep up with them when they were blocked by the Azucar. They landed with a splash and swam toward the targeted Bubble. Quinn yanked the door open with ease.

Brice heard a clink-clank. Bullets were flying past them and hitting the Bubble's surface. Their grace period was over. Quinn grabbed Brice and hurled her through the door.

From memory, she groped for a button near the doorway. She found it and the lights turned on. They were very bright.

"Shit!" She pressed another button and dimmed them. She fingered the panel.

"I hope I remember everything my Grandpa Daelan taught me. Here goes!" And she pushed the throttle all the way down. They heard the snap of the cord that had attached the Bubble to the main ship. In another second, the craft was flying through the sea. She pushed another button and the craft went even faster.

From a distance, they heard the sound of weapons being fired. Mallard's soldiers weren't giving up easily.

It was time to go back to Suvarnadvipa and meet up with Hari, Jae, and her sister Ira.

"God help us all," Brice said. On the panel, she input the Bubble's directional path – Suvarnadvipa, Indonesia.

"Agent Brice, look!" Quinn was pointing to the view in front of the ship. The skies had darkened and the ocean was swirling in giant waves. They were heading right into a huge storm.

"We'll survive this, Agent Quinn. Keep the faith.

Fasten your seatbelt, it's going to be a bumpy ride!" Brice shouted as the water shuddered and bobbed, and then it sank and twirled to the deepest abyss of the ocean.

Chapter 19

Suvarnadvipa Island

Indonesia
Asian River Coalitions
23 August 2071
23 days after the Drone Strike

The wind became stronger as the Bubble flew on and soon Brice realized she was flying right into the chaotic winds of a raging typhoon.

Her father had taught her the Lord's Prayer. "Our Father, who art in heaven..." and she started saying the prayer. The sound of thunder flattened her against the bubble wall.

Brice continued to check the correct location of Suvarnadvipa and pressed "Proceed" for the Bubble's final destination.

Brice knew that her uncle had prepared the Bubble, and would have swept it free of any kind of surveillance.

She calculated that she and Quinn had a short lead time before their movements were tracked.

Round and round the craft went, in dizzying circles, and then the centrifugal force was too much and she lost consciousness.

She awoke, but didn't sit up. Her eyes rested on the transparent ceiling of the Bubble. She could see that dark grey clouds still surrounded them. The Bubble was bobbing on the surface of the ocean now. The bad weather had passed, or perhaps the Bubble had traveled through it. She sat up, and saw Quinn staring at her.

"Brice, I almost fainted from the turbulence of the storm and the dizzying speed we were traveling. Miraculously, I think we're in Suvarnadvipa. It was the last navigational area you programmed," Quinn grinned, and helped her stand.

"Since when were you a part of Uncle Avila's clandestine team?" she asked.

"Diego recruited me at the hospital ship USS Golden Wattle. He explained President Mallard's plans to annihilate the Sollus and the AQs. I can't still believe it till now."

"Why didn't you give me a tiny bit of hint?" she asked.

"It's better no one suspects," Quinn said. "In the end, I'm the one who's in danger and Diego, Avila and you saved me."

"How long was I out?" She touched her head, and felt for bruises. She felt a bit shaken but otherwise was all right.

"Around five hours," Quinn said.

The Bubble gave a shudder, like a monster about to split in two. Grandfather Daelan had warned her that when damaged, the Bubble would self-destruct.

"Uh oh... this doesn't feel good..." she said, and the Bubble stopped moving forward. She opened a panel nestled in a side wall and extracted two packages. With one push of a button, she inflated them into personal floatation devices. Then she pulled out two big boxes and rummaged inside until she found what she was looking for: a pair of burn suits, which came standard with each Bubble, like the flotation devices.

"Please suit up, Quinn. I'll give you three minutes. Then we need to disintegrate the Bubble." They wouldn't leave their pursuers any evidence of their presence.

The material of the suit was thinner than the suits she'd used previously in Suvarnadvipa. She hoped it was made that way for swimming.

"Are you ready?" she asked Quinn, then returned to the control panel and swiftly manipulated several buttons. It worked: the Bubble shuddered and as it collapsed, she pushed Quinn out the door and followed him.

The floatation devices had small motors and she and Quinn switched them on, as they paddled through the choppy waters.

She struggled as she encountered the bigger waves.

"I can help you, you know," Quinn teased, as he floated away.

"I hope you know I hate you right now," she said back, but he was too far away to hear her.

When they finally reached the calmer waters near the shore, she saw the mouths of caves looming out of the water. She felt a simultaneous feeling of relief and anxiety.

Was it the right cave? Avila had given Quinn coordinates and some instructions and she trusted him not to waylay her.

She and Quinn bobbed onto a part of the beach hidden by boulders. They crawled out of the water, hugging the sand, waiting for whoever was there to leave. And finally, they did.

Quinn held two fingers and tapped them on the back of his hand. He was telling her to follow him. And he stood up and ran toward the opening of one of the caves.

He stopped in front of it, and then he groped at the rock. He seemed to be looking for something. Apparently, Avila had given him very detailed instructions. With relief, he finally found what he was looking for — a rope — and motioned for her to hold it and enter the cave. Gripping it tightly, Quinn led the way, quickening his pace once he was inside. When she was a little girl, her feet had become bloody as she tried to master the sharp rock of the cave path in Concordia. She felt suddenly like she was walking into a memory.

She counted as she walked. Three hundred. This was the magic number of steps, Hari had told her, to get to the hidden room in the Palawan cave. How many steps would she take inside this Suvarnadvipa cave?

She was nearing step two hundred ninety-nine when she saw a tiny bit of illumination. It was a just a speck...

Brice heard the sounds of crying babies first, then saw the people. There were, she estimated, two thousand people there, more or less, mothers cradling infants to their breasts, children playing tag, fathers talking and smoking. But many had started rolling out mattresses to sleep, family members bunched together, sharing sleeping space however possible. Clearly, they sought harbor from the harsh wind outside the caves.

But this chamber wasn't Quinn's targeted destination.

She was beginning to wonder if they were lost when she heard her name called and saw a flicker of light. The kerosene lamp that had appeared from the darkness illuminated wavy hair and a thin, athletic frame. She suddenly felt like her heart was about to explode.

"Hari?" she whispered.

The figure stopped walking. No. Not Hari.

"Amil!" She ran and embraced him.

Amil looked contrite. " Hari and Jae wanted to spirit you out of London, but Mallard bombed the Memory Banks with drones in London so he could frame Hari and Jae. Gabriel also had you in a chokehold underneath Victoria Station. It's great Quinn joined the cause," Amil said. He reached out to Quinn and shook his hand.

"It's an honor, Sir," Quinn grinned. "I hope that mission wasn't a complete loss."

"Come on, they're waiting for you." Amil motioned for them to hurry, and then turned and trotted into the darkness.

"Follow me, please," he called to them. The kerosene lamp he held illuminated passage after passage. The cave was an underground warren.

Amil's voice came again. "Walk fifty steps toward me, and follow my voice," he said, and Brice did as she was told. "Now, stop."

She couldn't see anything at first in the darkness. But then she saw a faint glow. Her eyes picked out two figures huddled near each other. One was smoking. The other was standing facing them, his arms akimbo. Then there was a third figure, a flash of dark brown hair and green eyes.

When Amil gave a long, low whistle they looked up and smiled. And then Brice recognized them.

She started running, nearly blinded by floods of tears. Hari was running toward her as well. As they met, they embraced each other so tightly that for a moment, she couldn't determine where his limbs started and hers ended.

"My God! I was so afraid I wouldn't see you again," Hari said, kissing her. Then he faced Quinn. "Thanks for helping her out from the Wahoo, Quinn..."

She wasn't able to finish her words when a body hurled into her. "Brice, Brice," Ira cried.

"Shhhh, there, there. You're safe." She kissed her sister.

"I don't want to go to the International Space Station, Brice. Please, I want to stay with you here," Ira pleaded.

"Hush, Ira," she soothed her sister. "You know Uncle Avila and I wouldn't ask this of you if there weren't a threat to your well-being, right? But you need to leave till the threat is gone."

"But I haven't said goodbye to Mum and Eilish properly," Ira sobbed and she was inconsolable.

"It's not forever," she said.

"Promise?" her sister asked.

"I do. Hey, I've long wanted you to meet Quinn." She turned away from Ira to return to the group of people waiting for them to finish their conversation.

Quinn shook Ira's hands, and it was clear he was mesmerized by Ira's beauty. "I'm... in love," he said in a hypnotized voice. Hari chuckled, while Ira giggled.

"Brice?" she heard Jae's voice and turned.

"Jae, beloved brother, I was so worried about you and Hari all this time," she wept when they hugged each other. Her heart seemed to soften every time she saw Jae. The need to protect him since she saw his Reformation would remain always. "So, are you prepared for your great adventure?"

"No, not yet. But come," he beckoned to everyone, "I'll show you something."

As they started to follow him, she noticed a number of soldiers from different parts of the world securing the premises.

They reached the end of the walkway, and entered another door. When Jae opened it, Brice saw a runway, and at its end, a silver silo around six stories high. A space transport vehicle was sitting at its top. A line of people was going inside it. But it was the figure standing alone near the base of the silo that caught her attention.

"It's an international concern to spirit out the Homo Roboticus genus. It's all possible because of this man. Look who's here to greet you?" Hari grinned as he said this.

"Brice —" but she ran toward her uncle and embraced him.

"I'm glad you escaped unscathed, Brice. I would never forgive myself if something happened to you," her uncle's voice caught in his throat.

"Thanks for choosing Quinn. He helped tremendously, Uncle Avila," she said.

Avila walked back from the base of the silo toward the main door and shook Quinn's hand, then hugged him.

Quinn appeared flustered but took the embrace with humor.

"You have my eternal gratitude, Quinn." Avila thumped his back one more time and then faced the group.

"Here it is, Everest. It's lent to us by the French government. It's a space vehicle that can bring thousands of our people to LEO. From there, they can be brought to the moon colonies."

People of different nationalities were entering the silo.

"Many are AQs," Jae said, "but with the new rulings, the Sollus have started packing their bags to escape Mallard's dictums."

"How long have you been planning to do this? This is fantastic!" She was so excited about this and her uncle smiled at her.

"Oh, it was a lot of help from a coalition of our allies, Brice," Avila said. "The French government made it possible for the Everest to be here. And we have to thank the Japanese and Singapore governments for opening their moon stations."

"Will they be safe at the ISS?" she asked.

Avila nodded. "The International Space Stations have assured us they will. They've even expanded and started building an extra Buckmister Fuller dome on Mars, their eventual destination, to accommodate the new arrivals. They've called the new dome Daelan, after your grandfather."

"This is an incredible plan," she said. "Daelan. Grandfather will never be forgotten."

"We will build a community of like-minded Sollus and Aequilavums," Jae said. "Mallard might have created the first Drone War to frame the Roboticus, but we knew he was planning a second one to eliminate all sentient robots, and so Avila, with the help of the foreign ministers, had to work fast to help us escape."

"We had different missions for six months to track Mallard's plans. That is a story to be told our future kids," Hari laughed.

"I'd love eventually to live in Daelan – but Jae's words were interrupted by the sound of a loud blast.

A huge part of the cave wall had fallen down, and

George Mallard and a group of men dressed in grey were coming toward them through the opening. The army in grey started running toward the Coalition soldiers and with their guns zapped them in electricity.

" Suvarnadvipa!" Mallard said. "What a brilliant place to hide this little experiment, Avila. I knew you were up to something. It's illegal to harbor the Homo Roboticus." He turned to the squadron of soldiers behind him. "Arrest this man," he ordered.

The grey army started to advance, but a violent gush of water from the side of the cave flowed toward the runway. And yet, this didn't faze them. The waters subsumed them but they continued to move toward them. Was it a trick? Was it a hologram?

"They're holograms with electrical energy. Run away from them," Hari shouted. The soldiers were not there in physical form, but the electrical surge emanating from them was just as deadly.

"Fight with fire," Jae said as he ran to the weapons arsenal prepared to secure the Roboticus escape. He extracted a Flammatelun and opened it. A big gush of fire spewed from the weapon and some members of the grey army fell to the wayside.

She found herself near her uncle. Mallard was closing in on them when he jabbed the two of them with an electronic prong.

Avila fell on his knees while she was rendered stunned by the electrical charges.

Avila faced Mallard. "You unleashed the first Drone War, you evil bastard. You framed the Roboticus so you could get rid of sentient robots. You're the one who should be arrested."

But Mallard didn't respond. "Before anyone moves, and before I blast you, O'Rourke, tell everyone to stop boarding that spaceship," he commanded. He jabbed him again with the electronic prong.

Avila screamed from the pain. "You are a coward. You could not forget your fear of the Machinas from the first time you laid eyes on them. So you'd rather eliminate them."

"The Earth belongs to humans, not droids," Mallard shouted back. "Answer me!" Mallard jabbed Avila and and he screamed in pain.

"You never forgave Jae for humiliating you in Concordia, you heartless piece of shit," Avila spat at him and Mallard jabbed him with the prong until he lost consciousness.

Jae and Hari came running from behind and directed the Flammatelun on Mallard. The hologram spewed off its own electricity, fighting fire with fire, its colors brightening its intensity, then turning to white before the image disappeared before their eyes.

"Jae, hand me your weapon. Gather Ira and Quinn. Lead them to the Everest," Hari said.

"Are you sure, Hari?" Jae asked as he looked with concern at Brice who was still seated, and nodded faintly. "I'm conscious, I'm okay." He handed the Flammatelun to him.

"Please leave now. We we can talk to each other later when you're at LEO. Go," she urged. "There's no time to waste. Avila will be our problem. Go to the Everest," she begged Jae.

Jae embraced Brice. "See you, my friend," Jae Goo Loo teared up. "I'll keep in touch."

"You better keep in touch. Now run. Please take care of Ira and Quinn. Go. Go!" Brice cheered him on.

She heard Jae commanding all the AIPs including Quinn

and Ira to board the Everest. Ira was again in hysterics but Quinn embraced her hard and brought her inside the space shuttle.

"Brice, Brice, are you okay? Avila, what happened to him?" Hari placed his fingertips on Avila's pulse. "Oh my God, I'm going to do CPR on him." He placed both hands in the middle of Avila's chest and started pumping his chest.

"I couldn't even help you, Hari," she cried. "I couldn't even turn and see Uncle Avila," she sobbed. She held the Flammatelun higher toward Mallard. "Please, please don't let his hologram move."

Then she heard her uncle cough. It was the sweetest sound to hear. He was alive.

The explosive sound of a rocket launching pierced their ears and the heat from the blast pushed them three feet away from where they originally stood.

Avila, who had just stood up to regain his balance, was thrown again and lost his footing. He lessened the impact by hurling himself into a fetal position. Brice, who was seated, felt the jet propulsion's blast.

"Good God, that was a great launch! Attaboy, Jae," Hari cheered at the top of his voice. "Woooooohoooo!!!!"

The heat launch of the rocket ship seared the hologram images away and when she stood up, Mallard and the grey army were gone.

"Agent Hari, we need you to tend the injured," one of the Coalition soldiers ran to him, but Hari turned to her with concern.

"I'm good, Hari. Please help those who are far more injured than me," she said. Hari paused for a beat and then ran to assist those who were splayed on the ground a few feet from her.

The ground shook again. She heard the pounding of feet hitting the ground and running toward them. Was this Mallard's men coming to arrest them? There was no way to defeat this amount of military force. They'd have to surrender.

"Avila, m'boy, you look like a wretched dog, my friend. Sorry my cavalry was late. The SG army raised an alert as soon as Mallard and company entered this area." Ng Lee walked toward Avila as a group of other Coalition officers surrounded the runway. He walked toward the opening and stared upwards toward the sky. He whistled. "What a beauty!"

"Ng Lee, Defense Minister of Singapore, meet my niece Brice. She doesn't look too spiffy herself," Avila chuckled.

"I can turn my neck a little bit now, thank you," she whispered. "The electrical charges from the holograms were deadly. What weapons were they using?" she wondered aloud.

"Weapons-grade military hardware we haven't seen anywhere, for sure." Ng Lee crouched beside her and yelled for a medic to check her out.

"Did you catch Mallard?" Avila asked.

"Yes, Samagatse caught him just as he was about to leave the Mallard Building in Shinjuku," Ng Lee said. "His ass will be in jail for a long time. Did our Roboticus friends escape in time?"

"Yes, we held Mallard's men till they were able to board," Avila said as Ng Lee high-fived him.

"Ach, a success for the French. I won't hear the end of it from Melanie about her government helping our friends reach LEO," Ng Lee said. "But I guess it's a thank you to us for saving Paris during its hour of deep need."

"Yup, she can boast of the Everest till our ears drop, but boy, they're safe!" Avila said in gratitude. He stood up and together, he and Ng Lee walked around the runway and surveyed the damage brought by Mallard.

She felt Hari come near. He dismissed the medic attending to her, and sat beside her on the ground. "You still have to have a full check-up to make sure there are no long-lasting effects of the electrical charges," Hari said.

"I'd like to stand up, please." She tried to stand up and at first she was a bit unsteady, but found her footing and started walking toward the opening where Everest had been parked an hour ago. Hari held her elbow as they both stood and looked up to the sky.

"They're gone," Brice said with a sad tone.

"They're safe from madmen like Mallard," Hari said as he wrapped his arms around Brice.

"No more Hans, and no more devious plans of madmen plotting against the Roboticus. I can't believe we're at peace after thirteen years. We don't know what it means to be at peace," she said in wonder.

"After being away from you for six months, all I know is, I can't wait to be with you body and soul, O'Rourke," Hari said, and caught her hand and kissed it. "Marry me?"

She brought Hari's hand to her lips and kissed it.

"Hari, I knew I'd end up married to you the first time I saw you all those years ago," she said. He kissed her.

When they came up for air, soldiers from different Coalition forces started clapping and cheering. From afar, she saw her uncle clapping for Hari and her.

It was over. Really over. There was peace at last after thirteen years.

Chapter 20

Notre Dame Cathedral

Paris,

France

23 October 2071

83 days after the Drone Strike

The altar of Notre Dame was bedecked with a thousand red and pink roses, and tiny lights were flickering at the background, casting a magical scene in front of them. The floods had crept two feet inside the Cathedral, but the pews and the altar were raised so that church activities could resume for all the parishioners.

Avila and Analie were the most resplendent bride and groom she'd seen in a long time. The surge of weddings amongst friends, colleagues, and family members soared after E Day and the arrest of George Mallard. It was like the whole world started breathing again, and it seemed celebrations were happening every day, all day, all over the world.

Many of the Defense Ministers who helped topple Mallard were now her uncle's groomsmen. Melany Amady, the French Defense Minister was one of the bridesmaid. They were teasing Avila over something to which he leaned back and laughed.

"Well, it's about time," Hari smiled. "Tio Avila took a long while to get married."

"Just eleven years," Brice smiled. "There was one postponement three years ago because of me. So much tragedy, so much sacrifice to get to this happy day. Uncle Avila deserves all this," Brice said as she wiped away tears from her face. She heard a shriek as flower girls were chased by ring bearers and Eilish passed by, all gussied up in her gown.

"Paolo is such a naughty boy," she screamed as she was chased by a boy with the same height as she. Mira, who was standing beside Analie and fussing over her dress before another round of pictures, heard Eilish's voice and turned to her. She was about to say something, but shrugged her shoulders and smiled.

Tio Dio, who was seated behind her, caught Eilish's hands and whispered something in her ears. Perhaps for her to slow down? Tia Mira drew Eilish into her arms, then patted her cheeks. She ran away from their arms, giggling all the way.

"Will you miss Ira next month during our own wedding day?" Hari asked gently.

She nodded. "Do you think she'll be able to return here now that the threat from Mallard is gone?"

"I don't think so. The threat is still there, even if it's

invisible," he answered, shaking his head.

"Guess what, I got an encrypted message from Jae and Quinn from the International Space Stations this morning. The French have offered asylum to the whole Roboticus crew who escaped on Everest," she said. "They'll be sent to the moon colonies as soon as a vacancy pops up. Looks like Ira and Quinn are getting serious, and thinking of moving in together. I haven't told my mom yet," she chuckled.

"See, life goes on," Hari said and drew her nearer. "Time to get married and make babies, you agree?"

"I just want a simple life, Hari. You promised." She held Hari's hand and squeezed it.

"Yes, a simple life in Concordia treating those who are sick, while you..."

"Rest in a hammock and face the sea. That's the life for me," she laughed as she snuggled closer to Hari.

She rested in the crook of Hari's arms, at peace with the world, while watching family members joyously participating in the rituals of marriage, an act of love by two people, done by millions of people since the beginning of time.

It was a miracle to be even sitting here, in a wedding, inside a church built nine hundred years ago. It was unthinkable that Paris was an occupied country till its liberation five years earlier.

It was the sacrifice of many people present in this cathedral that made it possible for the world to be liberated from hate. The people present here were selfless, generous people serving the people they love, without thinking of a reward for their own selves.

It was love that freed them from tyranny. Love that will

protect them from any kind of selfish, maniacal leader in the future.

She knew that wars could still happen at any time. But she knew that they would be defeated since there were good people fighting evil every day. Hope would prevail. Forgiveness would prevail. Love would prevail. Peace would prevail.

"I can't wait to start a quiet life in Concordia," she smiled.

"You deserve a quiet, full, fulfilling life, Brice. You deserve it all." Hari kissed her.

T. H. E.   E. N. D

Acknowledgments

For being my literary guiding spirit, providing a beacon
of light as I undertook the journey writing Homo
Roboticus, I'd like to thank my editor Susan Krawitz.

For helping birth Homo Roboticus to the printed and
e-book world, Kimberley Hitchens, Elisabeth Hallett, Indy
Chatterjee, SM Savoy and Eduardo Plaza.

For their patience and kindness, their love and
understanding, my angels on earth, and an inspiration to do
my best. I am eternally grateful to:
Lily Cai, Paolo Cai Yuhico, Patty Domingo, Linda
Schweitzer, Yvonne Green, Sol Salao, Leah Escobal, my
brothers Raul and Gil Ligad and Lilibeth Lacson.
Chit Intal, Chichi Acsay, Hermeeh Florendo, Ditas
Martelino & Mela Tolentino

To my formidable advisers who've always brought their
A-game to the creative table: Bodi Yuhico, Eric Angelo
Yuhico, Mathew Yuhico and David Yuhico.

To my real-life superheroes:
Concordia Afable Ligad & Leoncio Ligad
Bonifacio & Elizabeth Yuhico
Ramy Diez & Dora Afable
Richard & Kate Gordon.

To my real-life hero & love of my life
Bons, this book would not be possible without your
love and support.

A Note About the Author
Mayet Ligad Yuhico was born and raised in the
Philippines. She has been based with her family
in Singapore since 2012.

Visit
Mayet Ligad Yuhico
www.mayetligadyuhico.com

Manufactured by Amazon.ca
Bolton, ON

17884659R00199